"Reden, down, up," ...

it's in you," kedrax said.

Bianca closed her eyes, concentrating harder, and looked into McManus to find the poison. She wove a spell to transform the poison particles into healing ones. Not just for his blood either, but to boost his immune system and speed up the healing process. She could feel the life flowing back into him.

When she opened her eyes, the wounds closed as if zipped from the inside, though the blood remained.

Confusion turned to accusation in his eyes as he looked up at her. "What've you done?"

She panicked. The magic, stronger than any she'd used before, backlashed.

Kedrax.

She kept hold of the energy to protect the dragon. Until a white light exploded behind her eyes . . .

By Tracey O'Hara

Dark Brethren Novels

NIGHT'S COLD KISS
DEATH'S SWEET EMBRACE
SIN'S DARK CARESS

TRACEY O'HARA

Sin's
Dark Caress

A DARK BRETHREN NOVEL

 HARPER Voyager

An Imprint of HarperCollins*Publishers*

HARPER Voyager

An Imprint of HarperCollins*Publishers*
10 East 53rd Street
New York, New York 10022-5299

First Harper Voyager mass market printing: August 2012

Harper Voyager and) is a trademark of HCP LLC.

Printed in the U.S.A.

10 9 8 7 6 5 4 3 2 1

For my boys
David, Corey and Seamus

acknowledgments

The road to writing this book was rather more difficult than others, but I have to say how much I love the result. Several people helped me along the way. So a big thanks goes to my editor, Diana, and all those people at Harper-Voyager who helped get this book out, and to my agent, Jenn, for her support.

With this book I had several readers who really stepped up when I needed it the most. So a big kiss goes to Heather, Nicky, Mel and Cathy—love you girls muchly. Without you I couldn't have done it. Also I would like to thank Karyn, who suggested the brilliant newspaper moniker for my serial killer on facebook. It was priceless and perfect.

And as always I would like to thank my supportive family—specially my husband, David, who is the love of my life, and my two wonderful sons, Corey and Seamus, who found their way into the pages of this book. Love you boys.

Sin's
Dark Caress

1
Rising Sin

BIANCA SIN STRODE past the flashing emergency-vehicle lights to the crime tape strung across the alley entrance and nodded to the uniformed police officer whose name she couldn't remember.

"Hey Dr. Sin," the young officer said, lifting the yellow crime tape. "He's waiting for you."

She smiled her thanks as she ducked under the tape, making her way to where the man who'd summoned her stood talking to a couple of uniforms.

"Hey McManus, you look like shit," she said.

He smiled and leaned one hand on the hood of the squad car as he dug into his coat pocket to pull out a pack of cigarettes. "Sweet talk will get you everywhere, Sin."

She painted on her biggest how-you-doing smile and slowed her stride. His square jaw was covered with at least a few days' growth, and by the circles under his eyes and his rumpled suit, he hadn't been home in a while either.

The shabby appearance might look unprofessional, but she knew it was most likely because he'd been working for several days without a break. His ice blue eyes, though somewhat bloodshot, still pierced with a sharpness few others possessed, reminding her why he was one of the city's top homicide cops.

Bianca turned her smile on the other two. "Barnes, Jones, how you guys doing?"

Officer Barnes returned her nod. "Not too good after seeing this one, Dr. Sin." He lightly tapped his partner on the stomach with the back of his hand and tilted his head to the crowd gathering at the perimeter. Jones nodded and the two officers moved off.

McManus pulled a cigarette from the pack with his lips and fished out his lighter. "This one's real messy," he exhaled in a cloud of smoke.

"Whatcha got?"

"A homeless woman, split like a can of corn for the baby surprise inside." He scrubbed a hand across his bloodshot eyes. "It's the second in as many weeks."

"So why'd you call me in?"

"You're the expert on that magic crap, and there's a symbol I need you to check out. It could be witchcraft, but there's something different about it," he said, his nose crinkling. They'd worked together for years, been friends for almost as long, and never once had McManus hid his dislike for thaumaturgy, or those who used it.

"Hey," someone yelled from behind.

They both turned as a blond reporter pushed forward past the yellow tape, only to have the two uniforms step into her path.

"Excuse me, Dr. Sin—Trudii Crompton WTFN News—can I have a few words?" the reporter yelled as she tried to force her way past Barnes and Jones.

"I'll give you two. *No comment!*" Bianca called over her shoulder, and leaned toward McManus, dropping her voice. "Get rid of her, will you?"

He flicked his cigarette butt on the ground and stamped on it before sauntering toward the reporter and her cameraman. "Come on—you know the rules—take it back to the perimeter."

"But Detective McManus—" the blonde protested.

"Move back, Miss Crompton, or I'll have you taken in for obstruction," McManus said.

She straightened her shoulders, defiance flashing in her eyes as she lifted her chin. "You can't do that."

"Maybe not, babe." He slid his hands into his trouser pockets, opening his crumpled coat to reveal a crumpled suit. "But where would you rather be when the story breaks? Here or downtown in lockup?"

The reporter's lips thinned and a deep frown creased her perfect brow. Bianca smiled and turned away. She didn't know what Ms. Crompton took offense to more, being threatened or being called "babe." McManus had a knack for deliberately pushing a person's buttons when they pissed him off, and the reporter was taking the bait.

As Bianca approached the cordoned area, her skin grew clammy, the hairs on her arms stood on end, and nausea washed over her. She rounded the corner and bright crime scene lamps lit the area in gory detail, turning the alley into a slaughterhouse. Blood pooled around a pale body lying amidst the congealing viscera, but that wasn't what made her stomach churn.

Burning bile rushed up her esophagus with a dark urgency. She ran, putting as much distance as possible between her and the crime scene so she wouldn't contaminate it. The contents of her stomach gushed out of her mouth and hit the filthy ground, just missing her shoes.

Footsteps came up from behind. "You all right?" McManus asked, genuine concern softening his expression.

She reached into her pocket for a tissue and her hands shook.

"I've never seen you pavement pizza at the sight of blood before. You're not going soft on me, are you?" He took the tissue from her hand and cupped her chin as he wiped her mouth, his brow creased in concentration. "We've seen a hell of a lot worse than this."

"It's not the blood." She pushed him away gently and bent over with her hands on her knees as her head spun again. "Something dark happened here, not just the murder."

The remnants of black energy radiated from everything surrounding the body.

"That's why I called you in," he said, rubbing gently between her shoulder blades. "How're you feeling now?"

Nausea and dizziness subsided. "Okay I think." She took back the tissue to clean herself up and smiled her thanks.

The smile he returned remained a little uncertain. "You had me worried there for a minute."

"You're not going 'soft' on me, are you, McManus?"

"Never." He winked. "Come on, I've got something to show you."

Bianca followed him back to the body and dropped to a squat. Dark blond hair was tacky with drying blood that pooled around the dead girl's head, and her lower abdomen was just an empty cavity. Her old clothing was mismatched and grubby, like someone who'd been on the streets for some time, but her frozen features held an innocent youthfulness, almost untouched by the squalidness of a homeless life in dark back alleys.

"Goddess, she's around sixteen or seventeen at the most." She looked up at McManus and swallowed the urge to puke again. "We got an ID?"

"Not yet," McManus said. "We're still questioning the other bums in the area, but no one is admitting to knowing her, let alone seeing anything that happened."

"What a surprise—" Bianca froze as she glanced past McManus to the wall behind.

"So whatcha think?" the detective asked when he saw where her gaze was directed. "Satanists?"

"I wish," she whispered, uncurling from her crouched position and pulling a cell phone from her pocket.

"What's up?" the deep voice rumbled through the earpiece after the second ring.

"How soon can you get the team downtown?"

"About a half an hour," Oberon replied. "Bad?"

"The worst," she said, then gave him the address and slid the phone shut.

"Why'd you have to call him in?" McManus asked.

The whole time her eyes remained firmly fixed on the symbol, painted in blood. "Because we've seen this before."

All too recently.

There was no mistaking the mark of the Dark Brethren.

2

ᴅarkness this way comes

THE HEAVY RUMBLE of a Harley-Davidson engine grew closer, a single headlight clearing a path for the large black SWAT van that followed through the crowd of onlookers and media. The team had arrived.

"You called him in, you deal with him," McManus said, and walked away slightly pissed.

Bianca sighed and made her way toward the newcomers as the buzz from the gathered press rose in renewed interest with their arrival. Oberon DuPrie pulled the motorcycle up beside a squad car and kicked out the stand before cutting the engine. Antoinette Petrescu climbed from behind him and smiled widely.

"God, Oberon, I really gotta get me one of these," she said, running her fingers through her newly shorn Nordic-blond hair.

Oberon swung his long leather-clad leg off the bike and stood to his full seven-foot height, towering over the Aeternus female. "I don't know what Christian would say about that."

"He can say what he likes, won't make any difference," Antoinette said with a grin.

Oberon turned to Bianca. "So is it what I think it is?"

Bianca nodded and dropped her voice low enough so it didn't carry beyond them. "Looks like we might have another Dark Brethren death."

Antoinette's expression sobered as she looked over her shoulder at Kitt Jordan climbing from the passenger side of the black van. "Same M.O. as the campus killer?"

"No, but just as bloody." Bianca glanced over at Kitt. "Does she know?"

Oberon nodded, his own eyes filling with concern for his surrogate sister. "I gave her the chance to stay behind."

"Do you think she'll be able to handle it?" Antoinette asked, looking at the forensic pathologist. "The campus killer was so close for her."

Kitt swept her silver white and gray-black-streaked hair out of her eyes with one hand and raised the other in greeting, her smile a little strained.

"It's been several months since Nathan's death." Oberon pulled the Bluetooth headset from his ear and glanced over his shoulder. "And she's a lot stronger than she looks. Besides, Cody's here if things get too bad."

"Let's hope it doesn't come to that," Bianca said, her eyes flicking to the blond surfer boy climbing out of the van's driver seat. "Because I have a feeling this one's going to get real messy."

"I think I'll go check out the surrounding area," Antoinette said as she walked off.

"Hey," Bianca called after her. "I thought you were flying out to meet Christian?"

"Tomorrow night." The Aeternus's smile beamed as she skipped a backward step and held up two thumbs. "Two glorious weeks of sand, sea, and sex in Miami."

"Okay." Oberon put his hand on Bianca's shoulder. "Show me the body."

"This way," she said, and led him through the crowd, past the crime tape and into the seemingly normal alleyway, until they turned the corner.

The dark magic pressed in on her again, bringing on the same nauseous feeling. But this time the dark energy seemed to move back, as if pushed away by some invisible force field. Her cobalt blue pendant grew quite warm against her skin.

Weird. She wrapped her fingers around the stone encased in a gold fitting and looked at it closely. It seemed to hum with energy.

"Bianca?" Oberon said with some force.

"What?"

"I asked when the body was discovered," he said, a frown creasing his brow. "Are you all right?"

"Um . . . yes." Her voice shook a little. She cleared her throat to shake off the odd feeling and gather her thoughts. "When . . . ?"

Oberon dropped to look at the dead girl.

"Just over two hours ago now," McManus said, coming up behind them, still not looking pleased. "The owner of a nearby diner found her when he was closing up."

An azure luminescent tear beaded in the corner of McManus's left eye. Luckily, Oberon was still focused on the body and not on the detective.

She leaned closer to McManus. "You have something in your *eye!*"

McManus turned his back to them and took a handkerchief from his pocket.

"Any sign of the infant?" a voice asked.

Oberon stood and turned around. "Chancellor Rudolf, you didn't need to come all the way down here. I'd have sent you a report first thing in the morning."

An elderly man stood with his hands behind his back, looking up at the symbol on the wall. "I wanted to see for myself." He turned to Bianca, his gaze drawn to the charm around her neck. Then he lifted his eyes to hers and smiled. "It's good to see you again, Dr. Sin."

"You too, sir," she replied.

"And this is?" He smiled quizzically at the man by her side.

The detective stepped forward and held out his hand, everything appearing normal again. "Detective McManus, Homicide."

"McManus, I'd like to introduce Chancellor Rudolf, who's just been promoted to the Five in CHaPR," Oberon said.

"Promoted! Ha! That Akentia can be very persuasive." A strange expression flashed across the old man's face as he took the detective's hand. He frowned, then covered it with a smile. "More like bullied into it."

"Princess Akentia, the Aeternus?" Bianca asked.

"Um, yes." The old man recovered his composure quickly, but not before another rather nervous glance at her pendant. "The same."

She touched the necklace protectively. Why was he so interested in her family heirloom?

"Rudolf is the closest thing there is to an expert on the Dark Brethren," Oberon explained. "He helped us out on the campus killer case several months ago."

"Good to meet you, sir," McManus said.

"So, young man," Rudolf said. "What do you think happened here?"

McManus straightened and looked around. "One theory is it's a black market baby-stealing racket."

"But you don't think so?" Oberon glanced between them.

McManus shook his head again. "I don't know why, but it just feels . . . off somehow."

"And you'd be right." Rudolf nodded to the bloody symbol painted on the wall. "This has the seal of the Dark Brethren."

"And you say this is the second victim?" Oberon asked.

McManus nodded. "The other was found down by the tracks, several blocks from here, but we're pretty sure she was killed elsewhere and dumped. The scene was nowhere near as messy as this one."

"Can you send both the reports to my office?" Oberon handed him a card.

McManus took it. "You can have them tomorrow. Okay?"

"I guess it will have to be." Oberon turned to the chancellor. "I'd like to get your input too, Rudolf."

The old man nodded. "I'll do what I can."

"Excellent, let me walk you to your car."

"Thank you, Oberon." The old man's eyes fell to her pendant again, then he smiled before turning away.

"Creepy old man," McManus said as soon as Oberon and the chancellor were out of earshot.

Bianca turned and punched him in the arm. "What the fuck, McManus? You're doing *Neon Tears* now?"

3

once upon a midnight weary

"I'M HOME," BIANCA called, throwing her keys on the hall table before kicking off her shoes.

It'd been a hell of a night and she really needed a hug.

"Vincent, sweetie?" she called again. "Mama's home."

Bianca walked into the kitchen and opened the refrigerator door. She took a bottle of white wine from the door, pulled the cork, and grabbed a glass from the dish drainer beside the sink. As she began to pour, her hand paused. Maybe she was drinking too much lately. *Maybe a coffee would be better at this time of the—*

She glanced at the clock. It was almost dawn.

As she recorked the wine and put it back in the fridge, she thought of McManus. His drinking problem went as far back as she'd known him, but the drug use was new. Fluorescent-blue discharge was a telltale sign of a Neon Tears user. The most effective way into the system was through the multitude of tiny veins in the sclera or white of the eye. However, overuse could lead to permanent damage, even blindness. It was only one of the several new designer drugs hitting the street recently. No one knew where the narcotics came from, only the chaos they left in their wake.

Movement blurred on the windowsill above the kitchen sink as Vincent finally appeared and began cleaning his ebony velvet coat.

"There you are," she said, picking up the huge black cat.

He acknowledged her with a sharp meow, his yellow feline eyes shining.

"Hello, baby. What've you been up too, hey?" She kissed him on top of his slightly misshapen head. She'd rescued him as a battered week-old kitten from a Dumpster a few years back. He was so tiny then, with only one ear intact and half his tail missing. She'd hand-raised him with a bottle, cleaning and caring for him like a baby until he was able to look after himself. The bond between them was still strong.

He let out a drawn out, half purr, half mew—his way of saying, "I'm happy to see you too, now where's the food?" While she'd never formed the familial bond with the orphaned cat, she'd learned to interpret his ways.

His single intact ear pointed toward her, then he suddenly hissed and struggled out of her arms, landing on the countertop with his half tail burred. Her pendant warmed against her skin and she could've sworn she felt it move.

"What's the matter with you?" she asked, moving to pick him up again, but he came up on his toes with arched back and hissed even louder at her pendant.

Bianca sighed and unhooked the clasp behind her neck. The necklace slid into her hand, and she took it into the living room. Vincent followed her, still looking spooked and puffed up; he eyed the pendant warily as she placed it on the table by the sofa.

"There you go, you silly thing. Is that better?" She scooped him up and rubbed his soft tummy. "Let's go find you something to eat."

"M'ow," he replied, and craned around her arm, keeping both eyes on the pendant.

BIANCA WOKE ON the sofa, dressed only in her robe. The television spewed the latest news into the room in brilliant high-def. The streaming headlines flowed across the bottom of the screen while a far-too-chirpy reporter chatted about the abysmal state of the economy. Her shoulder pinched from the awkward position she'd fallen asleep in. She wiped a sheen of sweat off the back of her neck.

Why was it so hot in here?

The imitation fire with glowing fake logs blazed in the fireplace. She hadn't turned it on, at least not that she remembered. But then again, she'd been pretty wiped after a warm shower.

Vincent purred madly in front the flames. She stretched to ease the tension in her aching muscles from sleeping on the sofa, dropping her hand to her chest.

My pendant!

It wasn't on the table where she'd left it, and she dropped to her hands and knees to search the floor under the table and the sofa.

It had to be here somewhere.

But where? Vincent lifted his head and looked at her. His what-the-hell expression almost made her laugh, until she saw the gold chain protruding from under his left paw.

Weight lifted, she laughed with relief and crawled over on all fours. "What're you doing with that?"

The cat's only ear flicked back and his eyes narrowed as his head dropped a little lower. The purring stopped.

"Come on, puss," she said, reaching for the chain. "Let me have it."

He growled and swiped at her hand with sheathed claws.

"You're a crazy cat. One minute you can't stand to be near it, now you won't give it back."

A strange low hum pulsated through the apartment, making it feel like every molecule in her body was vibrating. It came from everywhere and nowhere at once. The unsettled sensation she felt last night returned and unnerved her even more than before. She crawled to her feet and looked down at the stubborn cat.

"Go on, then. Keep it while I get ready for work." She walked over and switched off the fire and the thermostat.

He'll have lost interest by the time I finish dressing.

Bianca went into her room and opened the closet door. At one end hung the gothic clothes her mother bought her before her bonding. Since she never bonded with a familiar, the cultural badge of her race stayed in her closet unworn, but for some reason she'd never been able to throw them away.

She reached for a pair of navy pants and dressed quickly. She twisted her hair up and secured it with some pins before picking up her shoes. Vincent still lay where she'd left him, curled up and purring again. He still had the pendant.

"Come on now," she said, bending down. "Give it up."

This time the cat didn't sheath his claws when he swiped. Three parallel crimson streaks stung the back of her hand. He'd never struck her before. Not in anger.

Her phone rang.

"Are you coming in tonight?" Oberon asked.

"Sorry, I slept through my alarm." She didn't want to tell him she'd fallen asleep on the sofa. He'd worry.

"I need you to go over that data from the crime scene. We're getting some heat from above."

She glanced at the cat and sighed. The pendant wasn't going anywhere for now. Though feeling a little naked without it, she pulled on her coat and gathered up her keys.

"Be good," she said to Vincent on her way out the door.

BIANCA HAD SPENT most to the night and half the day going over the thaumaturgic data she'd gathered from the crime scene. The photos were the worst, though. While she'd become more accustomed to the sight of dead bodies over the years, she knew it wasn't something she would ever get used to. And if she did, well, that would be the time to change jobs.

Now she just wanted to collapse in a heap.

A blast of hot air greeted her as she opened the apartment door. The heating was cranked up to the max, and the fake fire blazed away again. It was a miracle the whole place hadn't gone up in flames. A dirty paw print dusted the wall next to the thermostat.

Vincent? Since when had he known how turn up the heat? *And why?*

It wasn't exactly the weather for it, given the typical late spring day with a balmy seventy-one degrees outside. She turned down the temperature and switched off the fire, but Vincent was nowhere to be seen.

Her pendant lay where she'd left it that morning, only now it was in two pieces. How had the cat managed to break a solid piece of stone in two?

When she picked up the pieces, she found them to be hollow, like . . .

An egg?

She walked over to the kitchen counter, and Vincent suddenly appeared on the windowsill with a dead mouse dangling by its neck in his mouth.

"You that hungry, baby?" she said, moving toward him.

He ducked her hands, jumped and raced off into the living area before she could catch him. The cat dumped the mouse on floor, which wasn't as dead as it first appeared. He placed a paw on its tail and started to mew strangely, almost as a mother cat would call her kittens.

The mouse tried to crawl away, but the cat held it fast.

"Let's put this poor thing out its misery," Bianca said, getting closer.

But the cat crouched low over its prey, ears flat and a low growl rumbling in his throat. Bianca backed away and he began mewing again, then something flashed past her foot, hardly bigger than the captured mouse.

She sat down heavily on the lounge, her brain trying to comprehend what she was actually seeing.

A dragon. A tiny, perfectly formed, baby dragon.

Cobalt blue to aqua scales shimmered along its body and a pair of metallic maroon and crimson tipped wings spread awkwardly from its back as it tried to keep balance on four tiny legs that ended in black-tipped talons. The minuscule beast greeted Vincent by rubbing its head against his cheek. The cat answered with a happy purr, then lifted his paw and let the mouse go.

It scurried away, but Vincent pounced on it again before it could get too far. He flipped it in the air and caught it under his front paw before meowing at the miniature dragon. The creature scampered on unsteady legs as Vincent lifted his paw again, releasing the mouse's tail. The hapless mouse ran, but the baby dragon fell upon it this time, instinct taking over as teeth and talons shredded the rodent. The creature ripped the mouse's body apart and threw back its glistening blue reptilian head, jaws working to position meat so it could swallow it, the same way a lizard or alligator might. Yet, it was definitely neither.

The tiny mythological creature devoured a dead mouse on her living room floor while her cat looked on like a proud parent. She sank onto the floor, crawling slowly and cautiously closer, afraid she might be hallucinating. The creature eyed her warily as she drew nearer but seemed more worried that she was after its meal than afraid of her.

Bianca reached out a shaking hand.

The second her fingers made contact with the little creature, a jolt ripped up her arm and through her body, the force throwing her backward into the sofa and snapping her head back.

THE BLACKNESS RECEDED. Vincent licked the side of her face and purred in her ear, but there was another strange sound, an excited jitter.

Bianca opened her eyes and blinked, turning her head to stare into a vertically slit, molten gold eye looking at her intently. It almost seemed to smile at her. She sat up so fast her head spun, then leaned forward on the sofa.

The dragon tilted its head and looked at her through intelligent, liquid-gold eyes. And yet, every molecule in her body buzzed with a peculiar energy, unlike anything she'd felt before.

"What happened?" she asked, her voice sounding strange and shaky.

"We bonded."

"Bonded?" She rubbed the back of her smarting head, then froze. "You can speak?"

The little creature crawled up into her lap, and she tentatively ran her finger over his tiny, jeweled body. He was warm, almost hot, yet soft like kid leather. "That's part of the gift," he said in a childlike voice.

Bianca wasn't as freaked as she knew she should be. She'd often dreamed of dragons and flying, especially when she was younger, but this was just weird. "I feel I know you."

"You do. I'm Kedrax."

The name surprised her. She used to have an invisible friend she called Kedrax. "You can't be the same one." As soon as she said it, she knew he was.

It all started to make sense. The reason she couldn't bond with another familiar was that she'd already mentally bonded with Kedrax as a child. She'd just learned to suppress it. Now that his physical form existed, the bond was complete.

The question was, *why* now? And more importantly, did it have anything to do with the Dark Brethren?

4

smoke and mirrors

MCMANUS PUSHED HIMSELF away from the wall as a bald man in a dark maroon T-shirt crossed the lobby to meet him.

The man held out his hand. "Detective McManus, Antonio Geraldi. Oberon sent me to meet you."

"Didn't you work for VCU with DuPrie, Antonio?" McManus asked.

"You have a good memory." His handshake was firm. "And please, call me Tones."

McManus followed Tones to the elevators, and the doors opened immediately when he hit the down button. "Do you know why DuPrie ask me to come here?"

"Sorry. You'll have to ask the captain that yourself."

McManus glanced at him out of the corner of his eye as they entered. The T-shirt showed a pair of lush lips surrounding fangs and bore the slogan MEAT IS MURDER–BITE A VEGETARIAN. His jeans and the basketball shoes were of the expensive designer kind, but purposely made to look shabby. If he remembered correctly, this man was an Aeternus. He must be one of those weirdos from the humegitarians movement who only fed on vegetarian blood.

Tones leaned over to swipe his ID card across the panel

and punched the lowest floor button. He stood back and smiled the uncomfortable smile of someone who wasn't sure what to say but feels he should say something anyway. McManus hoped he didn't. He hated small talk, especially elevator small talk.

"So . . ." the Aeternus said at last. "You work for Homicide."

McManus groaned inwardly and kept his eyes front. "Yup."

"And you've worked quite a bit with Bianca?"

McManus blinked slowly and let go a weary breath. "Yup."

"Hmm, a man of many words I see," Tones said. "I can see why you and Oberon get on like a house on fire."

Smartass.

The elevator chimed and opened, saving McManus from any more inane comments. He followed Tones through the only door in the short stark white corridor into the security guard's coffee lounge. A couple of guys in uniform sat in animated discussion over some game, and three more played cards while watching TV. Another guard had his feet up on the desk. He gave them a cursory glance and went back to reading his paper.

"Please wait here," Tones said, and disappeared through the door marked CHIEF OF SECURITY.

A few minutes later a buzzer sounded on the desk and McManus heard DuPrie growl, "Send him in."

The guard behind the desk dropped his feet, sat forward and indicated the hand-shaped panel on the wall. "First, place your right hand on the reader."

After a human U.S. senator was almost assassinated by a facimorph masquerading as one of his aides, the facimorphic test had become standard in most major organizations and government departments. McManus hated the fucking things.

The office was small and dingy, not exactly what he expected. Oberon DuPrie's massive bulk sat behind the desk shuffling through papers while Tones was nowhere to be seen. There was only one other door to the right. Without looking up from what he was doing, DuPrie indicated the empty chair opposite him with a wave of his hand. McManus waited for him to finish. And waited. And waited. He glanced at his watch and realized it had been nearly ten minutes since he'd entered the room. Much more than was polite without acknowledgment.

DuPrie used the tactic McManus himself used to put people on the back foot. Make them wait.

If that bloody bear thinks he can intimidate me, he has another thing coming.

McManus rose from his chair and headed for the door.

"Where are you going?" DuPrie asked, still not looking up.

"*You* asked *me* here." The doorknob was cool against the palm of his hand. "I came as a favor to Bianca. But I'm not into playing these games."

"Really?" DuPrie said. "I could've sworn you were, given that you're playing us. You've been dodging my calls."

McManus turned. "What're you talking about? What calls?"

"Every time I called your office, I got the brushoff," DuPrie said. "And you never sent me those reports either. I assumed you were getting territorial. Then Bianca tells me that you'll be happy to see me."

"I never received any calls, or even any word that you received those copies I emailed yesterday to the address you gave me."

The ex-VCU captain put down the document and leaned back with a raised eyebrow. "Sit."

McManus held his ground. He'd dealt with tougher nuts than Oberon DuPrie before.

The large male relaxed his posture and indicated the chair opposite. "Please."

He relented and walked back to the chair.

DuPrie stared at him several seconds longer then hit a button on the intercom. "Tones—Plan B—see if you can get me those reports."

"No need." McManus pulled a crumpled buff folder out of the inside pocket in the front of his coat. "I made a copy."

DuPrie arched an eyebrow and took the file, tilting his head. "Why'd you bring me this?"

"I didn't, I was taking it home to go over myself." DuPrie reached for the file, but McManus kept a firm hold on it. "I want this back."

The large male leaned forward, his eyes narrowed for a moment before he agreed with a nod. McManus let the folder go.

DuPrie opened it and picked up a crime scene photo. "Someone's stonewalling us on this case. Any ideas who?"

The newspapers had taken to referring to the killer as the Womb Raider. Good to see DuPrie wasn't. "How about VCU?"

DuPrie shrugged his shoulders. "Could be. But last I heard, they're all but disbanded. Too many mistakes have made it hard for the higher-ups to ignore them. The best and brightest have moved on. The rest . . . well." With a sigh as large as the man himself, he met McManus's eyes. "No, this is something else. To hack into either our email system or yours and stop this report smacks of someone with much more competence than the VCU I know."

"Maybe you have a mole," McManus said.

DuPrie's features hit Defcon 3. "Hell no," he spat. "Not in my team. I've handpicked every single one and I'd trust all of them with my life. No—this is either someone in your department or someone external."

Interesting. Bianca was right about DuPrie's loyalty to his people. "So what do you need from me?"

DuPrie leaned back and linked his hands behind his head. "Just do what you're doing and keep Bianca on your side."

McManus was under no illusions; he was being interviewed. The question was why. A dizzy spell washed over him. He'd tried to ignore the lethargy creeping into his limbs and the blurring of his eyesight, but the tingling in his tear duct indicated a Neon Tear bleed.

I can't let him see the tear. "Can I use your bathroom?"

DuPrie's eyes narrowed for a moment before he flicked his head toward the only other door. "In there."

McManus rose from the chair, trying to stay calm and unhurried. The bathroom was a small dank room with a tarnished mirror and a rust-stained basin. It looked like their budget was in even worse shape than the New York City Police Department's. A water droplet fell from the leaking faucet with a fat plunk, and the cistern of the toilet continuously flowed.

McManus leaned against the basin and looked at his reflection in the speckled mirror as the iridescent tear squeezed from his duct. Thankfully, he felt this one coming. Not like yesterday's when he'd been too preoccupied. Must be more careful in future, he told himself—the effects were wearing off sooner each time. The water from the faucet was bracingly cold. It washed away the drug residue and shocked his senses back into gear. But he needed a hit and needed it soon. He fingered the vial of the drug in his pocket and was tempted for a moment. The risk wasn't worth it.

Leaning closer to the mirror, he searched his features. God, how he hated what he'd become. The hollowness behind his eyes reflected the emptiness he felt in his soul, like something was missing—*or long dead.*

"Are you all right in there?" DuPrie called from the other side of the door.

"Be out in a minute," he replied, and with one last look in the mirror to make sure all traces of the drug were gone, he opened the door.

DuPrie stood behind the desk, his face cast in a suspicious slant as McManus took his seat.

"Actually, I think we're done for now."

"Okay." McManus stood and straightened his coat. "When will I get my file back?"

DuPrie shook his head. "I'll give these reports to my people to take a copy, and give it to Bianca to drop off."

"I assume she'll still be available to help on the case with the magic crap?"

"She's still the recognized authority on that 'magic crap.' " DuPrie's features almost relaxed into a smile.

"All right, then, if you're finished, I'm going." McManus walked to the door. He stopped and turned back to DuPrie. "Tell me something. If that's the only door out of here—where did that Tones character go?"

The large man's smile deepened. "That's something for another time."

"Right."

MCMANUS WATCHED THE floor numbers light up as the elevator rose and fingered the cold thin glass vial in his coat pocket. He pulled out an empty hand and held it in front of him, palm down. The shakes were getting bad; his skin felt damp and clammy under his clothes. There was no way he could function enough to drive like this. He curled his fingers into a fist and shoved it back in his pocket. He'd have to risk a hit before he went anywhere.

The doors opened onto the semideserted lobby. Class was still in. Using in public was always risky, but if he didn't get a hit soon, temporary blindness would be next.

The elevator stopped on the first floor and he made his way to the public bathroom. A toilet flushed in a far stall and a student gave him a polite yet wary nod as he crossed to wash his hands. Kids were always cagey around cops, especially college kids, and the kids at NYAPS were no different on that front. They seemed to smell him out just like he could tell that the guy who'd been in the stall was an Animalian of some sort.

McManus stood in front of the mirror, checking the stalls behind for feet. Luckily, they all appeared empty, and the kid hurried from the room with a slight scent of nervousness. McManus could recognize a fellow user, even without knowing the kid's poison of choice.

He went into the cubicle farthest from the door, turned the lock and dropped onto the seat. Nausea groaned in the pit of his empty stomach, his sight swam in and out, and everything shook. Every molecule in his body vibrated like it was about to fly apart. His fingers were so numb he could barely feel the glass of the vial, and as it cleared his pocket, it slipped from his grasp.

Time stopped.

He held his breath, watching in horror as it hit the floor with a plink of glass against ceramic tile and then bounced.

Once, twice, three times.

Each time, he braced himself for the sound of breakage, but none came. He fell to his knees on the filthy cubicle floor, bumping his hip on the toilet paper holder on the way down and lunging for the vial of Neon Tears, sending it skittering away. He managed to slap a palm over it just before it disappeared under the stall door. His breath expelled in relief and he dropped his head, then stumbled upright to sit on the toilet seat again.

The outer bathroom door squeaked open and McManus froze. Had Oberon followed him after all? Fear and jonesing-for-a-fix paranoia doubled the tremors in his hands. He closed his eyes and breathed again as the sound of someone whistling as they pissed noisily into the urinal came from beyond the toilet door.

A cold sweat broke all over his body. His legs shook, his shoulders shuddered, and his fingers quivered as his vision dimmed—the final symptom of the drug comedown. He needed this hit.

NOW!

He unscrewed the top and squeezed the rubber dropper, pulling the phosphorescent liquid into the tube, and tilted his head back. The blurred droplet hung suspended above his eyeball. Then it dropped.

Pain seared right through to the back of his head. Then his

sight returned and the ceiling zoomed closer, the cracks becoming more defined as his senses honed to the drug. Steeling himself for more of the inevitable agony, he repeated with the other eye and then leaned back to rest his head against the cold tiles. The drug worked its way through his system, chasing away the aches, shakes, and blindness. Pain stopped as suddenly as it hit, and his senses moved into a more enhanced normalcy. He brought his head up, replaced the vial's stopper, and put it back in his coat pocket.

While he waited for the drug to take full hold, McManus slid a pair of sunglasses from his shirt pocket and slipped them on, then floated to his feet, once again in control. Well, as much as one could, in the grips of a mind-altering drug.

Even with the sunglasses, everything seemed bright and shiny. He moved to the mirror and leaned against the counter. The bathroom was completely empty now, he hadn't even heard the last guy leave. He lifted the shades and checked his eyes. The drug's swirling luminescent film covering his eyeballs slowly dissipated as it was absorbed into his system.

The bathroom door opened. He quickly dropped the sunglasses back into place and turned on the faucet. Two guys entered, joking and shoving each other, but stopped dead when they saw him washing his hands. He watched them in the mirror as they crossed to stand before the urinals as far from him as they could get.

"Cop," one whispered.

"You sure, man? He looks high," the other replied.

He looked back at his reflection, at what he'd become. An empty shell. Not because of his vices. They were just what he used to try to fill the void. But the drugs or alcohol couldn't fill the emptiness inside, only numb the pain for a little while.

Kicking Neon Tears wasn't easy. He'd tried. Numerous times. The worst was when the neon blindness had him trapped in his apartment for three days—helpless until he'd finally lost it and called his supplier. Maybe the only thing worse than being helpless was death—and even that was only a maybe.

If his superiors got wind of his addiction, he was toast. He'd already given them enough fodder to put his ass in a permanent sling.

5

DOWN to BUSINESS

OBERON PUSHED AWAY the papers and leaned back in his chair. He'd have bet a week's pay McManus was the one obstructing the case. Cops didn't like their jurisdiction questioned, and he obviously had a thing about parahumans. But McManus seemed on the level, just like Bianca said he was. Which left two questions. Who'd been behind the attempt to hack the Bunker's computer system? And why were they trying to impede the investigation?

Luckily, Tones was all over it. That Aeternus was worth his weight in computer chips. Oberon rose and placed his palm on the panel behind the strategically placed plastic plant. The back wall slid aside to reveal the secret entrance to the Bunker, his real headquarters. He picked up McManus's report and started for the spiral staircase when the freight elevator in the secret alcove pinged behind him.

"Captain!" the janitor said with a cheery smile as he backed his cleaning cart out of the elevator.

"Chad," Oberon returned as the janitor wheeled out into the office beyond.

The panel slid shut behind him, leaving Oberon alone. He descended the circular staircase into the Bunker's open plan office to find Bianca and Cody bent over some photos laid out on the table, while Kitt and Tones sat in front of a computer screen. The Aeternus rubbed the back of his neck and hunched over the keyboard again.

"Go get some rest, Tones," Oberon ordered. "It's well past midday and you've been at this for nearly thirty-six hours straight."

"Just a few more minutes," the bald-headed tech said with an absent wave of his hand.

Kitt placed a hand on Tones's shoulder. "He's right. I can work on this some more while you sleep."

"I need you at the top of your game." Oberon placed the folder down on the nearest table. "Later, I want you to access the Homicide mainframe and compare this report to theirs. Bianca, I'll need you to make copies of everything, McManus wants it back ASAP."

Bianca picked up the buff file and began to skim though it, smiling. "I told you he'd come through."

Oberon crossed his arms. "He seemed pretty adamant that he'd emailed us the original report, and I couldn't smell any lies. He's definitely hiding something, that's for sure, but I'd say it's just his drug habit."

Surprise flashed across the witch's face. "You know?"

"Sure. I saw what happened the other day. As long as he does his job and doesn't jeopardize this investigation, his Neon Tear addiction has nothing to do with me. Now let's get into the conference room and go over what we've learned so far. Not you, Tones. You go rest, and that's an order."

"But Captain—"

"And feed too," Kitt added. "I've put some blood on to warm in the kitchen."

Tones sighed and kissed Kitt on the cheek. "Thanks."

As he headed off toward the kitchen, Kitt's cell phone rang. She glanced at it and smiled. "Excuse me a minute."

Oberon followed the others into the conference room. He took a seat and looked at Bianca, who seemed preoccupied.

Cody leaned over and whispered something in her ear. She grinned and playfully punched him in the arm. The two of them were usually partners, but not when she worked with Homicide—the Incubus tended to make some cops nervous.

Kitt came in a few minutes later with a smile still plastered on her face and sat at the computer keyboard.

"I take it from that smile Raven was on the phone," Cody teased.

She blushed as she nodded. Oberon smiled back at his surrogate sister. It was good to see her so happy again after all this time. Raven was a good man, and she deserved a good man after all she had been through.

"When are they due back from the Adirondacks?" Bianca asked.

"Not for another couple of weeks," Kitt said, her smile dying a little.

Cody leaned forward in his seat. "So, how are the twins doing?"

"Exceptionally." Her smile returned and widened into a proud parental grin. "Raven said they've taken to the training much better than even he anticipated. He thinks the new Draconis Nocti will be ready for action very soon."

"I'm glad they're doing well. And I want to hear all about it later, but now we need to discuss this case," Oberon said, bringing the meeting back on track. "Why don't you start with the forensic pathology?"

She straightened her shoulders and put on her professional face as she tapped the computer keys. Gruesome images of the crime scene appeared on the large computer screen at the far end of the room. "As you can see—it was very bloody. The parahuman medical examiner, Tez O'Connor, and I examined samples taken from the scene. We were able to identify the victim's blood, amniotic fluid, and viscera. We have even determined that the sex of the baby was a girl."

She picked up a remote and stood next to the screen as it filled with a shot of the symbol painted in blood on the alley wall. "I've been getting updates from the OPCME. They assumed the victim's blood was used here, but that's since been proven incorrect. DNA tests show the blood is male and human, probably painted at least an hour before the victim's murder. We found dried flakes in the victim's hair from brushing against it."

"So where did the blood come from?" Bianca asked.

Kitt clicked the remote again, and a shot of a pale male body taken at the morgue appeared on the screen. "Tones did a cross-reference against several other crimes that happened around the same time. This one was a twenty-something male mugging victim just a few blocks from the crime scene who'd had his throat slashed only an hour or so earlier. We got Tez to run a comparison on the blood samples and it came back positive."

"Were there any other links between this boy and the victim?" Cody asked, a frown creasing his surfer-boy good looks.

Kitt looked at him. "We haven't identified the girl yet so it's difficult to establish. The boy wasn't from the area. He was pre-med at NYU."

Oberon leaned forward on his elbows. "Was the murder weapon the same?"

She shook her head. "The boy's wound was inflicted with a long curved blade. Tez says it's like nothing she's seen before, and whatever it was, the blade was razor sharp. The girl's wounds are a little bit more difficult to ascertain. The wounds were quite bizarre, as if no blade whatsoever was used. The epidermis and subcutaneous tissue, muscle, and the womb wall were severed with no damage to the viscera or any other internal organs. There were also no blade marks or nicks of any kind."

"I might be able to shed some light on that," Bianca said. "I think the flesh may have been opened using black thaumaturgy."

BIANCA STRAIGHTENED UNDER her colleagues' scrutiny. Everything Kitt had just said only confirmed her suspicions and her findings so far.

"The magic used in the alley was the darkest I have ever seen. So dark it made me physically ill. Magic that black needs blood and death to feed it. When I went over the scene with all my instruments, I couldn't read any definable magic signature; it was too obscure even for my most advanced devices. I think the boy's murder could've been in preparation for the main event. They needed his blood and his death to fuel the spell."

"Why would they need magic that strong to murder a girl and steal a baby?" Cody asked.

"I think the real question is why would a black thaumaturgist want to steal babies?" Oberon asked.

"I don't know the answer," Bianca said. "But whatever it is, it can't be good."

"Right, looks like we have a lot of work to do. Bianca, when you've copied that report, get it back to McManus. I think his insight as a homicide detective may give us alternate views."

Everyone rose and gathered up their papers except Bianca. She stayed behind after the others left. She wasn't feeling like herself today, which wasn't surprising after what had happened. Was Kedrax okay? He was just a baby, after all. But he'd assured her that with Vincent to watch out for him, he'd be fine. Still, she worried.

Maybe she should've called in sick or something. Not that she felt sick, not at all; in fact she felt great. Her whole body tingled. She held up her hand, willing the energy to take form. Sparks and tiny bolts of electricity danced from one finger to the next, playing across them.

She shut her fist and dropped it quickly at the sound of a slight scuff at the door.

Oberon stuck his head in. "You coming?"

"Sure," she said, plastering a smile on her face.

The big man frowned. "Are you okay?"

"Yes, fine," she said a little too quickly. "Just a little tired is all."

"Okay," he said, his expression not entirely convinced. "Come on, then."

6
Happy Birthday

TIFFANY SWIPED A layer of crimson across her lush lips and pouted into the mirror.

Eat your heart out, Gregory Harris. She smiled and slipped the top back on the red lipstick before glancing at her watch. She'd kept him waiting for five minutes, and that should be enough.

Greg might be captain of the basketball team and the heir to this hotel chain, but she was damn well worth the wait. His dad had him bussing tables in the ballroom to build character. She giggled. He was furious his father had made him work this summer. Greg had ranted endlessly about being forced into menial labor instead of hanging with his friends. She finally got bored and left.

But tonight he'd slipped a note begging her to forgive him and give him another chance. He'd asked her to meet him by the restrooms for a surprise. *A birthday surprise,* and she just *loved* surprises.

Chi-Chi yipped in her sleep. Tiffany smiled and reached into the purpose-built pet bag and rubbed the silky cheek of the sleeping Chihuahua pup. Her tiny birthday present groaned, stretched, and rolled over, but remained asleep.

Tiffany adjusted the top of the three-quarter-length red satin fingerless gloves then ran her fingertips over the black lace choker around her throat, the crimson-painted fingernails gleaming under the harsh fluorescent lights. With a single thought, she made the cosmetics fly into the open purse lying beside the handbag. Her reflection returned a saucy wink as she patted the complex raven-black coiffure—jangling the gold bangles on her wrists. With a devilish smile, she ran her little finger along the free lock of hair at the front, turning it the exact shade as her lips.

A simple glimmer spell was much easier than dyeing her hair. She dragged her fingers down the other side, turning the lock purple. Thank the Goddess she'd bonded with Chi-Chi this morning. The little puppy twitched and yapped in her sleep again.

This magic stuff is such a buzz.

Today was one of the most important days in a young witch's life—the day she came of age and inherited her powers. Tiffany giggled and hugged herself, barely able to contain the excitement. With one final twirl she craned a look over her shoulder at her reflection to check how good her ass looked in the clingy red velvet skirt under the black leather and lace corset. Every bit the well-dressed witch.

If this doesn't get the poor boy panting . . .

She picked up her bag, slid the makeup purse in the side pocket, and checked in on the darling little Chi-Chi before leaving the bathroom, almost colliding with Greg. He leaned against the wall in his busboy uniform, his arms crossed against his chest and a sulky frown creasing his brow.

He grabbed her roughly by the wrist. " 'Bout time."

"Hey," she complained. How dare he manhandle her this way?

Music and laughter thumped down the corridor from the main ballroom behind her.

"Hurry up," he growled, sounding strange. He was also nowhere near as astounded by her awesomeness as he should be. In fact, he'd barely seemed to notice.

"Don't be angry with me," she said, dropping her bottom lip in the way that always reduced him to putty in her hands. "Not on my birthday."

"I don't have time for these games," he said, dragging her toward the kitchen.

The music grew louder as someone opened the door at the far end of the corridor. She glanced over her shoulder at the party, *her party*, going on in the ballroom. It wasn't easy keeping up with his long basketball player's legs in her brand new stilettos and tight floorlength evening dress. She almost tripped several times.

"Slow down!" she cried. "Where're you taking me?"

"Somewhere a little more private," he murmured, looking around cagily as he headed for the exit into the back alley.

Tiffany screwed up her nose. "But it's smelly and dirty out there. Can't you just give me my present inside?"

"No!"

What was wrong with him? Why was he acting so strange? Usually she had him ready to sit, roll over, and beg on command. Chi-Chi whined, as if even she sensed Greg's weird behavior.

All around them the kitchen bustled. People rushed around, preparing food, washing dishes, and shouting orders. No one seemed to notice them leaving through the back door.

"Greg, let go," she demanded, trying to pull her hand loose from his iron grip as they passed into the alley.

The bag was jostled and the tiny pup complained with a faint little yip from inside.

"We don't have much time," Greg said, pulling her farther along the semidarkened alleyway.

Tiffany finally yanked her hand free and turned her back on him to face the wall, crossing her arms. He hated it when she did that, but she was too mad to care. "Then maybe we should just call this all off right now. And maybe I don't want your present."

"Don't be so childish," he said, his voice growing strangely raspy.

The light seemed to change in the alley, becoming softer and more subdued, as if some weird sepia tone had covered all the lamps. A mist flowed out of the walls and poured onto the ground. As she stepped back away from it, her heel snagged and she fell, landing on a soft bulk, losing her familiar carry bag. The puppy yelped as she toppled out onto the filthy pavement, then scooted back into the safety of the bag. Tiffany climbed to her feet with disgust, germs all over her hand like minuscule bugs; she could feel them crawling and burrowing into her skin as she glanced down at the drunk passed out on the ground.

Except . . .

The bum didn't move. He hadn't even flinched when she landed on top of him.

She tilted her head for a closer look, squinting in the darkness. He wore a similar busboy uniform to Greg's. She looked closer. He was also roughly the same size . . . the same build . . . and even had the same hair color—

Greg?

"I think there's something wrong—" She looked up as the Greg she left the kitchens with advanced toward her, his eyes shining with a strange disturbing glow as he closed the gap.

Suddenly, his features blurred and wavered until "Greg" imploded with a pop.

A glimmer or doppelganger spell?

The fog became thicker—swirling and solidifying into a figure dressed in a white robe that dropped to the ground to become part of the mist. A cowl covered the face, obscuring any features, which made it hard to tell if the figure was male or female within the shapeless folds.

Chi-Chi whined and cowered, backing farther into the overturned bag as the moon emerged from behind the cloud cover, making the weird glow a little easier to see by. But even that didn't help determine the stranger's identity or sex. Whether a *he* or a *she* remained a mystery as the figure stayed shrouded in smoke and shadow, shifting and swirling to obscure it from the naked eye.

She raised her hands. A black stickiness covered her fingers, but the scent was unmistakable.

Blood!

The scream built from the pit of her stomach as she shook her head, trying to deny what she knew was true. Terror swelled in her chest, pushing the scream up her throat, but before it could leave her lips an invisible force smashed into her, forcing her mouth shut, silencing the cry as her body slammed against the wall behind. Her eyes darted to the body on the ground.

Oh God! Greg!

Help me, someone please help me. But she somehow knew her silent plea would go unanswered.

The ghostly stranger floated in the mist over Greg's body without so much as a downward glance. Tears of terror squeezed from the corners of Tiffany's eyes. The hooded stranger pulled a small glass vial from the folds of the robe. Fear burned the back of her throat as she tried to wrench her head away, but a dark unseen force pushed her arms out farther against the wall, the strain making it hard to breathe as she remained vertically immobilized, spread-eagled against the grimy bricks. Evil power crackled in the air around her, the fine hairs on her arms standing on end. The shrouded figure scooped the teardrops rolling down her cheeks into the thin tube and sealed it with a rubber stopper before concealing it again within the folds of the robe.

Her expensive birthday dinner churned in her stomach and rose quickly, burning her esophagus. The stranger deftly stepped sideways, avoiding the projectile vomit as it burst from her mouth. Some hit the pavement with a filthy wet splat, and the rest dribbled down the front of her brand new dress.

The harder Tiffany struggled, the tighter the invisible grip grew. She couldn't break free, couldn't call for help, and couldn't even use her own newly acquired powers.

Then the spell-weaver began to chant. Multiple voices spewed from within the cowl, male and female, all intoning old, dark, and powerful words in perfect synchronicity. The stranger wove the sinister spell, and an abominable black mist floated in the air around her, swirling, touching her hair, her skin, and pushing past her lips and into her nostrils. The black enchantment forced its way down her throat and twisted her insides like shards of broken glass.

The perspiration on her body turned to ice as one by one the hooks down the front of her corset popped open. The satin and leather garment fell away and the heavy velvet of her dress split open from hem to waist.

Tiffany's eyes widened.

Terror coursed through her veins.

Tears flowed, blurring her vision and burning her eyes.

And the chanting continued.

This couldn't be happening. *Not today. Not on my sixteenth birthday.*

She had looks, money, power, and talent, not to mention position. Her grandmother had practically promised her from birth that she'd be the future Domina of the New York covens.

This sort of thing just didn't happen to people like *her.*

The vile spell-weaver dipped a ghostly hand in Greg's blood and approached. She was helpless to get away as *he . . . she . . . it . . .* placed a bloody palm against her lower abdomen. She squirmed to get free of the loathsome evil touch, but all for nothing. The black magic held her fast.

The chant rose in tempo. The words chilled her blood. The figure pulled back and Tiffany glanced down, watching the bloody hand imprint disappear, absorbed into her body along with the dark words.

A heaviness started in the pit of her stomach and grew, becoming more solid as it filled her. The rate of evil words accelerated to an unintelligible babble—not that she understood any of it in the first place. The language sounded ancient and far beyond her comprehension, but she recognized their dark power.

Inside, something moved.

Turning and twisting and alive.

Her abdomen swelled with amazing speed. The stranger, still chanting, pointed a finger toward her stretched, distended stomach. A ripple ran across the surface, a bulge pushed out the side. Then again. It wasn't unpleasant. Actually it felt kind of nice . . . kind of natural. The bulge appeared again and she almost got an impression of a tiny foot.

A baby. *My baby.*

The knowledge was sudden and absolute.

Somehow, a child grew in her womb. A girl child. An innocent, untouched by the vile evil that created it. Tiffany could feel a connection to her daughter and a strong maternal instinct kicked in. She wanted—no, *needed*—to protect her unborn child, whatever its origin.

Tiffany closed her eyes and reached down deep inside herself, drawing on all her strength to call on her familiar. Chi-Chi still cowered in the bag, shaking in terror. With a sweep of the hooded figure's hand, the zipper closed, locking the tiny puppy inside. If only the Chihuahua pup could've run, raised the alarm, maybe someone would've come to save her. But now all hope died as the bag skittered across the ground, taking her terrified familiar with it.

The baby flipped and dropped heavily into her pelvis. The dark magician shifted the pointed finger downward. The skin just under her ribs at the top of her rounded abdomen opened with a small split. There was no blood, just pain that bit deep and sharp as the finger moved down, extending the split in her skin. Then the muscle and flesh split, exposing her insides.

The fiery pain ripped through her, a pain so unbearable she longed for the oblivion of unconsciousness, yet she remained totally aware. A scream silently tore from her lungs, as if her very voice had been stolen. Then the child—her child—slipped free of the gaping wound with a sucking pop and a shower of warmth down her legs. Her daughter's large eyes squinted, blinked, and opened—appearing black in the strangely muted full moon light as the babe floated in the air between Tiffany and the dark magic wielder.

The tiny girl blinked again and looked around before her little face screwed up, filling the night air with a newborn cry. The stranger plucked the floating child out of the air before severing the umbilical cord and wrapping her within the folds of its robe.

The figure slashed the finger sideways opening a cross cut and the law of gravity suddenly reinforced itself. Tiffany's viscera dropped from the gaping abdominal wound with a wet splat and she fell to the filthy alley into a pool of quickly cooling blood, intestines, and amniotic fluid.

She couldn't make her eyes focus no matter how much she tried. The cold numbness of her extremities crawled toward the center of her chest; even the pain of her eviscerated stomach had dulled to an icy nothingness. With one last ditch effort she reached out to catch the bottom of the robe with bloody fingers, but they just slipped through the incorporeal mist.

The last thing Tiffany saw were Greg's cold dead eyes staring at her as the stranger floated back into the fog, crooning a multivoice lullaby to the newborn snuffle of her baby daughter.

Then even Greg's face dulled as the final vestiges of life bled from her body.

7

Babes in the Wilderness

BIANCA GRIPPED THE steering wheel and accelerated as the light changed from red to green. All she wanted was to get home and check on the little dragon. The creature had been playing on her mind all day. And it'd been a *very* long day.

The tinkling ring tone of her phone ripped her out of autopilot, and she glanced at the caller ID before answering on her hands-free. "Hey McManus, what's up?"

"Where are you?" The detective's voice had a familiar urgency.

"On my way home," she replied, looking around to get her bearings. "Is there another one?"

"Could be. Meet me at the Langford Plaza on East 53rd." There was a pause. "Officer Jones rang me direct and hasn't even called in yet. How soon can you get there?"

She glanced in her rearview mirror for traffic. "I'm not that far. I'll see you in a few minutes." She hit the end button and merged right to find somewhere to turn the car around.

BIANCA PULLED INTO the drive of the ritzy hotel. The valet in a Langford Hotel staff vest approached, and McManus stepped forward, holding up his badge as he opened her door. The valet turned to help a beautiful young woman climb from a flashy black sports car instead.

"So where's the body?" Bianca asked in a low voice. No use starting a panic.

"This way," he said solemnly.

"Let me grab my case first." She popped her trunk and took out her forensic thaumaturgy bag.

He took her past the hotel to an alley where a squad car was parked, blocking any entry.

"Thanks for letting me know first," McManus said to Adam Barnes, who stood beside the black and white car. "Have you called it in yet?"

"Not yet." Barnes crossed his arms, leaned against the squad car and nodded over his shoulder. "Jones is waiting for you with the kid who found the bodies."

"Thanks," McManus said, slapping the uniform on the shoulder as he passed. "You call it in now while we take a look."

"You got it." Barnes gave Bianca a friendly wink as he leaned in to grab the radio.

An oppressive darkness gripped her insides and twisted as she followed McManus down the service lane. She closed her eyes and swallowed, concentrating on pushing back the sick black sensation.

It worked.

She could feel Kedrax's presence. With a little more concentration, she kept the corruption at bay. It was amazing how all the theory of spellcraft she'd learned as a teenager came flooding back now that she was able to put it into practice.

They found Jones on a cement loading platform outside the building's side door, his thumbs hooked into his police utility belt, the universal stance of a cop. A young man in an apron sat on the bottom of four steps with his head in his hands.

"Jones," McManus said, climbing the steps to the small loading dock.

The two cops talked in hushed tones as Bianca sat down beside the young man and extended her hand. "Hi! My name's Bianca Sin. What's yours?"

He just looked at her hand for a moment, and then shook it weakly. "Mickey." His Adam's apple bobbed as he swallowed nervously.

She noticed that the clothes he wore were similar to those on the nearest body. "Do you know this guy?"

Mickey glanced over and shrugged. "Bit hard to tell without seeing his face."

Good point. "You work here in the kitchen, don't you? Did you notice anyone missing?"

"You're kidding, right?" The boy tilted his head. "There's a big function going on. Do you know how crazy it gets in there?"

"I can imagine." Her smile seemed to relax him a little.

"It's a madhouse. In fact my boss is probably screaming for me right now." He ran a hand through greasy hair and tossed a glance over his shoulder at the cops. "I hope I don't get fired."

She glanced in the same direction. "I'm sure it'll be fine."

McManus was on the phone, frowning in concentration. He put the cell back in his pocket and approached.

Bianca placed her hand on the boy's shoulder. "This is Detective McManus," she said, and then to McManus: "Mickey here is a little nervous about getting fired."

The detective gave her a slight nod. "Everything's going to be okay, Mickey," he said. "I'll square it. Someone will be along soon to take your formal statement, but I just want you to run me through what happened."

"I didn't do nothin'," he said, holding up his hands, terror masking his face. "I just found them like that."

"I know that, Mickey." McManus used the boy's name again, keeping his tone soft and consolatory. "I want you to tell me about how you found them."

The kitchen worker's shoulders relaxed a little. "Oh.

Right." He rubbed his open palms hands along his thighs and stood up. "I came out the door to throw the trash away over there." He pointed to the Dumpster just beside the loading platform. "I didn't see nothin' at first. It was dark, like the lights weren't working properly, they was kinda dim. When I looked at them, they got all bright again and then I looked down to see . . ." He waved his hands at the bodies.

McManus stood up and pulled her aside. "The medical examiner is on the way. Why don't you quickly check over the bodies and do some preliminary readings?"

She set her case down on the ground. "Do you want me to orb him too?" she asked.

"I have a feeling we're not going to get too much more than what he's already told us, but I'll let you know after I talk to him some more." McManus turned back to the boy.

Bianca pulled the thaumaturgic scanner from the bag, moved to the first body and turned on the device. It went off the charts, then settled back down to a more normal frequency. She ran the reader over the dead boy. There was some trace spell residue, but nothing dramatic enough to send the scanner into overdrive.

The girl's body was half hidden in the shadows, but before she got within ten feet, the thaumaturgic scanner went crazy again and the sick feeling returned, even worse than before.

The scanner had trouble getting a fixed reading on the magic signature. Multiple colored strands twisted together and blurred as the frequency patterns intertwined across the LED readout. She'd only seen something like this once before—the other day when she attended the other murder. Even with group caste magic, the signatures usually remained different from one other, separate and distinct. But this . . . *this was weird.*

And she didn't need a piece of equipment to tell her how black the spell was. The loathsome corruption oozed out of the very air around her, making her head hurt and her stomach churn.

Bianca dropped to a squat beside the victim's body. A sense of recognition washed over her as she looked at the dead girl, but the light was too poor to see properly.

"Anyone have a flashlight?" she called over to the others.

Jones pulled the police issue flashlight off his duty belt and passed it to McManus, who came up and shone it over her shoulder. Some of the black hair escaped the elaborate hairstyle framing the pale lifeless face, making the bright crimson lips stand out in stark contrast. But it was the trademark violet eyes, even if clouding in death, that truly gave up the girl's identity.

"Shit!" she spat.

"You know her?" McManus asked.

"What's the date?" she asked.

"May fifth."

"Shit," she said again, and turned around. "This is bad. This is real bad."

"What do you mean?" he asked.

Bianca moved away from the body. "If tonight is the fifth, then right now there's a gathering of covens in this hotel celebrating the Age of Enlightenment for the granddaughter of Gayla Hilden—Domina of the East Coast covens."

"And the CEO of the Hilden Group—one of the biggest investment management corporations in the country. I know who she is," McManus said. "What of it?"

Bianca stood. "Well, I'm pretty sure this is the granddaughter."

8

The Delicate Taste of Grief

MCMANUS KNEW THAT if Bianca was right, this was going to turn into a mega shit storm fast.

He turned to Jones. "Why don't you put young Mickey here in the back of the squad car for now and get him some coffee. I'll be inside talking to the staff."

The officer helped the young man to his feet.

"And Jones, call for more backup. Lots of it. I have a feeling we're going to need it before the night's out." He turned to Bianca. "Coming?"

"You bet," she said. "You're really going to need my help for what comes next."

McManus banged on the door and it opened from the inside. The kitchen buzzed—people ran around yelling orders across the room, and delicious odors made his mouth water, reminding him that he'd forgotten to eat again.

A jumped-up little man in a tuxedo confronted them with hands on hips. "What's the meaning of this?"

"Detective McManus." He held up his badge. "Is there somewhere more private where we can talk?"

"I'm a little busy right now. You may not have noticed,

but there is a very important function going on tonight."
The man's dismissive arrogance was really starting to piss
him off.

He leaned in close. "If you want me to shut this place
down here and now, I can and I will."

The man pursed his lips and frowned. "Follow me."

McManus leaned over to Bianca and dropped his voice.
"Keep an eye on this lot."

The tuxedoed man led him to a small office and closed
the door on the hubbub outside. "I'm François, the manager.
Now what is the meaning of this?"

"There's been a double homicide just outside. It looks like
one of your staff and a party guest have been murdered."

The pompous man deflated. "Oh."

"I need you to find out which of your staff is missing,
apart from young Mickey, who found the bodies. It's very
important we keep this contained. Several police officers
will be arriving soon to start the questioning and I'd like
your full cooperation."

"Of course, Detective." The man twisted his hands together nervously. "Though I'm not sure what I'm going to do
about the party guests."

"You just leave that to me," McManus said, and slapped
him gently on the shoulder. "When you've worked out who's
missing, come find me or my partner, Dr. Bianca Sin."

François glanced down at his hands. "Is Mickey a suspect? He's a troubled kid, but not a murderer."

"Right now he's a witness, but we can't discount any pos-
sibility."

The manager nodded and squared his shoulders as Mc-
Manus opened the door. People stood around in the kitchen,
some in stunned surprise, others whispering as the rumors
started to circulate the room. François clicked his fingers to
the nearest girl in a service uniform. "Show the detective to
the ballroom."

McManus followed the server through the kitchen, down the corridor, and out into an unusual gathering. People milled around, drinks in hand and casting suspicious glances in their direction. Most of them had their animal familiars with them, which made things even more interesting in the noise department. He scanned the crowded room, looking for the person in charge and suppressed a shudder. *Of all the parahuman races, it had to be witches.*

Bianca appeared at his side. "I called Oberon. He's going to send Cody over to help keep the emotions of a room full of witches under control."

"Good," he said. "Now let's find this Domina of yours."

She touched his arm and nodded in the direction of a formidable dark-haired witch with a large eagle perched on her shoulder. "That's her."

"Right," he said.

"McManus." Bianca kept hold of his arm. "Tread carefully with this one, okay?"

"What are you saying, Sin?"

"Darling, I thought you weren't coming." A red-haired stunner in a tight black velvet dress and an albino python wrapped around her shoulders leaned in to kiss Bianca's cheek.

"I'm here for professional reasons, Artemisia," Bianca said, and turned to him. "Detective McManus, I would like you to meet Alto Artemisia Sin. My mother."

The woman extended a delicate hand toward him. "Nice to meet you at last, Detective. My daughter has spoken of you often."

"And you, ma'am." Her palm was warm against his. Very warm. "But she left out how beautiful you were."

"Artemisia, please. Definitely don't call me ma'am." She smiled at him. "Bianca tends to keep her family at a distance these days, since she took up with that team at the Academy. We hardly get to see her." The python wrapped around her shoulders hissed at McManus. "Play nice, Matilda," the witch said, stroking the snake's head.

The reptile's cold pink eyes kept him in a dead stare as its head rose to rest on the woman's shoulder. She placed her hands on her slim hips, emphasizing her tiny waist. His hands would fit easily around that waist. He could picture it clearly . . .

Oh God.

His face warmed and he pulled his coat closed over the front of his suit. He hadn't had such lack of control since he was a teenager, when even the accidental glimpse of a bra strap would send him hard. But this was Bianca's mother and disturbing on so many levels.

"Stop it, Artemisia." Bianca's voice had a sharp edge.

"What?" The witch feigned innocence and winked at him. "Sorry, Detective, but it's just you have quite the . . . delicious aura."

"The Sin's succubus blood is strong in *my* mother," Bianca explained, giving Artemisia the same look she gave him when he'd done something wrong.

She just smiled and a shrugged. "Sometimes I just can't help myself."

He felt the erotic sensations subside and got the impression she was playing down her abilities and her control. He'd no doubt that what just happened had happened on purpose, and that he'd been tested. Question was, had he passed or failed?

Artemisia Sin's smile lit him up inside like a jackpot winning slot machine.

Bianca's frown deepened. "We're here on business, Artemisia. We've got some news concerning the Domina's granddaughter."

"Tiffany?" Bianca's mother glanced over her shoulder at the tall severe woman and then leaned in with conspiratorial delight. "Is she in trouble? It'd really piss that old witch off if her pride and joy was—"

"Dead," Bianca said.

Artemisia's head snapped up and she pinned her daughter with an intense stare. "No! She can't be."

"I'm afraid it's true," McManus confirmed.

"But I saw her only a few moments ago." Artemisia craned her neck, searching the crowd. "Over there. Look."

McManus followed her finger to the girl moving through the crowded room, dressed in identical fashion to the body outside. He would've sworn it was the same girl. Except this one didn't have her guts spilled all over the floor or the pale mask of death.

"Look how she's moving and how carefully she's not engaging anyone much," Bianca said. "I think that's a doppelganger."

"A what?" he asked.

At that moment the girl turned toward them—almost as if she knew they were talking about her—and then her body seemed to shrink inward, folding in on itself until, with a pop like a bursting balloon, she disappeared.

Those nearest turned to look but found nothing there. They returned to what they were doing with odd nervous titters, but no one seemed to realize a girl had just imploded nearby.

"What the fuck was that?" he asked.

"The illusion shattered when we realized it wasn't real," Artemisia explained. "A doppelganger spell can only be maintained as long as the illusion isn't questioned. You'd think it would be easier to get a facimorph—a doppelganger spell that complex requires a lot of power, and close proximity to maintain it."

"Not if they're using the black," Bianca said.

"Besides, a facimorph would be just a loose end," McManus added.

Her mother's jaw dropped, her face horrified as she looked from one to the other. "Black magic? Here?"

A sharp commanding tone interrupted their conversation.

SIN'S DARK CARESS   51

"Artemisia, I see your daughter has finally made an appearance in society."

Both women turned as one and bowed deeply.

"Your Eminence," Bianca said.

He'd never seen her so . . . deferential. Not even to Oberon DuPrie, and he knew she respected him a lot.

"She could've at least dressed more appropriately," Gayla Hilden said as the eagle on her shoulder screeched and flapped its massive wings. The witch dipped into a pouch around her waist and held out a tidbit, which the bird snatched gently from her fingers.

Quite the piece of work, this one.

"She has always been inadequately respectful," the Domina continued, narrowing her unusual violet eyes.

Artemisia straightened her shoulders and placed herself slightly in front of Bianca. "My daughter is entitled to wear whatever she pleases, Gayla."

Obviously, no love lost between Bianca's mom and the Domina.

"I can handle this myself, thank you, Artemisia," Bianca said. "I'm sorry, Your Eminence, but we're not here for the festivities."

McManus stepped forward and held up his badge. "Now hang on a second, you can't talk to her like that."

He glanced over at Bianca's tight-lipped expression, but saw a slight twitch playing at the corner of her mother's mouth.

The Domina of New York straightened and wrinkled her nose as if he were something nasty she'd stepped in. "You can't tell me what to do. Please leave. At once."

"Apologies, Mistress Hilden," Bianca said, pushing him aside and shooting him a death stare. "My colleague seems to have left his manners at home. Is there somewhere we can speak privately?"

"You have nothing to say that I want to hear," the Domina said.

"Gayla, please! Listen to her," Artemisia pleaded.

"This is my granddaughter's enlightenment ceremony, and for passing her entrance exams into the Isis Institute this morning."

Bianca mouth's dropped and her eyes went wide. "Oh my Goddess, now I know what the spell was for."

"What?" McManus asked.

Bianca waved him off with a touch of irritation. She did that when she was on to something. "Have you seen Tiffany recently?"

"Yes, she's just over . . ." Gayla Hilden scanned the room with more than a little desperation. "She was there a few minutes ago. I saw her."

"But have you actually spoken to her recently?" Bianca asked.

"I've been very busy," the Domina said, sounding pissed again. "There are some very important people in attendance that have demanded my attention."

Bianca glanced at McManus. He nodded.

"Your Eminence, a young woman was found murdered in the alley behind the hotel. We think it might be your grand-daughter."

"Tiffany?" The Domina's hand fluttered close to her throat as she took a staggered step back, desperately search-ing the room again. "That's impossible!"

"It's been a few years since last I saw her," Bianca said. "Do you have a recent photograph just to make sure?"

The Domina regained her composure and snapped her fingers for her manservant. "Bixby, bring me my purse and find Tiffany." When the servant disappeared, the Domina turned back to them with her mask of arrogance back in place, although somewhat shaky. "I'm sure there's been some sort of mistake. Tiffany will be here in a moment to clear things up."

"I wish that was true, Your Eminence," Bianca said.

THE UNCOMFORTABLE SILENCE extended as they waited. Bianca looked at her mother, her expression carefully guarded. Artemisia and Gayla were far from the best of friends, but even her mother would not wish this on anyone.

Bixby returned and leaned in to whisper in the Domina's ear. Her face grew panicked and her gaze flicked to Bianca as she slid a photo from her wallet. "This was taken last week." She sounded less sure than she had a few minutes ago.

A grinning dark-ponytailed cheerleader waved from the snapshot. So young and full of life, not drained of blood in some dark filthy alley, but it was definitely the same girl. The eyes were a dead giveaway. She passed the picture to McManus, who glanced at it. The tilt of his head said he agreed.

The Domina's expression was expectant. "Well?"

Bianca could not make the words come.

McManus handed the picture back to the Domina and inclined his head with respect. "I regret to inform you that your granddaughter has been the victim of a murder, and we will need someone to formally identify the body."

"No." Gayla Hilden shook her head with astonished denial, and then her mouth thinned with determination. "This is some kind of cruel joke. She's here somewhere. I told you, I saw her."

"It was a doppelganger, Gayla," Artemisia said. "I saw it too. But it expired when we looked too closely."

A female uniformed officer came over carrying a tiny, shivering Chihuahua puppy, the tail tucked firmly between its legs, its ears laid flat with terror.

"No." All the blood drained from the Domina's face. "Not Tiffany."

McManus waved the officer away. A man approached with a woman who looked like a younger version of the Domina.

"Mother, what's going on?" she asked.

"Marcus, take Astrid up to the room," the Domina commanded.

"No," the younger woman said. "Tell me what's happened."

The Domina's face fell. "There's been an accident."

Bianca tried to school her features into a neutral expression but failed. It was definitely not an accident that had killed Tiffany Hilden.

Astrid Hilden's eyes widened as she saw the puppy the policewoman carried away and her expression crumpled. "That's Tiffany's Chi-Chi? Where's my baby?"

The Domina took her daughter's hand. "Go upstairs with Marcus, Astrid. I'll be along shortly."

"No, Mother, I need to know." Astrid's voice rose an octave, hysteria creeping in. "Where is my baby?"

The blood had drained from Marcus's face. Something passed between him and his mother-in-law as he placed his arms around his wife's shoulders. "Come on, sweetheart, let's go upstairs."

She wrenched herself out of his embrace and stood shaking. "Tell me now." She screamed. The whole room stopped and looked their way.

"I'm sorry," Gayla said. "She's gone."

"No." It was hardly more than a hushed breath. "No, not my baby. Not my little girl."

Marcus wrapped his arms around his panic-stricken wife again, but she fought him, beating him with both fists until she collapsed, burying her face against his chest as heart-wrenching sobs wracked her body.

Cody appeared out of nowhere at that minute. "Oberon said you might need some help."

"Perfect timing," Bianca said with relief.

He approached the Domina but she waved him off. "Don't worry about me, Incubus, just take care of my daughter." She turned to McManus with a stony expression. "So what are you doing to find my granddaughter's murderer?"

"First, we're going to get statements from your guests," McManus said, and turned to signal one of several police officers arriving at the entrance. "And if you don't mind, I'd like to start by asking you a few questions. When was your granddaughter due?"

The Domina's brow creased. "Due?"

"Ah, McManus . . ." Bianca said, shaking her head. *He didn't know.*

He just ignored her, bumbling on. "The baby," he said. "When was the baby due?"

The Domina's brow creased deeper in confusion. "I'm sorry, I don't understand."

"No, I'm sorry, Your Eminence, I should've explained," Bianca said. "Tiffany was killed for the fetus she carried inside. They took the baby."

"Impossible," the Domina said. "There was no baby. I told you, she passed her entrance exams to the Isis Institute."

"I know," Bianca said.

"Then, can someone please fill me in?" McManus asked.

Bianca sighed and turned to him. "It means this morning—on the dawn of her sixteenth birthday—Tiffany Hilden was certified as a virgin."

9

TIME TO PUT AWAY TOYS

"How CAN THAT be?" McManus asked. "Do we have the wrong girl?"

Bianca shook her head. "A doppelganger spell takes massive amounts of energy, and black magic is the most potent. But I still couldn't work out why so much dark magic was needed to kill the girl, until the Domina told us about Tiffany passing the exam to enter the Isis Institute."

The animals seemed as unnerved as their owners. The python hissed, coiling and uncoiling its tail around Artemisia's arm while the eagle screeched and flapped its wings.

Artemisia placed her hand on her daughter's shoulder. "So it's a mystic pregnancy through black magic. To what end?"

"I still haven't worked that out yet," Bianca said.

"But does put a bit of a different spin on the case," McManus said.

"My granddaughter was killed by a magic wielder, maybe even one of my own kind?" The Domina, looking a little lost, glanced at her daughter and son-in-law, the worried frown marring her marble smooth brow. And there was something else, which McManus couldn't quite read, but it looked a little like fear or suspicion.

"Your Eminence." He glanced at Bianca and back to Domina Hilden. "I'm sorry for your loss, but right now I need to do my job."

Bianca's face relaxed into a smile. He could play nice. *For now*. But there was something off here—he could feel it in his gut. And he wasn't the only one, if the expression on Artemisia's face was anything to go by.

"If you'll excuse me," the Domina said, "I must see to my daughter. You can ask your questions later." She turned with a sweep of her heavy velvet skirt and headed for the hysterical younger woman.

"I should go as well," Artemisia said to Bianca. "Your father is calling in an hour." She turned to McManus. "My husband is the world renowned parahuman anthropologist, Theron Hunter."

"I know," McManus said. "Bianca's spoken of him often"

"Speaking of Daddy, when's he due back from New Guinea?"

"You know your father. He's found some new witch doctor to talk with and wants me to join him. But you know how I feel about the jungle."

"Yes." Bianca smiled. "But you end up having the best time when you get there."

"I was thinking about it, and in light of tonight's events, I think I'd best stay close to home." Artemisia Sin held out a black lace gloved hand to McManus. "I can't exactly say it's been a pleasure, Detective . . . but it has been interesting."

He shook her hand. "Thank you, Your Eminence."

"Actually it's Your *Honor*," the flame hair beauty corrected. "I'm the Alto of my coven, that title is for the Domina."

She held his hand for a few seconds longer than was polite or necessary, searching his eyes with hers, before she dropped it and turned to her daughter, leaning in to whisper in her ear.

Bianca blushed. "Mother."

Artemisia laughed, kissed Bianca's cheek, and with a quick wink at McManus, walked away. He couldn't help but watch her, and tilted his head at an angle for a better look.

Mmmm, mmm . . . nice.

"McManus!" Bianca hit him. Hard.

"What?"

Her eyes flashed dangerously. "That's my mother you're ogling."

Shit. "Sorry, Sin, but that woman oozes sex, and I'm a red blooded man, after all." He adjusted his belt.

Bianca sighed. "I've seen men fall to their knees in front of her when she turned on as much 'juice' as she just hit you with."

"What is it with witches? Always testing their powers?" he grumbled, then realized what he'd just said. "Sorry—no offense."

"It's okay," she said. "We've been friends a long time. You've never kept it secret how you feel about my kind. Besides, it was technically her succubus side."

"Now I know why you get on so well with that incubus. By the way, what did she say to you just then?"

Bianca scowled and looked away, blushing. "Nothing."

"Come on, you can tell me."

"I think I want to take another look at the murder scene," she said, avoiding his question.

Best not push.

The mood in the room had turned rather anxious. The animal familiars picked up on their masters' fear and confusion and chaos reigned. Squawking, screeching, and the general noise level increased as the animals got more and more agitated. The beginnings of a headache pinched behind his eyes.

"I think I'll come with you," he said, following Bianca.

Jones still stood guard beside the door, and he nodded as they came through. The alley was now a hive of activity, with forensics moving around, tagging evidence and taking photos.

The air was ripe. Trash, rotting food, and fresh spilled blood assaulted the senses, but he could breathe much more easily than he did in a room full of magic wielders. He pulled the pack of cigarettes from his pocket and lit one.

God, that's good.

"So." He dragged in another lungful of delicious smoke. "That Domina really has it in for you and your mom."

Bianca shrugged. "I don't function properly, which reflects poorly on my family and their standing in the community. My people don't really forgive failure. If not for me, my mother would probably be the Domina of New York, though she's never held it against me."

"Thou shalt not suffer a witch to fail?" he said as he exhaled a stream of smoke.

She laughed. "Something like that."

Her smile totally transformed her face, into something almost angelic. He loved that smile. He took another drag on his cigarette and kept his eyes locked with hers. "I'd hardly call head of forensic thaumaturgy at the Academy of Parahuman Studies and top consultant to all the law enforcement agencies in the tristate area a failure."

A shade of pink flushed her cheeks. She was never good at taking compliments. "In my culture, any witch who can't wield magic is a failure."

He placed a comforting hand on her shoulder. "It's hardly your fault that your powers failed to manifest. Besides, you would never have been as good at your job if they had."

"No—you misunderstand," she said, locking eyes with his. "If my powers had failed to manifest it would've been a blessing. I wouldn't be seen as a witch then. I have everything I need to be a practicing thaumaturgist—the power, the theory, and the knowledge to use it. The only thing stopping me is my inability to *bond* with a familiar."

He frowned. "I don't understand."

She sighed. "For all intents and purposes I'm a fully functioning witch, but without a connection to an animal conduit I can't draw on the thaumaturgic essence to weave it into spells. Some in my situation have been known to turn to black magic as a way to access their power."

"Instead, you turned it to good use as a forensic thaumaturgist. Win-win for us, I say." He dropped the cigarette butt and ground it underfoot.

The medical examiner, Tez O'Connor, stood up from beside the girl's body and pulled off a pair of bloody latex gloves as she walked over to meet them. "It's a real fecken messy one, this."

McManus looked at the wall brightly lit by the crime lamps where the same symbol as at the other two crime scenes was barely visible on the dirty brickwork.

"We're pretty positive the girl was a virgin," Bianca said to the M.E. "Can you check that when you're doing the autopsy?"

"You're fecken joking, right?" Tez said with her usual Irish lilt. "You know a wee babe was cut from her gut, right?"

"I know, but we are thinking there was dark magic involved. Let me show you my readings." Bianca led Tez away.

Both women had beautiful pale skin and a slight build, but the similarities ended there. Tez had midnight black hair compared to Bianca's pure snow-white locks. The medical examiner's eyes were a brilliant azure blue, where the witch's were pale, almost colorless. And Tez had a mouth on her, loud and foul in her Irish way. She said what she thought, which put off a lot of people, but McManus liked her.

Shit, that succubus mojo Bianca's mother had used still had his libido humming like a high wire.

McManus stood up and stretched. Several hours of taking statements from ungracious guests and suspicious staff was starting to take its toll. His back cramped. Thank God they were nearly done. *Finally*. The Neon was beginning to wear off and he'd need a hit soon. A drink wouldn't go astray either.

His pocket buzzed and he reached into his coat for the cell just as it began to ring.

"McManus," his captain said on the other end. "I need you back at the precinct ASAP."

"Just finishing up here," he replied with resignation. "I'll be done in about an hour or so." *That drink would have to wait*.

"No, now, McManus. And bring Bianca Sin with you."

10

oxygen thieving a'hofe

BIANCA FOUND A parking spot in front of the precinct, something that usually only happened on television, but she wasn't about to dwell on her good luck—there was bigger fish to fry today. McManus seemed rather pissed by the summons, though she wasn't exactly sure why, and his mood hadn't improved much when she found him waiting for her by the building entrance.

"What's up with you?" she asked.

He shrugged as he slid his hands into his pants pockets. "Something just doesn't feel right. Come on—let's see what my captain wants."

"Okay," she said.

As she followed him inside, she remembered Artemisia's parting words. *"While he may have responded to my influence, it was you he looked at, thought about, and his lust is delicious."*

Her cheeks heated again. The one time they got together had been a disaster—a drunken romp after a postcase drinking session. It had been messy and clumsy and something neither of them talked about again. Not that she hadn't wondered how things could've gone if . . .

No, it was better this way. They were professional and that's the way it should be.

Homicide was on the third floor, and they took the stairs.

"Hey there, McManus." A detective rose from his desk and leaned in. "Watch your back in there. Rumor has it someone is after your head."

McManus glanced at the captain's closed door then at her, and slapped the guy on the shoulder. "Thanks for the heads-up, Harry. Come on, Sin."

The office buzzed with the usual cop banter, but it all stopped as she followed McManus across the room. On the outside, he seemed relaxed. However, the set of his shoulders and the tightness of his walk told a different story, at least to her.

A great hulking shadow stood on the other side of the frosted glass. Only one man she knew could dominate a room like that, and if Oberon was here, then McManus was right—something was wrong.

McManus opened the door and held it for her to enter first. Tension crushed the air in the small room. Oberon's mood was as dark as the black leather coat he wore. And the reason sat only a few feet away.

"Finally." Agent Neil Roberts of the Violent Crimes Unit looked at his watch as they entered.

Captain Phillips, McManus's superior, frowned from behind his desk. Another man dressed in an expensive suit sat next to Agent Roberts.

The suit stood up and smiled politely. "Palatine Grace, legal liaison to CHaPR."

Bianca had heard of Mr. Grace's recent rise to prominence in the organization. He was one bright boy, from all accounts. So what was he doing here with this VCU idiot?

"What's going on?" McManus asked in a wary tone, eyeing both Palatine and Roberts.

Captain Phillips looked down at his hands. "This baby

snatching murder case has been taken over by the Violent
Crimes Unit."

"No," McManus said. "This is my case. I've been working
it day and night for the past three weeks. Now that Bianca's
working with me, we're making good headway."

A lie. They had nothing, but she understood his desperation.

"I'm afraid . . ." Agent Roberts steepled his fingers. " . . .
Oberon and his team are no longer involved in the Womb
Raider case. Any jurisdiction they may have had has been
revoked by CHaPR."

Palatine shifted uncomfortably in his chair. "The power
granted to the team briefly during the campus killer case
was always seen as temporary."

Sweat beaded on Oberon's brow, his jaw clenched tight.
She could see he used every ounce of self-control to stop
from exploding. Agent Roberts sat in smug silence, brushing
a piece of invisible lint off his crossed knee. The man was
enjoying every damn second of this.

"This is bullshit," McManus spat, and shoved his left hand
deep into his coat pocket.

Palatine Grace shuffled his papers and cleared his throat.
"There've been a few changes on the council recently and
it's been agreed that VCU are best suited to investigate
this particular crime. It's a priority that the stolen infants
are found and returned to the victims' families as soon as
possible."

"What do you think we're doing?" McManus leaned in,
his hands braced on Captain Phillips's desk. "Twiddling our
fucking thumbs?"

"Detective McManus." For the first time, Neil Roberts
looked up at him. "You're quite welcome to stay on in a limited capacity. As a consultant."

"And Bianca?" McManus frowned. "She's the most quali-
fied forensic thaumaturgist there is."

She knew Oberon well enough to see how much he struggled to keep his temper. His hands balled into tight fists, the knuckles white with the effort. *Just hang in there a little longer, Captain.*

"We don't require any of Oberon's people to assist in this case," Roberts said with that same condescending smile, then stood up. "We have our own thaumaturgic expert."

A powerful wave of anger washed over her. Though she struggled to keep it locked away, a cup flew off the desk and smashed against the far wall, painting it with coffee.

All heads turned to the sound. She stood there, just as shocked as everyone else. It was an instinctive emotional burst of energy, raw and unharnessed.

"Fuck," McManus said.

It was enough to snap her out of it. She hadn't meant to unleash the energy, but it was safer than making Agent Roberts's head explode, which is what she'd pictured. Oberon looked at her, one eyebrow raised.

He knew. Somehow, he knew it was her. Well, too late to take it back now. She straightened her shoulders as if nothing had happened. The crash had been enough to release some of the tension in the room until Roberts opened his mouth, destroying the illusion.

"As I was saying, Detective, Dr. Sin will not be needed on this case." The agent watched Oberon. "So you will agree not to share any information about the Womb Raider with her or anyone else."

"And if I don't agree?" McManus asked.

"Then you will be removed completely," his captain answered.

"I see." McManus nodded sadly and glanced at Bianca. "Sorry, Sin. But it's my case."

He's going to do it. He's going to work with VCU. His betrayal stung, leaving a foul taste in her mouth.

The agent's malicious grin deepened and he couldn't help another gloating glance at Oberon as he held out his hand to McManus.

When he took it, Roberts's knuckles turn white as he gripped hard and his gloating smile deepened. "Actually, it's my case."

McManus frowned. His shoulders tensed as he tried to pull his hand back, but the agent held tight.

"Ah, fuck it." McManus smashed his forehead against the bridge of Roberts's nose.

It happened so fast, she hadn't seen it coming. Neither had Agent Roberts. Blood burst from his nostrils as he dropped to his knees, ripping his hand from McManus's grip to cup his face, the dark crimson seeping through his fingers.

All hell broke loose. Captain Phillips yelled, Roberts screamed, Oberon howled with a deep rumbling laughter. Palatine Grace just stood in stunned silence, though she suspected by the slight twinkle in his eyes that he was secretly pleased. He didn't like Neil Roberts any more than the rest of them.

"Enough!" Captain Phillips bellowed above the din, and the noise died.

"I want this man charged with assault," Roberts said, his head tilted back, a crimson spattered white handkerchief pressed to his nose.

"I'll take care of this, Agent Roberts," the captain said. "Please don't let me hold you gentlemen up any longer."

The agent's eyes narrowed over the bloody piece of linen. Then he stormed out, leaving the office door wide-open.

"I'll try smoothing this over," Palatine Grace said. "But unfortunately we'll need you to get all the case files to VCU by tomorrow." He turned and followed Agent Roberts out of the office.

Captain Phillips sat back in his chair and put his hands behind his head.

"OTA," McManus murmured, not even caring whether the two men were out of hearing range.

"Damn straight," the captain agreed.

"What's ota?" Bianca asked.

"O.T.A.," the captain said. "Oxygen thieving asshole. And that Agent Roberts is one of the biggest I've ever met."

Oberon barked out a sharp laugh. "That's the best description of Roberts I've ever heard."

"Yes—but that's beside the point." The captain linked his fingers together and leaned forward. "McManus, you—"

"I know." He sighed. "Hand in my badge and gun, I'm on suspension."

"Let's just hope I can talk him out of pressing criminal charges. Couldn't you have just played nice for once?"

McManus shook his head. "The only reason he wanted to keep me on this case was to get under DuPrie's skin."

Oberon crossed his arms over his chest.

"Still," the captain said. "My hands are tied. Sorry, McManus."

"I know." McManus slammed his gun and badge down on Captain Phillips's desk and stormed from the office, slamming the door behind him.

Phillips raised his head to look at Oberon. "So now Roberts has us bent over the table without even the courtesy of a reach-around."

"Pretty much," Oberon said. "What about McManus?"

"If I know McManus, he's more pissed at himself for losing control. He'll go off, get drunk, and calm down in a few days." The captain leaned back in his chair. "And I'm sure he's not the first to pop that a'hole one."

11

Draconis Familiaris

BIANCA STEPPED FROM the shower and slipped on a white fluffy bathrobe. With a swipe of her hand, she cleaned the steam from the mirror, then wrapped a towel around her wet hair and padded barefoot into the living room.

The sun shone brightly outside the kitchen window. It was so nice to see daylight again after working so many nights. She poured a cup of coffee and took it out to the terrace. Vincent and Kedrax were also out playing in the garden and enjoying the warm weather.

Bianca closed her eyes and leaned her head back to catch the late morning warmth. The scent of flowers and aromatic herbs planted in pots around the sheltered terrace relaxed her in minutes. She adored her little garden. When she moved into this apartment a few years back, this terrace had been bare concrete, but she'd seen the potential immediately.

Some of her herbs, while good for medicinal purposes, were also good at attracting insects and birds. Bees buzzed from flower to flower, and it made a lovely spot for relaxing and enjoying her morning caffeine hit while she watched them.

Vincent jumped onto the patio table and began cleaning himself.

"Hello, mister," she said, scratching behind his ear. "Where's your new friend?"

The cat stopped cleaning for a moment to answer with a soft "M'ow."

A blue head appeared on the other side of the little table, claws scrabbling for a grip on the weathered teak tabletop as wings beat furiously. Gravity won. The little dragon landed on the floor with a fat little plop. It had doubled in size since yesterday. He came around to her side and looked up with a sheepish tilt of his head. He flapped his thin leathery wings desperately trying to get enough lift to reach the table. She laughed and helped him up, then he walked across the table to Vincent.

"So, you're trying to fly," she said as he folded his wings against his back while the cat gave him a consolatory lick to the side of his head.

"Vincent's teaching me to hunt. Today we caught three mice, five rats, and a pigeon and I thought learning to fly will help."

"No wonder you're getting so fat. I hope you're being careful," she said. "We don't want anyone seeing you."

"People only see what they want to see. The lady downstairs calls me kitty-kitty and feeds us cream." The dragon licked his lips in obvious delight. "The homeless man down by the Dumpster calls me Spot and keeps throwing a piece of tree branch, saying 'Fetch.'"

Bianca laughed. So did the dragon. Even Vincent purred.

She stopped. "You're just a baby, but you're growing so fast, and your speech is getting better too."

"I've been watching late night television," he said, and she could swear he grinned. "But while I'm in my juvenile state, I'm still very vulnerable."

Kedrax tenderly pushed away the solicitous feline who'd continued to clean him and walked closer to the edge of the table near Bianca. He stood up on his hind legs, sat back on his tail, and crossed his reptilian front legs like arms across his chest. "Even though I've only just hatched, I'm older than I look. Older than the Hanging Gardens of Babylon, older than the Great Pyramids of Giza, older even than Stonehenge. I've mostly slept for nearly eight millennia in a petrified egg, but there've been periods of consciousness. Even more so lately."

"Why now?" Bianca said.

The dragon shrugged his shoulders. "I don't know. Something is stirring. I can feel their presence."

"The Dark Brethren."

"No, I sense their presence, but something else is waking." He scooted back across the table, craning his reptilian neck to watch her over his shoulder. "This is something else, something familiar."

He circled and lay down beside the cat, resting his chin on his crossed front claws, but his eyes never left her face. Vincent twisted over onto his back, legs stretched out and purring as the warm spring sun toasted his ebony belly. The cat reached out one paw to make contact with the little dragon and Kedrax closed his eyes with a contented sigh.

The two animals had become inseparable. Even though the feline was easily three times his size, Kedrax was fast catching up, and quickly gaining the upper hand in the relationship.

Bianca breathed in the vibrant floral scent deep and looked around her garden. Marigolds and petunias added a flush of color—but that was nothing to what her little terrace would be like in full summer.

Kedrax lifted his head. "Why don't you try something?"

She smiled down at him. "I thought you were asleep."

"You have to use your power sometime. Why not now to make your garden come to life the way you want it?"

I've survived this long without magic. When all her friends were practicing at school, she'd had to hang back and do things the old-fashioned way.

You're afraid.

"No I'm not. Hey, did you just say that in my head?"

Just like when you were younger.

He was right. The familiarity of it was strangely comforting. Bianca touched one of the rose bushes she'd pruned a few weeks ago. It would be nice to see the blooms. Up until a few days ago she'd never dreamed of putting her power into practice. Now, the energy flowed into her as she drew it from the sleepy dragon, and she began to spin the threads into a growth spell. As she touched the nearest bush, she opened her eyes again. The reddish-tinged new growth unfurled, enlarged, and darkened to green leaves. Tiny buds swelled and burst open with exquisite color and scent—smelling sweeter than they ever had before.

"Oh my." Her breath stuck in her throat.

The dragon's childish laugh tinkled in the spring sunshine. It felt like her whole body was smiling.

"More?" the tiny creature asked.

Yes more. *Much more.*

Shrubs and vines, trees, flowers and herbs. She wanted it all. While she could make things grow and bloom, she couldn't make things appear out of nothing. Magic didn't work that way. She closed her eyes and pictured what she wanted—a tropical garden paradise to rival the Garden of Eden. She went through in her mind what she'd do, palms here, orchids there, giant ferns with curly fronds. Energy tingled through her body as she practiced weaving the magic it would take to create the image of her little piece of heaven.

When she opened her eyes, her terrace had been transformed. Gone were the pansies and petunias, and in their place were the bird-of-paradise and lush ferns she'd imagined. Banana trees, palms, and leafy trees provided shady protection. Wisteria tangled in branches and along the supports. It looked just like the garden she'd always wanted. The sight of it unnerved her. She cut the energy off suddenly. The tree that had been twisting and growing seconds ago, withered and died. She fell back, a wave of exhaustion washing over her.

She glanced at Kedrax. His brilliant scales were dull and he seemed exhausted. "Are you all right?"

"You panicked," he said, closing his eyes. "It released a backwash of energy . . ."

Seeing his weakness, Bianca was horrified. The amount of power it took to do something like this was astounding, and yet she'd done it so easily . . . almost without thought, as the spell weaving theory came back so naturally and instinctively.

She'd have to rein it in future. Witches' familiars were conduits—used to draw in the thaumaturgical energy for use by the magic wielder. Careless handling of energy could damage, even kill, a familiar. He was just a baby.

"I'm so sorry," she said, hovering over the little dragon.

Vincent came over and gave Kedrax a nudge with his nose.

"It's okay," the dragon said, reaching out to the cat with what she was coming to think of as his arm. "My body is not yet strong enough to take that much backwash." He looked back up at her. "But it will be. The faster I mature, the faster I'll be able to reach my full potential, including my ability to handle the thaumaturgic energy."

The cat turned tail and disappeared.

"I'm sorry, I really didn't mean—"

"Can you please stop saying that? It's as much my fault. I have to learn to protect myself as much as you, and now we both know there are limitations." The little dragon's body quaked and shivered.

Bianca held his velvet soft body close to her chest. He felt a lot colder than he had a few moments ago. She carried him inside. "I'm so sorry," she whispered as she turned on the fireplace and cranked it up as high as it would go. She placed his cold little body on the mat she'd laid out just for him.

Kedrax sighed and closed his eyes. He was definitely

smiling. She sat back on the sofa just as Vincent raced in through the open doors carrying a large dead rat that he dropped in front of the pale dragon. Kedrax lifted his head and struggled to his feet, then ferociously fell upon the carcass. His color began to return as he fed, and Bianca sat back with relief and awe.

Then a loud banging at the front door startled her. She sat bolt upright and braced her hands on the edge of the sofa. "You'd better hide while I get this."

She switched off all the heating and turned to check that the dragon was gone. Both he and Vincent were nowhere to be seen, but a bloody mess stained the mat where the dragon had fed. She folded it over and kicked it under the sofa to clean up later.

The banging grew more urgent, and she peered through the peephole. McManus leaned one hand against her door frame and swayed.

What's he doing here?

He lifted his hand and banged again.

"Hold on." Bianca tied the belt sash on her robe a little tighter, then slid back the security chain and opened the door.

"About time," he slurred, falling through the threshold and landing face first on the floor.

12

Drunk and Disorderly

"DON'T YOU DARE barf on my carpet," Bianca said, kicking his feet out of the way to shut the door.

He mumbled some incoherent abuse into her carpet as she stood over him and tucked her hands under his arms, trying to lift him off the floor. His body went limp as he passed out. She let him go and he groaned as his nose smacked into the floor.

Serves him right, she thought with a perverse satisfaction.

Bianca sighed and shook her head. Better get him out of that soiled coat and off her floor. The strong stench of vomit hit her as she rolled him onto his back. He'd puked all over the front of his coat, but it was already half dry. She tugged at his left sleeve, slowly working it off his dead-weight arm, but it caught under his body. As she tried to roll him back onto his stomach again, he came to and staggered to his feet, slinging his arm around her shoulder and leaning against her. She threw her arm around his waist before they both went down.

He clumsily shook the coat off his arm and staggered with the effort. "Are you trying to get me into bed again, Sin?" His hand dropped to her ass and squeezed.

She pushed it away. "Not even in your best wet dream."

"I've had plenty of those." He moved dangerously close, lips puckered. "Some were even about you." The alcohol fumes were almost enough to make her pass out but she easily ducked.

"Good for you, McManus," she said. "Why don't I call you a cab?"

He pushed away and pulled his wallet out of his pocket. "I don't think I got any money."

Something slipped out and fell to the floor as he searched the wallet. He staggered forward to pick it up and dropped the wallet as he almost lost his balance.

"Now be a good boy and sleep it off," she said, catching him again before he fell.

She'd seen him like this a few times and knew to pay little attention to what he said. He pushed away again and tried to stand on his own, shaking his coat loose from the remaining arm and then fumbling with his belt. "C'mon, I can show you a good time."

He gave up trying to remove his pants and stumbled forward, reaching for her.

She ducked under his clumsy attempt and moved toward the sofa. He followed. If she could just get him to . . .

He overbalanced. With a little push in the right direction, he landed not so gently on the sofa, moving it back a foot. He struggled to regain his feet but she pushed him back down.

"Don't you love me?" he asked as he reached and snagged her around the waist.

"Not right now," she said, pushing his hands away. "You stink."

"Nobody loves me," he murmured in drunken self-pity as she wriggled out of his grasp. "They fired me."

"They only suspended you, McManus," she said, helping him to turn on his back and lifting his head to place a cushion under it.

He waved his hand dismissively. "Ahh, that's what they

say now. But what if they don't let me back? What'll I do
if I can't be a cop?" He looked up at her with genuine fear.

She stopped. He was a cop through and through. It's what
made him so good at his job. It'd kill him to lose it.

"It'll all blow over," she whispered, but his head lolled to
the side as he passed out again. Bianca slipped off his shoes
and went into the bathroom to wet a towel.

After cleaning him up a little, at least getting the sick off
his face and shirt, she pulled the throw rug from the back of
the sofa over him.

The small of her back ached. "Sleep well, you heavy son
of a bitch." And smiled as he threw his arm over his head
and snuggled into the sofa.

Bianca scooped up his coat from where McManus had
shaken it off. A vial of bright liquid fell out. She shook her
head and put the Neon Tears on the kitchen counter, then
picked up his wallet and the piece of paper that had fallen
out, which turned out to be an old newspaper clipping. The
edges were tattered, the ink blurring in the creases as if it'd
been unfolded and refolded many times.

FROM TRAGEDY, A HERO IS FORGED

The headline screamed above a photo of a preteen boy,
his face smudged with black. He held the hand of a young
girl, no more than six or seven. Her thumb was in her mouth
and tears marked tracks down her dirty face. One EMT held
an oxygen mask over the boy's face, while another treated
burns that looked to cover most of his body. Behind them,
firefighters battled a blazing building.

The thing that pulled at her most were the boy's eyes;
there was no mistaking that same haunted look he had to
this day.

"Oh McManus," she said softly, and reached out to smooth
his hair back. "Why didn't you tell me?"

As if answering her, McManus let out a loud snort and

rolled onto his side, his breathing quickly falling back into a steady rhythm. She'd had no idea he was one of the surviving orphans of the horrific fire that wiped out a special group of witches known as the Sisterhood.

Suddenly, so many things about him made sense. His utter lack of regard for authority, the drive to solve the case no matter what, and the constant emptiness he tried to hide, even from her.

In her own bedroom, she quickly changed into her pj's and slid into bed beside Kedrax, who lay on her pillow. She found it hard to sleep. The thought of what McManus had been through broke her heart. When Kedrax started to hum, she found herself nodding off as the dragon curled into the crook between her shoulder and her neck. His hum turned into a purr.

He must've picked that up from the cat . . .

BIANCA POURED STRONG black coffee into a mug and pushed the lever down on the toaster. She felt surprisingly rested, given the events of last night.

A groan floated up from the sofa. "Do you have to bang around so loudly?" McManus croaked, and sat up cradling his forehead with his hand.

"What, like this?" She picked up a saucepan from the dish drainer and banged it with a wooden spoon.

"You're an evil woman, you know that, Sin?" He crawled to his feet, looking around and patting his pockets, and then did a kind of half circle as he searched the floor.

"You looking for this?" she held up a glass vial with a tiny amount of phosphorescent blue liquid in the bottom.

His momentary relief quickly morphed into a frown. "You snooping through my pockets?" His accusation hung in the air like a foul smell. "Would you like to do a strip search too?"

"Like I told you last night—" The toast chose that minute to pop up. "Hell no, and here, take your fucking drugs."

She threw the vial at him as hard as she could, but he still snatched it out of the air with ease.

"And for your information, it fell out of your coat pocket." The blade dug deeply into the toast as she spread butter with a little more force than she intended.

McManus headed for the bathroom without another word, and Bianca bit into her mangled toast. It was all she had in the apartment since she hadn't had time to shop recently. Working in Oberon's team had her doing as many nights as days even though she and Cody were supposed to be the day shift.

She was on her second piece of toast when McManus wandered back down the corridor, his hair damp and his eyes much brighter. *Too bright.*

"Look, I'm sorry," he said softly. "You know what I'm like when I have a headache."

"Hung over, more like," she muttered, taking another vicious bite. "And there's no need to take it out on me. I was only trying to help."

"I know, and thanks for the bed . . . well, couch." He sighed. "Don't look at me like that, I have it under control. Okay?"

"Sure you do, just like your drinking," she replied. "And because all junkies have their addictions under control. Right?"

"I'm not a junkie," he growled.

Even he had to hear the lie in his statement, she thought as she placed more bread in the toaster with her free hand. "Look, I'm not here to judge. I just don't like seeing a friend do this to himself."

Just as she was about to take another bite, he snatched the toast out of her hand and shoved half of it in his mouth, giving her a cheeky wink.

"Hey."

"I know, and thank you." His eyes crinkled in the corners when he smiled. She didn't see it often enough.

She poured him a mug of coffee and handed it to him just as more toast popped.

He took a large swallow, his eyes closing in appreciation. "I hope I didn't behave too badly."

She looked up at him from under her eyebrows as she poured another cup for herself.

He huffed out a breath and rolled his eyes. "What did I do?"

"You tried to get me into bed," she said.

"You're kidding, right?"

She arched an eyebrow.

"Oh shit, I'm really sorry. Especially after last time."

"Was it that bad?" she asked, hurt that he found it so disappointing, even though she regretted it herself.

"I didn't mean it like that. Fuck. You know I don't really think of you that way."

She arched her brow even higher and dropped her chin. "That's not what you said when you had your hand on my ass."

Bianca had never seen him look so flustered and embarrassed. A blush crept up his cheeks to the top of his ears.

"Besides, never tell a woman you don't think of her 'that way.'" She grinned. "And never tell her you think of her that way either, especially if you're not involved. It's best just to keep your mouth shut."

"Oh fuck." McManus put down his toast untouched.

"Don't worry, I won't hold it against you," she said, and smiled. "Much. Come on, get some food into you. You'll feel better."

"Thank you," he mumbled.

She picked up her coffee and leaned back against the counter. "Why do you do it?"

"The drugs or the drinking?" he asked, looking directly at her again.

"Both, I guess."

He shrugged. "I don't know, sometimes to forget and sometimes to remember."

"Remember what? The something in your past that you're not telling me about?"

"It's not important," he said, avoiding her eyes. "Now what are we going to do about this case?"

"It's not going to work, not this time," she said. "So don't even try and change the subject."

"I don't know what you mean."

"Something fell out of your wallet too." She held up the newspaper clipping.

Blood drained from his face. "That's all in the past, let's leave it there."

"When you told me you grew up in an orphanage, I had no idea it was the Sanctum of the Sisterhood." She put her cup down. "Or that you were raised by witches."

Shutters dropped in his eyes. "It never came up."

This time she wasn't going to let it drop. "Fuck, McManus. You were there . . ." The words caught in her throat and she moved closer, touching his shoulder. "You were there at the end of the Sisterhood and their sanctum."

13

sanctum of death

WHEN MCMANUS CLOSED his eyes, he could still feel the heat of the flames, hear the terrified screams, smell stench of burning flesh. It haunted him now as much as it did when it happened almost twenty years ago.

He glanced at Bianca's sympathetic expression and moved away. His fingers ached from gripping the coffee mug too tightly. He didn't want pity from anyone, especially not her. He swiped up the newspaper clipping from the kitchen counter and shoved it into his pocket. As if that could shut away the pain.

"That kid in the picture," she said. "It's you."

He turned away. "The papers were ordered by the courts to protect our identities and keep our names out of it, but it didn't stop them from printing that one shot."

Bianca led him to the sofa and pushed him down gently. "I'll get you some more coffee."

The cup shook in his hand. "Don't suppose you have anything stronger?"

She placed her hands on her hips. He rarely saw her in jeans, without makeup and her professional mask. He liked it. She looked fresh, like a girl.

"I'm all out of wine, sorry."

There was no way he could tell her this without a little fortification.

"Are you sure you want to do this with your hangover?"

"There's no better cure."

"All right. I'll see what I can find," she said, throwing up her hands.

She disappeared behind the counter and he could hear her rummaging through her cupboards.

"Ah, perfect," she said aloud, and appeared with a bottle of dark green liquid. "But if we're going to do this, we have to do it right."

She handed him the bottle and returned to the kitchen.

"What's this?" he asked, pulling the cork stopper.

It was herbal-like, almost medicinal, and he upended the bottle to take a swig. It slid down his throat like broken glass yet coated his tongue with a thick liquorish taste.

God that tastes like shit. But a warm tingle spread out from the center of his chest.

Bianca returned carrying a tray with four small glasses and a bowl of sugar cubes, which she put on the table in front of him. "Hey!" She snatched the bottle away. "I said if we're going to do this, we do it right. I just need one more thing."

She went back and rattled through more cupboards. Moments later she returned carrying a strange looking contraption, a brass stand with little spigots and a glass bowl on top filled with ice and water. She placed it in the middle of the table.

"What the hell is that?" he asked.

"That is an absinthe fountain. And this is absinthe made from an old family recipe with anise, fennel, and wormwood grown in my mother's very own garden."

"Isn't it illegal?"

"Probably. Good absinthe is around seventy to eighty percent alcohol. This is the best kind—homemade. It's the wormwood that made it illegal—it's poisonous."

"Sin, you surprise me. I'd never have guessed you were into homemade illegal hooch."

"There's a lot you don't know about me, McManus," she said, filling two of the antique glasses with three fingers of the green spirit. "Anyway, my mother gave me this. Like I said, it's an old family recipe. Witches have been doing this for centuries, and we're going follow the old way, the proper way."

She took two slotted spoons from the back pocket of her jeans and laid one over each glass. On top of each spoon she placed a single cube of sugar and then positioned the glasses under the tiny fountain faucets. Water drops fell onto the sugar, dissolving it a little each time. As the cube melted, the green spirit slowly changed to a milky color.

"Everything is about ritual with you people," he said. "A man could die of thirst waiting."

"Ritual is everything to a witch." She glanced at him before returning her attention to the absinthe, regulating the water to drip at just the right rate. "Patience is a virtue. Anything good is worth waiting for."

"I'll try and remember that."

The silence dragged on for what seemed forever as the sugar cube totally dissolved and turned the liquid pale and cloudy.

Finally, she held out one of the glasses. "Here you go."

She set up another set of glasses before picking up hers.

"*À votre santé,*" she said, holding up her glass. "To your health."

"And yours." He closed his eyes and held his breath as he drank, but this time it tasted better—smoother, more subtle and slightly sweeter. "Mmm—not bad."

Bianca put her glass down and turned to him, all seriousness. This was the moment he'd been regretting.

"Tell me about it."

He had run from the memories for so long, it almost felt a relief to stop and think about them. He drained his glass before putting it next to hers. "The Sisterhood found me at their gates, wrapped in a woman's blue sweater, my umbilical cord still wet. A note was pinned to it with the words 'Lancelot McManus.' The sisters didn't know if it was my name or not, but that's what they called me."

"Lancelot?" she said, smiling with amusement.

"Go ahead, yuk it up."

The alcohol warmed his body and gave him the courage to keep going. Even if just for a little while. Maybe telling Bianca might help him rid himself of some of the demons haunting every sober moment.

"Life with them was good. Until . . ." He looked at his hands, searching for the words, but it was probably best to start at the beginning. He looked at the water dripping on the sugar cube over the absinthe and sighed. "The sisters took in orphans when required. They were devout, and didn't use magic."

Bianca nodded. "The Sisterhood believed that the best way to honor the Mother and their devoutness was to give up magic use."

She reminded him of the Sisterhood, a witch without magic. "Because most were familial witches, they wouldn't allow any animals in the Sanctum, in case they accidentally bonded. I remember when one of the other kids found a homeless dog with a litter of puppies. We hid them in the dormitory, but Sister Morgan found them and had them taken away. Some of the younger kids cried for a week."

"They must've thought that was cruel," Bianca said, glancing at a black cat cleaning itself on the kitchen windowsill.

He shrugged. "Not really. We knew the rules and it was never meant to be a punishment. The sisters never allowed animals within the Sanctum, pure and simple. Sister Morgan was just as heartbroken as the children."

"So what happened?" she asked, taking a sip from her glass.

"The sisters were gentle and good and kind. They took great care of us. When I was about thirteen, there were eleven kids in the orphanage, including me. I was the oldest and had been there the longest, so I could sense the undercurrent of tension in the sisters. We were restricted from going outside the Sanctum without supervision. Two sisters began watching over us during the day, and then one night . . ."

A lump formed in his throat, choking the words. He swallowed. "I woke to the smell of smoke." It was as clear in his mind today as that night.

"We can stop if you want to," she said, taking his hand in her warm, comforting ones.

He shook his head, trying to get the words out. Bianca handed him the remainder of her own drink. He gave a quick nod of thanks and drained it. The cloudy spirit went down as smooth as honey. His head started to feel light. With a little more fortification, he continued.

"I climbed out of bed. The smoke was everywhere, and I woke the older kids to organize the little ones up while I ran to fetch Sister Morgan. She was our dorm mother, the one who got up for the kids who had nightmares. But her room was empty." He swiped a hand across his face and looked at her. "I was so young and I didn't know what to do. I should've gone looking for the sisters. If I had, then maybe they would've survived."

She sat beside him on the sofa and squeezed his hand. "But you saved the kids instead."

The words lodged in his throat as the memory of those kids hit hard and fast. Their terrified faces all turned to him, huge eyes looking for answers. Answers he didn't have. He was just as terrified as the other children. But he was the oldest. The next eldest, Gavin, was eleven, and was just as scared. Tiny Isabelle, who looked younger than her eight years, was twice as brave as the rest of them and kept the younger ones calm.

"They would've died without you," Bianca whispered, as if reading his thoughts.

The derisive laugh escaped before he could stop it. "Maybe?"

"No maybe," she admitted. "I studied all the reports, though your names were left out of them. From all accounts, the children would've been trapped if you hadn't led them to safety. They would've died, just like the sisters."

He could hear the frightened sobs as they made their way out of the dormitory, the terrified screams as they came across Sister Morgan's body, her throat cut and blood pooling around head, frightening them. Memory after memory assailed him all at once. The cracking of burning timber crashing around them as they ran out of the building; the sight of Sister Elaine jumping from the fifth story window, flames engulfing her nightgown and the sizzling pop of her eyeballs exploding as the fire consumed her broken body where she lay in full view of the children.

He'd tried to open the door to reach the rest of the sisters inside, but the heat was unbearable as the flames seared his skin and the overpowering stench of his own flesh burning stopped him. It all became too much. He needed to make it stop.

He reached for the bottle of absinthe on the table and guzzled several mouthfuls before Bianca was able take it away, pulling him against her in a fierce hug.

McManus became aware of her warmth. "The sisters, they all died." His voice was muffled against her shoulder, and he clutched her with a tightness that bordered on desperation. "I tried to save them, but I couldn't. I was too afraid."

"McManus, you were a thirteen-year-old kid. You witnessed more than any kid should have, you helped nearly a dozen other kids to safety and you were suffering severe burns." She stroked his hair. "You did more than I could possibly imagine."

"But it wasn't enough."

"There was nothing more you could've done."

He wiped at his damp cheeks, feeling a little stupid. "Fuck

me." It'd been almost a decade since he last cried over the Sisterhood, and the tears surprised him. He drew back and looked at Bianca. She was so close, so soft, and so warm. Her moist eyes were filled with pride, not pity. He wiped away a tear with the pad of his thumb and moved closer. Her lips parted.

He stopped and pulled back before he did something stupid, and caught what looked like a flash of regret in her eyes.

Clearing his throat, he looked away. "When I became a cop, I looked into the police records leading up to the fire and found some strange incidents the sisters reported. Spot fires, stones thrown through windows, threats against the sisters and the orphans. But no one would listen. Even the report on the final fire said it was an unfortunate accident caused by a gas leak. But the sisters never used the gas. No one believed us about Sister Morgan either. They said it was just the trauma of everything that happened."

"That's why you became a cop?"

He nodded. "And I found out that a rival coven corporation was trying to buy the land. They purchased it for a song after the fire and put up a housing development. Nothing I turned up could prove they were involved with what happened to the Sanctum, but I know they were. I know it. *Fucking* witches."

He looked down at his hands, which were no longer shaking. "I became a cop so I could make sure this didn't happen to anyone else."

"Good ambition. Impossible, but still a good ambition." Bianca smiled and the tension went out of him. "You were burned pretty badly."

"Turned out to be not as bad as they first thought. When I was admitted to the hospital, they diagnosed severe second, third, and fourth degree burns to seventy percent of my body. I healed too quickly for that."

"What about the other children?" she asked.

"By the time I was discharged, the others had been sent to different foster homes and institutions. Me and Gavin ended up at the Cedar's Home for Boys."

Bianca sucked back her breath. "Oh, McManus, I'm so sorry."

He hated thinking of that place. "I was there three years, until just before I was sixteen when I met the cop who saved my life. He and his wife took me in. Gavin was smart and only in Cedar's for six months. Last I heard, he's changed his name to Wayne Gray and is some high-flying lawyer type on the West Coast. I lost touch with most of the others. But Isabelle . . ."

Sweet, brave little Isabelle . . . Her broken body surrounded by candles and other thaumaturgic paraphernalia.

"That little girl from the newspaper clipping?" she asked.

He nodded. "When I was fresh out of the police academy, I attended a disturbance call." The image of her body in that fleabag motel was burnt into his brain forever. "They weren't witches, just wannabes. When I found her in that room, her innocence had been stolen, her face all swollen and mottled with bruises; her naked body abused, raped, and stabbed over a hundred times."

"Oh, McManus," she said, squeezing his hand. "I'm so sorry."

"I saved her once, but I couldn't save her when she really needed me."

The memory of her death reminded him of their latest case. There'd been so much blood. Yet the murder scene of the first eviscerated girl had been surprisingly clean. The coroner surmised she'd been murdered somewhere else and dumped.

"Hey," he said, sitting forward. "Do you think that first murder would've had as much black magic as the last?"

"Probably, why?" Bianca asked.

"If the body had been moved, would there be any way

of tracking back to the original kill site using the residual energy?"

The white witch's eyes widened, catching where he was going. "It's very possible, but I'd have to visit the scene to see."

"You doing anything right now?"

14
Dark Secrets

BIANCA FOLLOWED MCMANUS into the yawning entrance under the old rail bridge. She knew people lived down here, but like others, she'd chosen not to think about it. Someone coughed; there was a distinct rustle of plastic bags; a child cried and a newborn howled.

"My Goddess, McManus, there's children down here."

The detective didn't answer.

"How could they live down here with babies? It's unhealthy, unsanitary, they should go—"

McManus turned on her, his eyes narrowed in the glow of the flashlight. "Go where, Bianca, where the fuck do you think they should go?" His voice dropped to a harsh whisper. "A homeless shelter? They're overflowing as it is and can't cope with more. Or maybe they should check into a cheap hotel full of junkies, hookers, and pimps. Surely that will be safer by far. But even that takes money they just don't have. Or maybe it would be best to just ship them off somewhere else—make them someone else's fucking problem. Do you really think they want to be down here in the cold and dark?"

"No," she said, stepping back. "I'm sorry, I just—"

"You know nothing until you've had to live like this."

A child coughed nearby. A woman with haunted eyes peered out cautiously when he scratched on the outside of the makeshift cardboard hut. When she saw McManus, she slid the cardboard "door" open some more.

"How you doing, Maria?" he asked.

"All right thanks, Detective," she said as a little girl, about two or three, dressed in a vest and a nappy, climbed into her mother's lap. The woman opened her coat and wrapped the child against her so only her head was visible between her breasts.

"Hey there sweetness," McManus said, gently tapping the toddler under the chin with his finger.

The woman smoothed down the little girl's dark curls and caught sight of Bianca. Her smile slipped and her eyes grew cagey. Bianca realized the woman was some sort of Animalian, probably canian.

McManus looked over his shoulder at her. "Don't worry, she's with me."

"She's not with Children Services, is she?" the woman asked.

"No."

Maria cast another suspicious glance in her direction and then turned to McManus. "You here about Angel again?"

"That's right." McManus squatted on his haunches to meet her at eye level and placed the backpack he carried on the ground. "Do you remember anything more?"

The homeless mother hugged her daughter closer and shook her head. "Sorry."

"You said Angel hadn't been here long, and you didn't realize she was pregnant. Did she mention anything about witchcraft or magic?"

"Yes." Maria frowned in concentration. "I overheard her talking to Fast Jimmy a couple of days before she was killed. She told him she'd pay him back all the money she owed just as soon as she got her first paycheck from that magic shop he sent her to."

"What magic shop?" McManus asked.

She shrugged her shoulders. "Sorry, I didn't hear that bit."

"That's okay, you've been very helpful." He reached out and ruffled the little girl's curls. "You be good for your mommy, okay?"

She smiled around the thumb and then coughed.

"Thanks again, Maria," he said, coming to his feet.

"Wait." Bianca dumped her bag and peeled off her coat. "Take this for the little one."

Maria's eyes darted to McManus, who gave her a slight nod, then she reached out and took it. "Thank you, miss."

With a quick nervous smile from the mother, the two of them disappeared back into their cardboard home. The detective slung the pack over his shoulder again and steered her away, moving farther into the tunnel.

"That was a thing good you did," he said softly after a moment. "If you'd offered the coat to Maria for herself, she would've refused. But these people can't be too proud when it comes to their kids."

"I just had no idea they lived like this," she said, looking around. She kept the flashlight tilted to the ground, but her eyes had adjusted enough to see shapes. Then there was more coughing, more moans and snoring. She turned to find him staring at her.

"Okay, what now?" she asked.

He held up a finger. "One sec." He darted over to a lump of clothing by the wall.

"Hey Harry," he whispered. "I brought something for you and old Mae." He pulled a bottle of cheap liquor from his backpack.

The clothing moved and Bianca realized it was an old man lying on his side, wearing more clothing than she'd seen any one person wear. His lined face split into a toothless grin when he saw the bottle, but then it disappeared.

"Old Mae ain't here no more, son," he croaked.

McManus put his hand on the old man's shoulder. At least

it was around where his shoulder should be, but it was hard to tell with all that padding.

"I'm sorry, when did she pass?" the detective asked sadly.

"Hell, she ain't dead, county took her." The toothless grin returned. "Kicking and screaming she was too."

McManus hung his head for a moment and smiled. "So she'll finally get that bad leg seen to. You enjoy this whiskey, but save some for her when she gets back?"

The old man's gummy smile widened as McManus gave him one last pat on the shoulder and rose to join Bianca.

"Harry and old Mae have been down here a long time, more than most. Occasionally the county gets them into somewhere, but eventually they end up back down here. I don't think they like being told what to do." They glanced at where Harry now sat, gesturing to someone to come join him. "There's communities like this all over New York; some are a mishmash of humans and parahumans like this one, while others are a little more exclusive."

"Should you really be giving them alcohol?" she asked. "I mean, won't that just make the problem worse?"

McManus sighed. "I know it seems wrong—but these people have nothing. A bottle can brighten a few hours, and Harry gets the DTs real bad if he goes too long without." He hitched the pack higher on his shoulder. "Besides, there but for the grace . . . well, I'm sure you get the picture."

She did.

Bianca heaved her own bag on her shoulder. "Let's take a look at this crime scene."

McManus took her farther into the tunnel. A faint light came from the opening at the other end, just up ahead. They could easily have come in that way, but then McManus wouldn't have been able to talk to the "residents," and she got the impression that was just as important for him. There'd been genuine warmth in his expression, especially for the old man and the little girl.

"You come down here to help these people often, don't you?" she said.

He shrugged his shoulders. "I do what I can." Then he turned to walk toward the back of the tunnel and across the tracks.

She watched him go for a few seconds before following. The man was such a contradiction in terms. Drug user, alcoholic, and yet he took the time to help some homeless bums most people refused to see. She'd known him for years, but after tonight she was starting to think she didn't really know him at all.

Stretched and tattered remains of yellow crime tape hung from the support pillars about three hundred feet from where the squatters camped. The faint remnants of dark energy still tainted the air and ground where the body was discovered. She squatted to open her black instrument bag and grabbed the thaumaturgic scanner. Now that she knew more about McManus's past, she wasn't about to let on that she could wield power. No, she'd do this the usual way tonight. Even though she could sense the traces of energy that felt identical to the other crime scenes, she scanned the site with the instrument.

The readout screen lit up the tunnel with a cold blue light. She fiddled with the knobs until she got the readings right and then looked up at McManus. "We're good to go."

She held the reader in front and followed the readings. The signal stopped and she turned around until she caught it again.

McManus scooped up her bag, shouldered his own pack as he took the flashlight from her and gave a nod. The signal of the black spell moved away from the unconventional community and out onto the railway tracks. A rumble announced the imminent arrival of a train. The horn blasted from behind the bright mono headlight as the squeal of metal wheels on metal rails set her teeth on edge and they waited as the hulking train clattered passed.

The thaumaturgic signature led them along the line and back to the city streets. She lost it a couple of time, but not the sensation; her sensitivity to magic had been enhanced since she bonded with Kedrax.

The trail led through back alleys.

"You'd think someone must've seen something," she said to McManus. "There are some areas we've passed that are very public,"

"People only see what they want to see. Besides, there aren't too many people about now. We haven't seen a soul. I've been wondering why they just didn't dispose of her with magic."

"I was thinking about that. It's not as easy as you think to destroy living tissue, not even when it's dead. I think since this was the first time they used the 'black,' they probably didn't have the control over it that they have now. If they used their own magic, it would've left trace evidence for me to track. Whoever's doing this knows the magic signature is unreadable."

The black trace signature stopped at a door in a dark alley. Nausea hit her so suddenly, with a force that took her breath away and made her knees week. She reached out a hand to steady herself but stumbled. McManus caught her.

"You okay, Sin?" he asked.

"Yes." It came out in a hoarse whisper. "It's strong here."

He stilled and brought the flashlight up to examine the store. "This is it."

Bianca glanced at the silvered letters on the back door: WILLOW'S OCCULT AND APOTHECARY. "I'd say we just found Angel's magic shop."

15

trinkets, charms, and talismans

"I want to take a look around the front," McManus said.

"Okay, I'll come with you."

They followed the alley back around to the street. Willow's was the third store down.

McManus shone the flashlight through the window, only to see shelves of books and trinkets. "If we look inside I bet we'll find the murder scene. But we'll have to be careful." He stepped back and looked up.

"That's not likely to happen now with you suspended and me off the case."

"Follow me," he said, and walked back down the street to the alley. "Are you coming?" he asked when she didn't move.

"You're not going to do something stupid, are you?"

"Probably." He fished inside his pocket, pulled out a couple pairs of latex gloves and handed her a one.

"You carry gloves in your pocket?"

He smiled. "You don't?"

She followed him around to the back door again.

"I'd bet money that window up there isn't locked. Should

be big enough for someone small." McManus bent his knees and clasped his fingers together. "Here, I'll give you a boost."

"No, no, no," she said, backing away and shaking her head. "I'm not going in there."

"Do you want to find out what happened or not?" He put his hands on his hips. "You're the only one that will fit."

"We could just report this."

"Fuck that. That jumped-up asshole from VCU can find this out for himself. I want to find out what happened to Angel and the others."

He was right. She wanted to see this through too. "Okay."

Bianca put the scanner in her pack and placed her boot in the cradle of his hands. He lifted her easily up to the window, but it wouldn't budge. She closed her eyes and concentrated, reaching out with her mind. The lock clicked open and the window slid up. She hauled herself through the gap and into the store's bathroom, then braced herself for an alarm to go off, but nothing happened. Could be a silent alarm. If so, she'd better hurry, as they wouldn't have much time. She cautiously opened the bathroom door.

Cartons and crates were stacked in the room beyond, and the door that led out to the back alley. She unlocked it for McManus, who picked up her bag and passed it to her before entering the shop.

He went into the office to the right of the back room and after a moment came out. "There's no CCTV or alarm that I can find. Strange for this day and age. Let's take a look in the shop."

Bianca pulled the thaumaturgic scanner from her bag and turned it on. The readings were stronger as she moved toward the front of the shop.

Trinkets, crystals, potions, talismans, and new age paraphernalia, all of it completely harmless commercial crap for human witch wannabes.

"This isn't one of our magic shops," she said.

McManus turned. "What do you mean?"

"None of this has any power. The potions are flavored sugar water, the talismans are uncharmed trinkets made in China, and all these ingredients are innocuous."

"You've lost me," he said, stashing a few trinkets into his bag. "Why would the trail lead here if it isn't a place of power?"

"What *are* you doing?" she asked.

"Making it look like a break in."

"O . . . kay." She shook her head.

"So this stuff is for saps," he said, knocking some of the potions onto the floor, shattering them. "Fakes to trick the gullible." He smashed a few more.

"Not exactly. Some of this is real enough, but for a potion to succeed, it must be mixed by a practicing thaumaturgist. Even if a human were to mix a preparation to precise directions, it wouldn't work. And," she said looking around, "no self-respecting thaumaturgist would be seen dead in a store like this."

"So is it the right one or not?" McManus asked, getting more impatient.

"There's still a black magic presence coming from somewhere in the store."

She moved the thaumaturgic scanner around. She didn't sense much until she came to a bookcase filled with harmless books humans bought, like the *Moron's Guide to Spellcasting* and *101 Best Love Potions*.

"McManus," she hissed.

"What?" he said, searching through stuff on the shelves, not even looking at her.

She placed a hand on her hip. "Come here."

His eyebrows rose as he stopped what he was doing and joined her.

She touched a bookcase set next to the wall. "There's something behind here."

He tried to shove it aside, but it seemed stuck firmly to the floor.

"Here, let me." She ran her fingers over the shelves, searching for some sort of trigger. In the thin gap between the back of the bookcase and the wall she hit upon what felt like a latch, and a jolt shot up her arm.

"We should get out of here," McManus said. "Now."

She felt it too. An overwhelming urge to be somewhere else, but . . . "Wait."

The spell was complex, though it didn't have the same signature as the murderer's. She didn't even know where to start unweaving it.

I'm here. Kedrax's voice entered her head.

With the dragon's presence, her mind cleared and her training returned. It was enough to make unweaving the spell possible. Soon the urgent feeling to leave fled.

"What the fuck was that?" McManus asked.

"The reason they don't need security alarms." Bianca searched for any other security spells they might have inadvertently triggered, but there didn't seem to be any. The arrogance of them. Her fingers flicked the latch and the bookcase swung open like a door.

Images of the most vile things flooded her mind. She fought to breathe and staggered back, as she threw up a defensive spell around them both and she slammed the door shut before everything faded.

ARE YOU OKAY? A worried voice echoed in Bianca's mind.

"Kedrax?"

I felt your pain.

"Who is Kedrax?" McManus's voice asked from the darkness surrounding her.

Bianca opened her eyes and blinked several times. Everything came back into focus and the pounding in her head receded a little more. She turned to find McManus's ice blue eyes mere inches from her face. "I'm sorry?"

"You frightened the living daylights out of me, you know?" His tone was hoarse with concern, and he brushed her left cheek with his thumb, just like he had last night when he wiped away her tears. A tingling warmth flooded her cheeks and made her stomach flip.

"You and me both," she croaked, sitting up.

"Don't do it again," he said, the tightness around his eyes easing a little.

She found herself on the shop counter. McManus must've carried her.

"So who is Kedrax?" he asked again.

"Um," she said, thinking fast. "He's my new . . . cat. I thought I was at home and heard him meow."

"I only saw that big black one."

She placed her hand on her head to try to stop the world from spinning again. "He's shy."

"Careful." He wrapped both hands around her waist to keep her from falling off the counter. "What the fuck happened?"

"There was dark thaumaturgic energy trapped behind the bookcase doorway. I wasn't prepared for it, but I'll be okay in a minute."

"It really hit you that hard." His face was so close to hers, his breath brushed her cheek.

She closed her eyes and breathed in his musky scent. It was warm and comforting. "Do you ever think of the time we . . ." She dropped her eyes from his face. "You know." *Where had that come from?*

His hands softened against her waist. "To be honest, we were so drunk I hardly remember."

"Oh!" she said.

"But that doesn't mean I don't think about what we could do," he whispered next to her ear.

Her cheeks warmed.

McManus dropped his hands and stood back. "How come other witches don't feel that dark energy the way you do?"

She tried to squash her disappointment at his obvious

change of subject. "The Sins have a long history of being sensitives, something to do with the cubii blood. My mother is one of the most famous. A talent she passed onto me, thankfully. It helped me to calibrate the forensic thaumaturgic equipment I've developed."

She took a deep breath and held it in her lungs. Surrounding McManus and herself in a pure white energy field, she protected them from the dark thaumaturgic essence. He wouldn't even know she was doing it. *I hope.*

With Kedrax's comforting presence in her mind, she jumped from the counter. Her bag was on the floor where she must've dropped it, and she lifted it over her back and put both arms through the straps. "Okay, let's see what's in there."

"Are you sure?"

No. What she really wanted to do was go home and bury her head under her blankets. "I have to find out." With hidden rooms and magic locks, not to mention that much dark energy, it couldn't be good. "I'm more prepared now."

"Right," McManus said, unclipping his shoulder holster and pulling out his gun.

"I thought you handed that in."

He grinned, his ice blue eyes crinkling at the corners under his thick blond eyebrows. "It's my spare." The smile slid from his face as it set in a mask of concentration, then he gave her one quick incline of his head. "Let's go."

She opened the secret doorway again. This time when the dark energy flowed toward her, she could almost see it, but it washed over and around the protective shell she'd set up, leaving them untouched.

"Okay," she said aloud, and switched on the flashlight.

"Here, I'll go first," McManus said, gently pushing past her.

Just beyond the opening, a staircase led down into the darkness. As the detective took the first step, light burst into life on either side of them, negating the need for the flashlight. Sconces attached to the wall burned with a magical luminescence, marking the progress of their descent and pushing back the darkness.

"What the fuck is happening?" McManus asked over his shoulder.

"It's just an automatic response to our presence." Unease stirred in the pit of her stomach.

"This isn't right, it shouldn't be this simple to just walk in here," he said, as if reading her mind.

"Hmm . . ." She swallowed the knot of fear in her throat. "Just be very careful how you go, and if you get a sudden feeling that something is wrong, run."

McManus's brow furrowed in concentration and his steps became more cautious. He stopped as he reached the bottom step, and held her behind him with an outstretched hand as he pointed the gun into the room. Everything was veiled in darkness, except for the lights behind them on the stairwell. Bianca pushed his arm down and he let her past. As her foot hit the floor, the large room flooded with light, momentarily blinding her.

16
magic shop of horror

NEVER BEFORE HAD Bianca seen such an abomination or smelled anything so vile. Everything needed to practice the dark arts was stacked, hung, or piled around the dingy underground store. Her stomach churned as she looked at the jars containing the fetuses of different creatures, from fish to bird to mammal, but worst were the tiny human babies in bottles.

This was the real magic store, not the fake one above. An illegal black magic store.

Books filled the shelves to the left, heavy ancient tomes both in size and content. Some were even bound in what could only be human skin, while others were newer hand-bound texts. An archway led off to the side, and she moved through it into the next room.

A long altar stood at the far end, painted in the dark castings of dried blood. Beside the altar sat a large jar with a fully developed female human fetus preserved in fluid. It looked fresh, but it was difficult to tell from where she stood.

Is it the victim's missing baby?

A large banner with reddish brown symbols in an upside-down pentagram painted in blood hung behind the altar.

"I'd say this is where the girl was killed," she said over her shoulder, not taking her eyes off the banner.

McManus joined her. "What is this place?"

"A shrine of obscenity," she spat. "This is the blackest of the black. The pentagram is the symbol of protection, and an upside down one means the opposite. Each point had one of the five castes of magic—Natural, Familial, Divination, Focal, and Necromantic—all upside down in their darkest forms. The symbol in the middle should be of the Unari, the first ones, but it'd been replaced by the sign of the Dark Brethren."

"The same as at the murders."

"Yes, they're an ancient race of nasties, mystically imprisoned by our ancestors who are now trying to get back to our world by corrupting parahumans on this side to spill enough blood in their name."

"You're kidding me, right?" he asked.

She shrugged. "Afraid not."

McManus took out his cell. "As much as it shits me, I'll have to let that fucker from VCU know about this. Damn, no signal." As the words left his lips, the banner burst into flames.

"Fuck," he said.

Bianca ran back into the other room. "Double fuck."

The stairwell leading out of the underground room was ablaze. Books started disappearing from the shelves, evaporating into thin air. Flames erupted in their place and other dark magic objects started disappearing.

"What the fuck's happening?" he yelled above the roar of the fire.

"It's a trap. They mean to kill us while they magically move their inventory and destroy the evidence."

"How did they know we were here?"

"They had a security system after all," she yelled back, the roar of the flames making it difficult to hear even her own words. "A magical one."

He looked around the room as flames burned higher. "We have to get out of here."

"But how?" She glanced around. "The staircase is burning."

He swept her up in his arms and strode toward the stairs. Smoke filled her lungs, scorching her throat and throwing her senses into confusion. She coughed and gasped, trying to draw on magic, but disorientation muddled her senses. She looked around for an escape route in the chaos of flames and heat. A coughing fit took over and she struggled to draw breath.

"Hold on," he yelled as he got to the stairs.

The blaze had burned the first few steps, but he leapt over them. Bianca managed to gather enough of her senses to give him some extra lift so he could land on the lowest stair that the fire hadn't yet reached. She looked down. The wood cracked dangerously, the flames reaching for him. McManus's pants had caught, the fire burning up his legs, but he made another leap as the stair beneath them caught and collapsed. The heat sucked what was left of the air around them. He took the rest of the stairs two at a time until they reached the top, only to find the secret entrance closed fast.

Bianca wrapped her arms tighter around his neck as he slammed into the solid wood. It remained sealed tight. She pulled it together just enough to draw on the last of her reserves. As he geared to slam into the door again, she reached out and pushed with her mind. This time the bookcase door flung open. McManus toppled through to the floor, dragging her with him. Bianca managed to hook the bookcase with her foot and kick it shut before the fire escaped after them.

She sat up quickly and removed her jacket to smother the flames on his legs.

"Thanks," McManus said when the fire was out, sitting up and leaning back on his hands.

Her lungs still burned and another fit of coughing over came her. "No, thank you," she said when she was finally able to draw breath. "We would've died down there."

"Well we didn't. Now let's get out of here before help arrives and finds us." He climbed to his feet and held out his hand.

The room began to heat, and flames suddenly burst through the floor, cutting off the back of the shop.

"Quick, out the front," he said, dragging her to her feet.

As she and McManus ran through the front door, he stumbled and fell. Bianca stooped to catch him or at least break his fall. With the amount of flames she had put out, she knew his burns would be extensive.

She managed to push him out the front door as part of the roof collapsed behind them.

17

into the underbelly

SOMETHING EXPLODED IN the store behind her. "Come on, let's get out of here," McManus said, hauling Bianca to her feet. "Before the emergency services arrive."

"Your bag is in there," she said, feeling the familiar weight on her back.

"It'll burn with the rest of it, I'm afraid." He glanced over his shoulder. The flames from the building reflected in his eyes, making it look for a brief moment that they burned with an inner fire. Wailing sirens grew closer. "Time to go," he said, sweat slicking his brow.

"We have to get you to a hospital and get those burns seen to."

"I'm in no pain," he said, hiking up his tattered trouser leg.

"But your legs were on fire, I put out the flames myself."

The skin below was smooth and bare as if the hairs on his leg had been seared off, and that was all. "Ever since the fire at the Sanctum, I knew I had some resistance to fire. But I had no idea it was this much."

"It's miraculous," she whispered, looking closer at his legs in the glow of the streetlight.

Her phone beeped with a text message in her backpack.

She dropped the bag to the pavement and pulled the cell out of the side pocket.

"It's Oberon," she said to McManus. "He wants me to get those reports finished."

"Why don't you grab a cab, and I'll go back to where I left my car down by the tracks. I'll catch up later to work out what we do with this lead."

"Lead?"

"Fast Jimmy. He got Angel that job, he might know who really owns this store."

BIANCA FINISHED HER last email, hit the send button and wondered where McManus had gone. She'd been trying to call him, but his cell phone was probably in the bag destroyed by the fire.

A familiar knock at her front door made her smile. She closed the laptop and crossed to answer it.

"About time you . . ." Her words trailed off when she found a well-dressed man in a black suit and camel coat standing in her doorway. "Sorry, I though you were . . . McManus?"

He took off the dark glasses and grinned. "Yep." He looked good, real good.

"Why the fancy dress?" she asked. "Are you going to an early Halloween party?"

His grin slipped. "Something like that. Get dressed in something tight and sleazy. We're going down to Sin Town."

Bianca swallowed as McManus crossed her threshold. Sin Town was one place she'd managed to avoid her entire career, and she didn't relish going there now. "Why?"

"That's Fast Jimmy's territory. If we're going to find him, it's the best place to start. And I can't exactly go in there as a cop. Too many people know me."

"Okay," she said. "I'll see what I can find."

Her wardrobe consisted of conservative work clothes, jeans, and T-shirts. She really didn't have anything sleazy. Except . . .

She drifted down to the other end and the clothes her
mother had bought for her to come out into society. She
hadn't worn any of it. Now, she pulled out a black leather
corset with red lace trim, a pair of knee-high vinyl boots,
and a floor length multilayered red net petticoat.

McMANUS WAITED IN the living room while she changed.
The black cat he'd seen yesterday jumped onto the kitchen
windowsill and eyed him suspiciously.

"Whatchya lookin' at, puss?" he said.

The cat's eyes narrowed and his one ear flattened against
his head as he hissed. McManus was a little taken aback.
Animals usually liked him.

He caught movement out of the corner of his eye as something jumped onto the terrace behind a bush. *Probably a
gull or a pigeon.* The cat leapt down and raced toward it.

"Look out birdie, here comes the big bad pussy cat," he
whispered to himself, and chuckled, though the cat didn't
appear to be in stalk mode.

It disappeared into the lush undergrowth of the tropical
terrace garden, and he wondered how Bianca managed to
get some of the plants to grow, especially here in New York.

The cat raced out from under one plant and disappeared
behind another. Two seconds later something followed. A
lizard. A giant lizard.

"A giant blue lizard?" he asked the empty room.

"What did you say?"

He hadn't heard her return. "You have a—" McManus
looked up and completely forgot about the lizard. "Well . . ."
He plastered on a smile to cover his loss for words. His mouth
was drier than a desert storm even though his skin felt slick
with sweat.

"Will this do?" she asked, smoothing down the front of
the corset.

He couldn't even think for the moment, let alone talk, only
nod like an idiot. Her whiter than white hair was piled on her

head, spiked with a kind of messy punk chaos. Smoky dark makeup enhanced her pale blue eyes, and the scarlet tint on her lips highlighted their lush fullness.

A black lace choker surrounded her slender neck, with strings of black pearls forming shiny loops against her throat. The leather corset hugged her sumptuous figure, pushing her breasts up into magnificent cleavage. Under the corset, she wore a red net skirt down to her knees at the back and so short at the front it barely covered her. A red lace garter belt held up a pair of black lace stockings that highlighted her smooth pale thighs. To finish off the ensemble, she'd added a pair of chunky black knee-high goth style boots with silver buckles up the side.

She had a kind of edgy sleaze crossed with an almost angelic innocence, as if the perverseness highlighted her purity. In Sin Town, men would pay a fortune for her. He'd wanted something to divert attention from himself, and this was definitely going to do it.

"Um . . ." He cleared his throat. "Yeah, great. Perfect."

"Really?" She looked down at herself, self-conscious doubt written all over her face. "You sure it's not too much?"

She has no idea. "No, not at all. But we'd better get going if we want to get there before night fall."

SIN TOWN—THE DARK underbelly of the city—infested with the worst of both human and parahuman society. If it was illegal or immoral, Sin Town was where to find it.

Every now and then Vice would put together a task force and raid. The place shut down then, so all they managed to bag were a few minor drug dealers and whores, nothing more. Then Sin Town would be back in business within hours of the police's departure.

"Do exactly as I say," he said to Bianca. "And stick close to me."

"Okay," she said, looking nervous.

Riddle Street, the unofficial border between Sin Town and

the rest of the city. As soon as McManus stepped into the street, he could feel the corruption in the air. He could feel the eyes on them. Eyes from the street, eyes from the shadows, eyes of the damned.

Gang members leaned in apparent nonchalance, carefully scrutinizing all who came and went. Hookers stood on the corner dressed in bands of scant material, barely covering the flesh they peddled, while their pimp held court nearby in a fancy colorful suit. Drug dealers surreptitiously passed little baggies of chemical fun in exchange for cold hard cash. This was Sin Town.

The pimp pushed away from the wall and watched them, his hungry gaze drifting to Bianca. McManus took her arm and staked his ownership. She was his property and his alone. The pimp got the message and returned to his usual nonchalant stance. But McManus could still feel his hungry eyes on them as they walked away.

"Stay very close," he whispered. "You're a very valuable commodity in this town." *I just hope we don't have to fight our way out of here later.*

"Where're we going?" she asked quietly.

"The shadow arena."

"Why?"

"You're not supposed to be asking questions, you're supposed to follow me submissively."

"You did this on purpose." She tugged her skirt down in front. "I feel like every man is looking at me."

They are. He felt the comforting weight of his gun under his arm. "There's a big match on. Jimmy loves the games."

The entrance to the arena stood quiet and unassuming. "Are you sure this is the right place?" Bianca looked dubiously down the darkened tunnel.

"You'll soon see for yourself, but be prepared, it can get very ugly." He led her into the darkness.

They came out in a sewer junction where a beefy guy stood with his arms crossed.

"What's the password?" he growled.

"Ben Franklin times two." McManus held out two crisp new one hundred dollar bills folded in half.

The bouncer looked around then took the money. He folded his arms again, jerking his head toward the muffled rumble coming from behind a curtained entrance. McManus entwined his fingers in hers and led her behind the curtain.

Before they reached the end of the tunnel, he turned her to him, her face just visible in the glow coming from the exit up ahead. "Now listen. Do everything I say, without question. Keep your head down and don't look directly at anyone. Speak to no one. You must act like my property. If they're looking at you, they aren't looking at me."

She squared her shoulders, her mouth thinned in disapproval.

"Maybe this wasn't a bright idea after all," he said. He should've left her behind when he saw what she looked like in that outfit.

She let out a breath and relaxed. "Okay, I'll do as you say."

"Good," he said. "Be ready to run at the first sign of trouble. And whatever you do, *don't react to anything that you see in there*. It'll be hard, but vital. Be strong."

Bianca nodded and took a deep breath. "Let's do it."

McManus took her hand and led her though to the arena.

18
arena of death

Bianca wasn't prepared for the size of the arena below the surface or the noise level as she stepped through the veiled opening. A sound dampener spell kept the roar of the crowd from reaching the streets above. The cavern was as large as a football stadium and a natural amphitheatre. She couldn't see the center, only the teeming crowd surrounding a large pit, most yelling and cheering as they shook fists stuffed full of dollars.

All kinds made up the crowd, from ladies and gents to street gangsters and junkies.

"Head down," McManus hissed out of the side of his mouth as he casually placed his hand on the back of her neck to keep her close.

That's right. She was supposed to be his property.

He guided her through the crowd and nearer to the edge of the pit. Bianca assumed it would be a typical shadow combat match with illegal betting.

"KILL HER!" screamed a well-dressed woman dripping in diamonds. "RIP HER FUCKING THROAT OUT!"

The man with her, obviously her lover by the indulgent grin he wore and his possessive stance, reached around and tweaked her breast through the dress. Bianca's skin crawled. The ugliness of this place was even more vile than she imagined it would be.

Someone shoved against her. At first she thought it was an accident, but when it happened a second time, she felt something hard against her hip. She turned to find a man pressing himself against her. He leered and reached for her breast. She smacked his hand away and the leer turned nasty. His lips peeled back from yellowing teeth as he reached for her. She pulled her arm back and punched him hard in the mouth.

"Bitch," he sneered, and raised his hand to her.

McManus stopped the downward descent mere inches from her face.

"Get your own whore," he growled at the man.

The man grunted a derisive laugh and yanked his arm away. "She's too fucking skinny anyway."

As he turned to leave, McManus spun him around and slammed him against the nearby wall, his knuckles white with the grip on the man's throat. Patrons turned from the game to watch the new entertainment unfolding outside the ring.

"What the fuck are you doing? She's only a whore," the man gasped, his eyes bulging with fear and his face turning purple as he tried to pry open the iron grip.

"But she's *my* whore," McManus said with murder in his eyes. *"Mine."*

"Stop it," she said, tugging on his arm. "Let him go."

But her pleas went unheard. If she didn't do something quickly, the man was going to choke to death. Bianca placed her hand against McManus's cheek and turned his face toward her. "Please, let him go."

With his lips peeled back from his teeth in a feral sneer, his face was a stony murderous mask.

"Lance," she said softly.

That seemed to reach him. His shoulders relaxed and he opened his fingers. The hapless man dropped to the floor gasping for air, then rose quickly and disappeared into the throng. McManus's fingertips bit into her flesh as he wrapped his hand around her upper arm and challenged the onlookers with a scowl. "Anyone else want a piece of this?"

With the sideshow obviously over, they all turned their attention back to the arena.

Bianca looked at him, stunned. She'd never seen him like this. Possessive and dark. It scared her more than a little. Not willing to take him on, the crowd opened a path and they edged closer to the arena. Pit was a good word for it because it was little else. Nothing like the complex layout of the official shadow-combat matches held in the purpose-built arenas. While the detective stopped to talk to someone, she placed her hands on the rim wall and watched the game below.

Four people were in the arena. One pair grappled on the far side near a large boulder, while the other pair was just below where she stood. A pretty female in tight black shorts and a blood-soaked white tank top torn across the bottom cringed against the wall of the arena. Blood also streaked her face. A half-naked male stalked toward her, knees bent and arms open to keep her cornered. He'd taken a few hits himself, by the look of the cuts and gore caking his upper torso.

The girl quickly glanced left, then right, fear etching her face as she sought an opening. It looked like she was about to lose the match.

Bianca suddenly realized the drooling male appeared to be a dreniac. The player was good. He had the twitchy mannerisms and the junkielike desperation down pat, and whoever had done his makeup was a genius.

He lunged at the woman, but she managed to duck under his arms into a tuck and roll, snatching up what looked to be a discarded kukri knife.

A confident grin had now replaced the apparent terror. She seemed very comfortable with the large curved blade and held it loose, ready to strike. The mock dreniac advanced on her again, a little more cautiously this time. Bianca found herself holding her breath in anticipation.

A heavy roar erupted up from the other side of the arena where the larger of the two males threw back his head and bellowed again as the humanoid creature he battled bit down hard on his forearm, the blood spraying them both.

The cry distracted the female for a split second, giving the dreniac the opening he needed to strike. He rushed her before she had time to recover and raise the kukri, his fangs extended as he knocked her down, pinning her knife hand to the ground by her wrist before bending in to rip out a huge chunk of flesh from her throat. The woman screamed as blood sprayed the sand beneath them and the male dipped his head and appeared to be drinking.

"Noooo," the large man screamed from the other side of the pit.

He yanked back the creature's head, removing a chunk of flesh from his arm in the process. Then he transformed, his features twisting into those of a bear. A massive paw came down, long powerful claws slashed his opponent, and he bit into the creature's neck, completely severing the head, which rolled away.

Bianca straightened, her breath sucked back into her lungs.

The half-transformed ursian man discarded the body of his opponent and charged the female's attacker, reaching him in seconds. As he hauled the feeding dreniac off her body, he bought up another powerful paw and ripped the head off the creature's shoulders, throwing the pieces far and wide.

Then he dropped to his knees beside the woman's prone body and lifted her into his lap. Her hand twitched in a death spasm, as did her feet. Blood ran down her outstretched arm and dripped from the tip of her index finger onto the sand. He cried out and rocked back and forth, cradling her against him.

Oh no! This was *not* theatrics. There was no makeup or special effects. The blood was real. The gore was real. This was *all* real.

Bianca let out a cry, her hands shaking as the reality set in. She grabbed McManus's hand. "She's dead."

A man standing beside her smiled. "Great match." Then frowned at her obvious horror.

"It's her first time," McManus said to the man, and leaned in as if to kiss her neck. "Keep it together, Sin. Be strong."

The man grinned and turned back to the action. Bianca's shaking increased. She couldn't stop it. He squeezed her hand gently and turned her back to the pit.

McManus ran his hand over her shoulders and leaned in once more, toward her neck. "Pull yourself together, Sin," he whispered while his hands rolled down her body intimately. "This isn't the sanitized version of the game you know. It's the illegal version, fought by men and women forced into the shadow death match because they're slaves or owe money to some very nasty people. Only the victor walks away from this alive."

"Why didn't you tell me?" she whispered back, finding his touch comforting and oddly arousing. "How can you let this happen?"

"Believe me, I've tried to shut it down a thousand times, but they're always one step ahead of the police. I'm sorry, you've been around law enforcement long enough, I thought you knew. Right now you have to suck it up and pretend it doesn't affect you. Can you do that?"

She pulled away and nodded, keeping her back to the pit. A roar erupted.

"What's happening?" she asked softly, not daring to look for herself.

"The cleaners are coming in to carry out the dead, but the bear won't let them near the girl."

Bianca could hear the angry grief from the male in the pit and had to see. He'd returned to full human form, the dead girl's body still cradled in his arms, tears streaming down his cheeks.

"He loved her." The first of the bodies were carried out of the arena as two other cleaners approached the grieving male. One reached for the girl, and received a large fist smashed into his face for his trouble. The next approached more cautiously, talking in calm tones, though she couldn't hear the exact words.

Another man came out of a door in the rock face, carrying a gun. The distraught male went back to hugging the dead woman against his chest, her arm sticking out and shaking with his movement.

"Come on. You don't want to see this, Bianca," McManus whispered in her ear.

She blinked and turned to him. "What?" Something he said bugged her. It took her a few more seconds to realize it was the first time he'd ever used her first name.

His ice blue eyes held a compassion she'd rarely seen in him, the compassion he usually reserved for small children and the helpless. It was the second time she'd seen it in as many days.

The crowd erupted. Half cheered, while the other half jeered. Bianca looked back into the arena to see the ursian face down over the body of his dead lover, the cleaner standing over him with a gun.

McManus pulled her through the crowd away from the edge of the pit. She was too numb with shock to do anything but allow him to lead her away. He stopped so suddenly she almost ran into his back.

"If it isn't Detective McManus." A cool smooth voice flowed over her and snapped her out of her state of shock.

McManus's grip loosened on her hand and he smiled back, if somewhat tense. "O'Shea. I didn't expect to see you down here."

"You're looking sharp, Detective." The expensively

dressed man with dark hypnotic eyes smiled at her. "And if I'm not mistaken, this must be the eminent Bianca Sin."

She'd never seen this man before. He took her hand and bent to kiss the back of her knuckles. He was all grace and charm, yet there was something fundamentally dangerous about him. But she felt he was nowhere near as dangerous as the slim man next to him. His dark waist-length hair fell forward as he kept McManus firmly in his sight with the coldest deep gray eyes she'd ever seen. They were the eyes of a predator, and he was very hungry.

"Bianca, this is Corey O'Shea, the CEO of O'Shea Freight and Logistics, and Sin Town's biggest drug lord, and his brother Seamus," McManus explained, though he needn't have bothered. The O'Sheas' reputation for their stranglehold on most of the drugs, prostitution, and gun-running was notorious.

"You shouldn't listen to those nasty rumors, McManus," the elegant man said.

"Oh they're far from rumors, O'Shea, and one day I'll prove it."

Corey O'Shea's smile deepened, yet somehow he seemed even more menacing. She was wrong—the slim man might be deadly, but the older brother was definitely more dangerous.

"Are you here looking for your cousin too, O'Shea?"

The man's gaze wandered up and down her body before he turned his attention back to McManus. "Fast Jimmy? Now why would I be doing that?" There was a strange lilt to the man's accent.

"Oh, I don't know." McManus shoved his hands into his pockets and frowned. "I hear you two had a falling out, which, given that he's one of your biggest dealers in Sin Town, could be a bit of a problem for you?"

"I think you have me confused with someone else, Detective." Corey's smile twisted. "Besides, Jimmy is family."

"Enough games, O'Shea." McManus stepped in, close and menacing. "Do you know where he is?"

Seamus O'Shea reached into the front of his black ankle-length leather jacket and took a step closer, but Corey placed his hand on his brother's chest and smiled. "The detective's only doing his job, Seamus."

The slim man's black scowl still didn't leave McManus, his cold eyes showing no emotion as he obeyed his brother's command and stepped back, though he kept his hand inside his coat.

Corey turned to back to McManus. "I haven't seen my cousin in weeks. But if you find him, tell him that his family misses him and welcomes his return."

"You mean he knows too much for you to let him go."

"You wound me, McManus."

"So you don't have any idea where we might find him?"

"Like I said, sorry." O'Shea adjusted the front of his suit. "Now if you'll excuse me, I have another appointment to attend." He took Bianca's hand, brushing the back of her fingers again with his lips and slipping his card into her palm at the same time. "If there is *anything* I can ever do for you . . . just call."

Bianca didn't need her mother's succubus skills to recognize the wicked gleam of lust in the drug lord's eyes.

"Before you go," McManus said harshly. "If you're not looking for Jimmy, then what are you doing down here?"

"Enjoying the show, Detective." Corey's grin deepened. "Just enjoying the show."

Bianca watched the O'Shea brothers walk away, followed by three more men in suits. As she started to turn away, she caught a girl watching them with interest. When she found Bianca looking at her, fear flared in her eyes, she dropped her gaze quickly and turned away, pushing through the crowd.

"McManus," Bianca said, nodding in the retreating girl's direction.

The detective raced into action, catching her by the upper

arm before she could get much farther. "Well now, Billy. Where's your supplier?"

"I don't know," the girl said, her eyes darting nervously between them.

"You're hurting," McManus said, concern creeping into his voice. "You have any money?"

Billy shook her head. "I was hoping Jimmy would give me a little credit."

He pulled a bunch of folded bills from his pocket and counted off a couple of notes. "This should get you what you need."

The girl reached for the money.

He snatched back the cash and shook his finger. "First tell me what you know about Fast Jimmy."

The girl glanced nervously in the direction where Corey O'Shea and his entourage had disappeared. "He's staying out of the way of late."

"Because of O'Shea?" he asked.

She nodded.

"Do you know where he is?" McManus seemed to be getting impatient.

She shook her head.

"Then I guess you don't need my help." He palmed the bills and slid his hand into his pocket.

Fear and need filled the girl's eyes, and she scratched at her arms in desperation. "Wait," she said. "He's been seeing the druidess who works down at Madam Lo's."

"Well done, Billy." McManus handed the girl the money and turned to Bianca. "Looks like we about to pay a visit to the whorehouse."

19

Madam Lo's House
of Pleasure

McManus led Bianca into the unassuming building. She was still a little shell-shocked from the shadow death match. *Fuck*. He should've told her more about how it went down in Sin Town. He just assumed she knew.

The hostess, Mistress Luna, stood just inside the door wearing a red vinyl corset clinched impossibly tight over a black PVC floor-length skirt split to the hip, with a pair of seven inch black and red stiletto platform shoes laced up to just below her knee.

"Well, if it isn't my old friend, Detective McManus," the BDSM mistress husked, running a professional glance over Bianca. His disguise had obviously failed big-time. Not that it mattered now.

"I need to see Madam Lo, Luna."

She sidled up to him with a slow smile and pressed herself against him as she fingered the lapel of his suit. "I'm sorry, Detective, but the madam is . . . indisposed."

"Then . . ." McManus leaned so close their noses almost touched. " . . . tell her to get *disposed*."

Mistress Luna's gaze dropped to his lips as hers parted slightly. "I'll see what I can do."

The succubi sisters Luna and Lo had been running the House of Pleasure for as long as he could remember. A man entered, dressed in an expensive looking suit. He smiled nervously at them and sat down. Lili appeared dressed in her usual demure school uniform, crisp white socks up to her knees and her hair in ponytails. She gave McManus a saucy wink as she crossed to the seated man. As usual it disturbed him on so many levels.

"Hello, Daddy," she said, taking the man's face in her tiny childish hands and giving him a tender peck on the lips.

The man leered, his trousers unable to hide his excitement as the prepubescent girl took his hand and led him from the room.

McManus shuddered, feeling dirty. He could never get used to seeing that.

"My Goddess, she's only a child," Bianca said, her face mirroring his own revulsion.

"Actually, Lili is more than three hundred years old," he said. "According to the law, she's well past the age of consent."

"Aeternus?" Bianca asked.

He nodded.

"Still," Bianca said, turning to the doorway where Lili disappeared with her john. "That's perverted."

"I know," he said. "But still legal."

"You know a lot about Sin Town," Bianca said, tilting her head. It was good to see some of her confidence returning.

"Before my foster parents took me in, I lived on the streets for a while. In fact, I met Dan Murphy when he caught me trying to boost a car that belonged to one of the nastiest drug dealers in Sin Town. It would've literally cost me my balls, if not my life, if I'd succeeded." The memory brought a smile to his lips. "Not everyone who lives here is crooked, at least not back then. The Murphys took me into their home right here in Sin Town."

"And a right little smartass he was then too." An elegant woman stood in the doorway. "Hello, Lancelot."

She was the only one besides his adopted mother who ever got away with using his first name. Madam Lo's long red lace gown showed her immaculate figure to perfection, and her dark hair, streaked with purples and reds, hung past her waist. She looked as beautiful now as she did to a seventeen-year-old boy with a crush.

Madam Lo came into the room leading two seminaked beefcakes on leashes attached to the studded collars around their throats. She gracefully reclined on the chaise lounge and arranged the skirt to best show off her spectacular legs. Her pets kneeled on either side, one running his hand up her leg, while she stroked the other's head.

She looked at McManus with hooded seduction. "Now what was so important you had to interrupt my evening meal?"

"We're looking for Fast Jimmy."

She arched a perfect eyebrow. "What makes you think I know where he is?"

McManus could see she did. Now all he needed was to convince her she should tell him. "Two reasons really. First, you know everything that goes on in Sin Town."

She acknowledged this with slight incline of her head. "And the second?"

"He comes here regularly to see one of your girls that he's involved with."

Again the Succubus gave him a sage nod. "Myf."

"Myf?" Bianca said.

"Myfanwy, a druidess with a great talent for erotic plant manipulation."

"Erotic plant manipulation?" he asked.

Madam Lo grinned. "Yes, tentacles, vines, and all sorts of other fabulous tricks. I could get Myf to give you a demonstration, on the house."

"Um, no thanks," McManus said. "We're just after Fast Jimmy. So is he here?"

Madam Lo looked at her sister, dropping the seductive act for a more professional face. "Is he?"

Mistress Luna nodded.

"You didn't need to disturb me for that," the madam said.

McManus glanced at Madam Lo. "Do you think she'd tell me anything without your say so?"

Her musical laugh lit up the room. "How well you know us, my boy." Her bedroom eyes drooped again and she ran her hands over her ample, perfect bust. "In all ways possible."

"I've long ago grown immune to your allure, Madam Lo."

She gave the same throaty laugh. "Only because I've let you think you have."

She was right; he could feel the desire swelling with the Succubus's pull. And a man never forgot his first.

"Madam Lo, the whereabouts of this Fast Jimmy could be crucial in helping us find a killer," Bianca said, stepping between him and the madam, killing the rising desire in his blood.

"Well now, witch, aren't you a surprise?" The succubus rose from the lounge chair and stood directly in front of her. "I see you have the blood of my people flowing in your veins. Rest assured, if I really wanted your detective, I'd have him and there'd be nothing you could do to stop me. But as it is, I merely want to remind him who he was dealing with."

She swept her skirts around and headed for the door, taking her pets with her. "Luna, take them to—"

A piercing scream shattered the air.

20

Fast Jimmy, Dead Jimmy

BIANCA FOLLOWED THE others in the direction of the scream. Doors on either side of a narrow corridor opened as naked and near naked people peered out. McManus pushed past, shoving some roughly back into their rooms. Bianca struggled to keep up in the ridiculous boots she wore but managed to make it to the screaming woman only a couple of steps behind him.

As soon as she entered the room, she could sense the now familiar vileness. It permeated everything. She took in the scene with a quick glance. Plants and vines grew everywhere, in pots, in hanging baskets, and creeping up the walls. It looked like some sort of fantasy jungle. A sweeping arc of blood sprayed across the large bed in the center. Some of it had splashed the ferns beside the bed and now dripped like gruesome raindrops.

"Well, looks like we found Jimmy," McManus said, looking down at the dead man lying on the bed. "Unfortunately, I think it's going to be a little difficult getting him to talk."

The shrieking girl now whimpered as she stood shaking by the wall with her hands covering her eyes to block out the bloody horror. She was naked beneath a traditional druidic cloak of pale blue open down the front. Bianca wrapped her arm around the distraught girl's shoulders and gently steered her into the waiting arms of Madam Lo.

"There, there, sweetness," the madam said, pulling the girl into a warm hug and stroking the back of her head. "I'll look after you."

Bianca pulled a blanket from the end of the bed, with only a few spots of blood splashed on it. "Wrap her in this and give her some hot sweet tea if you have any. She's going into shock."

Madam Lo nodded and took the blanket as she continued to soothe the young girl. "*Shhh, shh, shh,* I know," she said, wrapping the druidess up and leading her out of the room. A crowd gathered at the doorway, gasping and gawking at the bloody scene.

Vultures. "Can't you get them out of here?" Bianca said to Mistress Luna.

The vinyl clad mistress turned and held her arms out. "Everyone leave," she commanded as she shuffled the people out. "Back to your rooms."

"Don't let anyone leave the premises, though," McManus called after her. "I want them all for questioning."

The body lay on its back, with feet still on the floor, pants around his ankles and flaccid penis lying against one leg. His face was frozen in blood-speckled terror. This man had died badly.

"So what do you think?" McManus asked when they were alone.

"It's definitely the killer. There's the same dark magic remnants."

"How can you tell? You don't have any of your equipment."

"I told you, my family are sensitive. The devices just enhance my ability." Or at least used to until Kedrax, she thought. "Besides, the signature is fresh, strong, and far too familiar not to recognize."

"I think Jimmy was killed because he knew something."
McManus ran a hand over his head.

"Or they're still tying up loose ends after we broke into
the magic shop," she said.

McManus nodded. "We'll have to question everyone who
knew him, starting with the girl."

"You could try the video," Madam Lo said from the
doorway.

"What video?" McManus asked.

"How's the girl?" Bianca said at the same time.

"I've left her in Luna's capable hands," she said, and
pointed to the camera mounted near the ceiling. "And we
keep them in all the rooms."

McManus shoved his hand in his pockets and arched his
eyebrows skeptically.

"For security," she said.

"And if you happen to catch the odd senator or prominent
citizen in a compromising position, it wouldn't hurt."

Madam Lo's brow creased as she placed her hands on her
hips. "Our house runs on a solid reputation of discretion and
confidentiality. It would be counterproductive to blackmail
our clients. Besides, they're made aware of the cameras
before they participate in any bedroom sport. Some even
request copies."

"Sorry," he said, holding up his hands. "Let's take a look
at that footage."

"This way."

Bianca followed the succubus back to the reception area,
through another door and into an office. The madam sat
down at a desk and tapped the keyboard in front of a computer screen with long manicured nails, then looked up at
them.

"This is Room 113, Myfanwy's room."

Bianca moved around so she could look over the madam's
shoulder. "She's the druidess who found the body and the
victim's girlfriend, right?"

"Yes. As you can see, this is in real time."

"Can you go back to when Jimmy arrived?" McManus asked.

The madam's talonlike nails flew expertly over the keys. "Luna said he arrived about twenty minutes ago."

The computer screen flicked to a black and white image of a man entering the room.

"That's Jimmy," McManus said, bending over Madam Lo's shoulder for a closer look.

Bianca tried to ignore the way his hand rested on the madam's shoulder with a casual familiarity, and keep her attention on the computer screen, but she found her gaze drifting back to them.

She shook herself. It was none of her business if McManus and this woman were lovers. She refocused on the screen as a whistling Jimmy sat on the bed, totally oblivious to the fact that he was about to die. He flicked off his shoes then stood up, unbuckled his belt and pushed down his pants. His erection stood out proudly, and he continued to whistle as he squeezed the tip between his thumb and forefinger. Suddenly, the whistling broke off and he just disappeared.

"What the fuck . . ." McManus said, peering closer at the screen. "What happened to the video? Has this been edited?"

"No, look," Bianca said, pointing to the timer in the bottom right hand corner. "It's still running."

Madam Lo took the video back a couple of minutes and let it go. They watched Jimmy unbuckle his pants, drop them, and fondle himself again. Then Lo slowed the video to frame-by-frame. Jimmy's head snapped up with his face twisting from a grin to utter terror.

Then poof, he was gone, and just like that the room was empty.

The video continued to play, showing an empty room.

"Can you fast forward it a little?" McManus asked.

Madam Lo took it to where Myfanwy entered the room, then slowed it as the girl looked around, frowned and placed her hands on her hips. The witch sat down at the dresser and started bushing her long raven hair.

Then, abruptly, Jimmy's body appeared on the bed just as they had found him. The blood was dark splashes on the bed and plants in the black and white video. Myfanwy leaned into the mirror, then spun and jumped up so fast she sent the stool over on its side as she raised a shaking hand to her lips and screamed.

Less than a minute later McManus's image rushed into the room and Madam Lo hit the pause button, looking at them both in surprised confusion.

McManus looked at the druidess who sat with Mistress Luna on a lounge chair in the corner of the office. "I think we better get that girl out of here and into protective custody."

Bianca shivered. Sin Town had been even worse than she expected. She just wanted to go home and take a really, really long shower and wash this filth from her skin.

"We'll get her a safe house." McManus removed his jacket and wrapped it around Bianca's shoulders. "And I know just the place to go. Someone owes me a favor and it's about time I collected."

21

no one can hear you scream

MYF FLICKED THE channel on the TV. An image of a lion stalking an antelope appeared. She flicked again. A daytime soap. Flick. Music videos.

Flick. Flick. Flick.

The woman came out of the bathroom dressed in a fluffy white bathrobe.

"Ah, that's better," she said, fluffing out her pale hair with her fingers. "That bath is wonderful. You should try it."

"No thanks." Myf flicked the channel.

"I can't believe McManus got us this room. Would you like something, Myfanwy? I can call down for some room service."

"Call me Myf, and no thanks."

"Right, Myf." She looked around uncomfortably and tugged at the robe. "I'll be glad when McManus gets back with my clothes."

Myf put down the remote and stood up. "I think I need a smoke. Do you mind if I go outside?" she asked. "Sorry, I can't remember your name."

"It's Bianca, and yeah, that should be fine."

Myf dug into her bag, frantically looking for the half a

pack she had left, and let out a sigh of relief when she finally found them squashed in the corner under everything else. She slid the glass door and went out onto the balcony, leaving it open behind her. The wind this high up was chilling. She pulled her jacket tighter and placed the cigarette between her lips.

Out of nowhere a fresh wave of grief washed over her again. It kept taking her by surprise.

Jimmy.

He might've been an asshole sometimes, but he was her asshole, and now he was gone. Her hands shook so much she had difficulty getting the lighter to work. Finally, the flame held. The tip of the cigarette glowed and nicotine-laden smoke filled her lungs.

She exhaled slowly and glanced at the woman inside flicking through a magazine. With her pure cream complexion and whiter than white hair, she'd be very popular at Madam Lo's. Especially dressed in that skanky goth outfit she wore earlier. The perfect mix of innocence and depravity that Madam Lo's clientele would eat right up. Maybe even more popular than Lili.

Myf dragged deeply on the cigarette and closed her eyes. Too bad it was just tobacco because right now she could really use a splif.

She frowned. The air changed suddenly, becoming colder and darker. She opened her eyes to find the night had taken on a strange hue, like a crimson scarf thrown over a lamp, muting the light with tinges of red.

"What's happening?" she asked the woman. *I wish I could remember her name.*

The woman ignored her and continued to flick through the magazine.

"Hey!" she said.

The woman glanced up from the magazine, her eyes going wide, darting one way then the other, searching. "Myf?" she said, standing.

"I'm right here you stupid woman," she said, and tried to walk back inside, only she couldn't move.

"Myf?" The woman's voice rose higher. *"MYFANWY?"*

A strange mist appeared just off the balcony and drifted toward Myf, growing thicker as it poured onto the floor, obscuring her shoes. The air filled with a faint buzzing noise. As the mist continued to thicken, the noise increased, crystallizing into voices. Total and utter terror solidified into a hard cold knot, twisting her insides.

The witch's name suddenly popped into her head. "Bianca!"

But the woman continued searching, unseeing and unhearing. Impending danger settled in the pit of Myf's stomach, cold and cramping like menstrual pain with nails in it. Something moved in the thickening fog.

The swirling mist solidified, becoming a white robed figure. The surrounding air became a grayish muted backdrop, almost fading from existence. The hood of the robe obscured any features within dark shadows, and it was impossible to tell if it was male or female. Even the long fingers holding a black chalice were no help.

Dark energy flowed from the figure, especially the cup. The almost inaudible chant grew steadily stronger from somewhere in the hood, except it wasn't a single voice, it was multiple, all harmonized into one monotonous intonation.

The figure floated just off the ground, using the mist to glide across the ground.

"Hello," she said, hoping the thing would answer, yet dreading it at the same time.

It just kept chanting as it floated toward her. And it was definitely not friendly.

Goose bumps rose on her skin. Her hair stood out as if charged with electrical energy. She turned and tried to run, but her feet felt mired in mud. She screamed.

The pale witch ran out onto the balcony, straight past her, and leaned over the railing, calling her name.

"BIANCA!" Myf screamed. *"HELP ME!"*

But it didn't do any good. She was invisible. No one could see her, no one could hear her, and no one could save her.

I'm going to die.

He . . . she . . . it . . . closed in. The malignant presence strangled the air, making it almost impossible to breathe. The chanting increased in volume and tempo. Fear churned her stomach, pushing burning bile into her esophagus. She bent over and let loose the sweet tea they had given her to calm her nerves.

Jimmy. This is what got him. She raised her chin to look the dark presence in the face. Except there was no face. It lifted a bone-white hand, palm up, and she rose off the ground. She was no longer in touch with Mother Earth, but she had the feeling it wouldn't have done her any good anyway. There were no plants nearby, the actual earth was buried beneath concrete, and even the air felt cut off to her. There was nothing from which to draw her powers.

The hooded stranger turned the hand on its side and her arms went out wide. Her jeans were cut away and her T-shirt cut open, not with a blade, but with magic. She couldn't move and was totally helpless to stop it.

The figure pulled a brush from inside the robe and dipped it into the challis. Using thaumaturgy, the brush lifted from the cup, the tip in dark crimson paint, and disappeared into the swirling mist beneath her feet.

She spat at the figure. "Go on, I'm not afraid of you. Do your worst." But it was a lie. She was afraid. Terribly afraid. Hanging in midair, helpless, dressed only in her underwear and the tattered remnants of her shirt. It tipped the challis, and crimson flowed over the pale hand and onto the ground.

Blood. Jimmy's blood.

The spilled blood twisted and flowed into some sort of symbol beneath her feet. Some fell onto the stranger and soaked into the cloth until it disappeared completely, leaving only the robe unmarked. The figure placed the bloody palm against her stomach, and the dark crimson print was absorbed into her skin like it had the robe.

Her stomach grew heavy and started to swell. Her abdomen continued to expand, growing larger and heavier. And then it moved.

A baby.

Her baby.

Hers and Jimmy's.

And then the tears came.

22

The Vanishing

BIANCA LEANED OVER the balcony and searched the ground fifteen floors below. No sign of Myf, alive or dead. She leaned back with equal parts relief and confusion.

The front door closed. "I'm back," McManus yelled from inside the room.

"McManus," Bianca called. "Quick. She's gone."

"How?" he asked, placing a bag on the sofa and joining her on the balcony.

Bianca's growing panic threatened to overwhelm her. "I don't know. She came out for a cigarette."

"Do you think she just took off somehow?"

"I don't know, one minute she was standing there, smoking and then . . ." Bianca looked around, then it dawned on her. "Oh no—what about Jimmy?"

McManus put his hands on her shoulders. "Tell me everything that happened."

"She asked if she could smoke and . . ." Bianca trailed off as an enormous wave of black energy washed over her and Myfanwy's broken body appeared in a pool of blood a few feet away.

She pushed past McManus and ran to the girl's side, almost slipping in the blood. "Myf! Myfanwy."

Myfanwy's chest rose and fell shallowly. Her breath rattled in her throat and her stomach lay open like all the other bodies they'd found so far. Bianca knelt and placed her fingertips against her throat to feel the faint, slow pulse.

"She's still alive," she said.

McManus talked on his cell. There was blood everywhere, and Bianca didn't know what to do with the girl's intestines. There was so much damage.

"I've called the paramedics." McManus took Myf's hand and brushed her hair back from her forehead. "Can you tell me what happened?"

Blood gurgled in her throat and coated her lips with crimson bubbles as she shifted her head to look at him. "The mist was so cold." She coughed and her eyes closed slowly and opened again. "So cold."

McManus looked at Bianca. His shoulders tensed and the skin around his eyes tightened. He was just as frustrated as her. He nodded at the ground under her knee. "It's the same killer."

The symbol painted in blood was still wet.

"How did he find her, how did they know where she was?" he asked. "I thought she'd be safe here."

"I don't know." The helplessness threatened to paralyze Bianca as she squeezed Myf's other hand.

"Our baby . . ." the girl croaked, and coughed again. "They took our baby girl . . ." Her eyes rolled and she licked her blood-smeared lips. Bianca's heart sank. The girl was dying.

"What baby?" McManus asked.

"Our baby, mine and Jimmy's," she said, and stared into the air with a far-off smile. "She was so beautiful."

"Where did you go?" McManus's voice took on a frantic edge. "Who took you?"

Myf's brow furrowed and she turned to Bianca. "I called for you."

Tears stung Bianca's eyes. "I'm sorry, I couldn't find you."

The girl shook her head. "I was here, I could see you, hear you." She swallowed. "In the mist . . . it came in the . . ."

Sirens wailed to a stop in the street far below. Bianca glanced away just for a moment toward the sound and Myf's hand went limp in hers.

BIANCA SIPPED HOT black coffee as paramedics and cops and Goddess knew who else moved around the hotel room. She placed the cup on the end table beside her and wrapped her arms around herself. Thank the Goddess they'd let her change out of that blood-covered robe and into some of the clothes McManus brought from her apartment.

McManus sat down beside her on the sofa and she leaned her head against his shoulder. "How're you feeling now?" he asked.

She shrugged. "I'm just going over and over it all in my head, trying to figure out what happened. How did they find her? I mean it happened right there and I couldn't sense her or the black magic at all."

He put his arm around her shoulder and his heart thudded in a steady soothing rhythm under her ear.

"Don't beat yourself up," he said gently against her hair. "There was nothing you could've done."

A tiny smudge of bright blue, no bigger than a raindrop, stained his shirt not far from the tip of her nose. Yet, she didn't have the heart to take him to task. Hell, she could use a little something herself.

"What the hell are you doing here?" Agent Neil Roberts said from just inside the door of the hotel suite.

McManus stood as Roberts sauntered into the room with a plaster across the bridge of his nose and lifted the shades he was wearing to the top of his head. "You were told to stay away from this case, not to mention you've been suspended. So why are you here at *my* crime scene?"

"Because I sent them," Oberon said from behind him.

23

little white lies

McManus smiled as Oberon DuPrie filled the doorway. Agent Roberts spun on his heel toward the door. "You were also ordered to stay away from this case, DuPrie."

DuPrie crossed his large leather-jacketed arms and smiled. "What case are you talking about, Roberts? Since McManus knows Sin Town so well, I asked him to help Bianca look into drug a dealer suspected of supplying the campus. The murdered girl was the dealer's girlfriend."

"That's right," McManus lied. "When Jimmy was murdered in a Sin Town brothel, we took Myfanwy into protective custody."

DuPrie nodded. "It's just a coincidence that she turned up as one of your victims."

Roberts's mouth opened and closed, and McManus could almost hear the wheels spinning in the man's head.

"So if you are quite finished—I will take *my* people now," DuPrie said, crossing the floor and placing a protective arm around Bianca.

Roberts whipped the sunglasses off the top of his head. "They're still witnesses to a murder and need to be questioned."

"You know where to find them," DuPrie said, steering Bianca toward the door. "They'll be writing up the report on the dealer's death."

"DuPrie, I could charge you with obstruction." Roberts's face took on a crimson and purple shade, making the white plaster on his nose even more conspicuous. McManus got a kind of perverse enjoyment out of it. He was starting to like Oberon DuPrie.

"Do your worst." DuPrie threw the words over his shoulder and disappeared out the door with Bianca.

McManus turned to the beet-faced agent, shrugged and followed.

McManus RUBBED THE needle prick from the facimorphic test as they entered DuPrie's dingy little office. Bianca was still in shock and had hardly said two words the whole trip back to the campus.

DuPrie stood behind his desk, arms crossed and thick black eyebrows creased in a deep scowl. "Tell me everything from start to finish," he said Bianca.

"Look, this is my fault," McManus said. "I dragged her into it."

"I'll deal with you in a minute," Oberon snarled at him, and leaned his hands on the table. "Bianca, I went out on a limb and lied to Roberts. Now tell me why you ignored a direct order from VCU and continued to look into the case?"

She just stood there looking at him dumbfounded.

"Back off, man," McManus said, moving between Bianca and her boss. "I told you, I'm to blame, not her. I talked her into it. There's something about this case I just can't let go of and—"

"Good," the huge ursian said.

McManus was sure he'd heard incorrectly. "What?"

"I said good." DuPrie reached behind a plant. "I needed to hear how committed you are to this."

A panel slid open to reveal an alcove, with a spiral staircase leading downward.

"Fuck me," McManus said.

"I'd rather not, if you don't mind." DuPrie's gruff tone lightened. "But thanks for the invitation."

DuPrie took Bianca by the hand. "Are you okay?"

She smiled sadly. "I will be."

She descended the staircase first, and McManus followed her into a modern open plan office.

"So this is your real base of operations," he said to Oberon.

"Welcome to the Bunker." DuPrie placed his hands on his hips and beamed proudly.

Tones stood up from behind a bank of computer screens. "Captain, our guests have arrived."

"Excellent, show them down. We'll wait for them in the operations room."

The Aeternus bobbed his hairless head. "Right, Captain."

DuPrie's enormous hand fell heavily on McManus's shoulder. "Come on, we've a lot to discuss."

The ursian guided him to a room with a long table ringed by high-backed leather chairs. A computer screen, larger than McManus's big screen television at home, dominated the wall at the far end of the room. The Department of Parahuman Services symbol turned lazily in the center of the screen.

He said, walking down the table, "Sweet setup you have here. Is this the department's doing?"

"Not officially," DuPrie said. "Let's just say we're an autonomous organization that answers directly to the Five of CHaPR."

McManus looked through the glass walls out into the office beyond. There were a couple of people talking and bending over notes. He recognized Cody with the former medical examiner, Kitt Jordan. The Incubus looked up at that second, as though he sensed McManus's gaze, then headed into the room.

"Dude. I see you've been invited into the bat cave," Cody said, knocking knuckles with him, a grin splitting his sun-tanned face. Most cops got funny around Cody, but McManus didn't mind him, as long as he kept that emotion shit to himself.

McManus glanced at DuPrie. "And your boss is about to tell me why."

"All in good time, we'll wait for our other guests to arrive," the ursian said.

Bianca entered the room with her hair pulled back into a neat ponytail and looking a little more together. She took a seat opposite McManus and glanced at him quickly before giving Cody a tight smile.

Movement caught the corner of his eye as Tones returned with three others. McManus recognized the woman imme-diately and stood as she entered the room, followed closely by a man even larger than DuPrie, with skin like polished obsidian. The old man from the other day brought up the rear. Even DuPrie seemed a little awed by the elegant dark-skinned woman in a figure-hugging white ankle-length lace dress.

"Princess Akentia," he said with deference. "Welcome."

Everyone in the room bowed low to the oldest and most powerful living Aeternus.

24

Trouble in Paradise

"OBERON DUPRIE." THE princess held out a regal hand, which he bent and kissed. "Thank you for agreeing to meet me here. This is the one of the few places I feel will be safe for us to talk."

"Chancellor Rudolf, it's good to see you again. Thanks for coming," Oberon said, shaking the old man's hand before turning back to the princess. "Your Highness, we appreciate you coming in daylight. Can we get you some refreshments?"

"That won't be necessary, I fed before I came." She clicked her fingers toward the large bodyguard. "But I'm sure Keith could do with a bite."

Oberon straightened his shoulders and squared off against the other male. He couldn't help it. Ursians were a territorial breed, and this one was invading his space. Keith's dark skin shone under the lights and his muscles rippled under the tight T-shirt. Politeness won out. Keith inclined his large boulderlike head as he deferred to Oberon's territorial right.

"This way please." Tones said, guiding the minder from the room while the princess sat at the head of the table with Chancellor Rudolf by her side.

Bianca stood by her chair, open-mouthed. McManus scowled.

"Sit," Oberon said to them.

That seemed to snap them out of it and they took their seats.

"So," the princess started. "There has been another murder."

"Yes, and this time right under our noses," Oberon said, and looked pointedly at Bianca. "Not that there was anything we could've done about it."

"There are very powerful black thaumaturgies at work here," Bianca said.

"What I'm about to tell you," Akentia said, "you *did not* hear from me. In fact, I'm not even here." She leaned forward with her fingers splayed in front to her and looked at Rudolf, who gave her a slight nod. "Reports are coming in from all over the world of more sadistic killings bearing the Dark Brethren symbol. Most have been proven copycats. The thaumaturgists are using this as proof that those here in New York are also just another hoax."

Rudolf sat forward. "They're using this to say the Five are incompetent and trying to shift the balance of power in the council."

"He's smart—for a human." The princess's mask of aloofness slid for just a second as she smiled at the old man. "The thaumaturgists are blocking us at every turn. They object to Rudolf's admission to the Five, saying all members have to be parahuman and they want their representative to be appointed instead."

McManus said, "Who's the representative?"

"Marcus Hilden," the princess said.

"The Domina's son?" Oberon asked.

"Actually it's son-in-law," Bianca said. "We're a matriarchal society, the gifts are passed from mother to offspring and the male takes the family name of the female he marries."

Oberon scowled. "I'd bet a year's salary I know who the

real power is behind the scenes. Marcus wouldn't have the balls to shit without his mother-in-law's permission."

The princess inclined her head gracefully. "We have also come to the same conclusion. It was through his instigation that VCU was made the lead in the case. Apparently there was some objection to you, Detective." She looked directly at McManus.

"Yes, I um . . . I pissed off the head witch," he said in his usually tactful manner.

"As have I. Frequently." Akentia's smile was forgiving.

McManus grinned. Akentia had that effect on people.

"You must continue to work on this. Don't stop. The Brethren are close; I can feel the corruption growing." Rudolf stood up as she spoke. "We will try to block the magic users as much as we can. Now if you will all please forgive me," the princess said as she rose to her feet. "I really must be going."

Everyone else stood.

"Thanks for sharing this information with us," Oberon said, taking her hand.

"Oh." She stopped at the door and turned. "There is one more surprising player in all this. He's sticking pretty much under the radar, but has recently started making donations to the thaumaturgists' campaign." Again she looked at McManus. "I think you've already had dealings with a certain drug lord in Sin Town."

The detective's frown deepened. "Corey O'Shea?"

Akentia's regal smile was all the acknowledgment any of them needed.

"That slippery bastard is responsible for several murders and most of the drugs in Sin Town," McManus said, "but I've never been able to pin anything on him. Not even so much as a parking ticket. I think it's time you took him up on his invitation, Sin."

BIANCA HELD UP her ID. "We're here to see Mr. O'Shea."

"Do you have an appointment?" the uniformed security guard asked.

"Yes," McManus said.

"No," Bianca corrected. "But he asked me to stop by and see him any time. Tell him it's Bianca Sin."

The guard took her ID and went to the other side of the room. He talked on the phone for about a minute then looked at her ID and nodded.

"Bright one, that," McManus whispered in her ear. "He does know they can't see him on the phone."

"Maybe they can." She pointed to the camera in the corner facing their way.

McManus smiled and waved. She read *Yes sir* on the guard's lips as he glanced at them.

He finally hung up the phone and returned, handing back her ID card. "Someone will be here to collect you shortly. Please come through and wait."

"Thank you," she said politely.

He hit a button in the desk and a glass door opened to the left of them.

"That was easy," she whispered as they entered a waiting room with the large stylized letters OFL painted on the wall opposite the security counter.

"Too easy," McManus said. "O'Shea's up to something."

"I never knew this place was so big," she said, looking at pictures on the wall.

"O'Shea Freight and Logistics is the biggest independent transit company in the country, perhaps the world. They have their own trucks, aircraft, even ships and dispatches worldwide," McManus said. "Which is how we suspect he moves the drugs."

"Shhh." She looked around nervously.

"Welcome to O'Shea Freight and Logistics, Dr. Sin." A man in a suit and dark glasses stood in the doorway with another uniformed guard. "And Detective McManus as well. I'm Mr. O'Shea's head of security. He's waiting for you in his office." The security head stopped at the desk and held out his hand to McManus. "But before we go—your weapon please."

"I don't think so," McManus said with a dangerous smile that never reached his glacial eyes.

The other man easily had a good six inches on him and outweighed McManus by at least one hundred pounds. "Your weapon please," he repeated as he looked through the door and nodded.

McManus stood his ground.

The uniformed guard who had come with the suit grabbed McManus from behind and pinned his arms behind his back.

"Let them have your gun, McManus," Bianca said. *He was going to get hurt if he fought them.*

The security head stepped forward, flipped open his jacket and took the gun from the holster under McManus's arm, then handed it to the guard behind the desk and patted up McManus's legs, searching for more weapons.

"Hey. The least you could do is buy me dinner first," McManus growled.

"You'll get your firearm back when you leave," the suit said.

"I'd better, or I'll be taking yours," McManus warned.

The suit smiled confidently and led them to the open Jeep waiting outside, where the uniformed guard who had been with them slipped behind the wheel. They drove through the complex, and as they passed one of the aircraft hangars, a strange sensation washed over Bianca. It wasn't like any thaumaturgic energy she'd ever experienced before. It was neither white nor black, and she had the sudden urge to get as far away from the hangar as she could.

A protection spell.

The magic was so subtle that another witch probably wouldn't have detected it, not even her mother, but her sensitivity grew daily.

She glanced at their escorts in the front seat and leaned close to McManus's ear. "There's some heavy duty spells at work here. Powerful concealment enchantments."

"What could a drug cartel acting as a transit company have to hide?" he growled in a harsh whisper. "Hmm, let me think. *Drugs?*"

"There's no need to get snippy," she replied.

He scrubbed a hand across his craggy features. "Fuck, I'm sorry, Sin. I guess I'm still a little pissed at the manhandling back there."

The car stopped in the designated security spot in front of the six-story administration building. The security detail got out first and waited with feet apart, hands clasped low in front while she and McManus climbed out off the Jeep. O'Shea wanted them escorted straight to him without any chance of a detour.

Inside the building, the uniform guard moved into the elevator first and turned around to stare ahead. Bianca entered with McManus, and then the security head, who stood in front with his back to them as he pushed the sixth floor button.

McManus stared up at the changing floor numbers, his expression neutral. "Just so you know. You touch me again and I'll break your fucking nose."

Bianca started to doubt she'd even heard him until the security head looked over his shoulder with an arrogant self-certain smile. "I'd like to see you try."

The doors opened onto the top level, dominated entirely by Corey O'Shea's extensive office suit. Most of the open plan space had floor-to-ceiling windows, giving them an almost 360-degree view of the vast complex. The furniture was expensive yet tasteful, and she got the impression that opulence and power were what the O'Shea brothers were all about.

The man himself sat behind and immense dark wood desk, leaning forward in his large, high-backed leather chair, resting his elbows on the arms. "Well now, the delicious Dr. Sin and Detective McManus. Or should I say *Mister* McManus?"

"So you've heard about my suspension," the detective said. "Which means you know I'm not here on official police business."

"Nor do you have their protection." O'Shea's smile was both charming and lethal.

Bianca no longer had any doubts this man was a killer. But looking at McManus, she was starting to get the same feeling about him.

Several men in dark suits stood around the room. O'Shea's brother, Seamus, dressed in the same ankle-length black coat he'd worn the other night, lounged in the corner, his fingertips pressed together, forming a steeple. His long dark hair fell over his face, concealing most of his features. Except those eyes—the cold gray eyes of a pure predator.

"Please take a seat," Corey said, indicating the chairs on the other side of the desk.

Bianca moved forward but McManus's hand on her arm stopped her. "Thanks, but I think we'll stand," he said.

"And I prefer you sit." Corey narrowed cold eyes.

The uniformed security guard took her elbow as the security head grabbed McManus. He spun, snagging the man's wrist, twisted it behind the man's back and smashed his face into the wall beside the elevator. She heard bones crack as McManus forced the security head's arm between his shoulder blades.

"I warned you I'd break your nose if you touched me again," McManus hissed. "Consider the arm a bonus."

The man brought his other elbow up and smashed McManus in the mouth, then slammed his fist into the detective's kidney, dropping McManus to his hands and knees.

The detective spat blood onto the floor. He looked over his shoulder as the head of security kicked him in the gut, sending him over on his side coughing and gasping for breath. Bianca didn't know what to do. Kedrax was too far away for anything but the simplest of spells.

The head of security pulled his gun, his lips peeling back in a snarl as he pointed the weapon at McManus's head. Hair sprouted on his hands and face. Animalian, probably canian.

The detective rolled to his feet in one fluid movement, leapt forward and slammed the gun hand back into the man's face, opening a gash on the cheek. It surprised them all. Two other men in dark suits rushed in and tackled McManus to the floor, one shoving a knee in his back, the other pinning his shoulders.

Corey stood then and came around from his behind his desk. "Stop struggling, McManus, and my men will let you go."

He nodded at his men, and when McManus finally stopped struggling, they climbed off and lifted him by his arms to his feet.

As Bianca moved toward him, one of bodyguards grabbed her upper arm and roughly pulled her back. In response, McManus struggled against the guards restraining him, his face fierce. "Don't you touch her."

"Let her go," O'Shea said as he moved back to his chair. "And calm down, McManus. If I wanted you dead, you would be."

The two bodyguards released the detective. A fly landed on the side of McManus's face, buzzed off and landed, then buzzed off and landed again. She watched mesmerized as it continued, shifting with jerky little movements to drink from the blood leaking from his bleeding eyebrow. Then it landed on the top of his ear as it rubbed its front legs together.

Strange. What was a fly doing in here?

Corey gave his brother a short sharp nod. In a blur of fluid movement Seamus stood, reached into his pocket, extended his arm, and sat back in his seat. A blade flipped through the air, skimmed past McManus's ear and embedded in the wall behind, pinning the fly. Well, what was left of it.

The detective straightened his jacket, his ice-blue eyes narrowing. "Is that supposed to impress me?" he asked as he pulled out a cigarette from inside his pocket and placed the butt between his lips.

It sure impressed the hell out her.

As McManus felt around his pockets for his lighter, a gun blast startled her. Only a tiny remainder of the cigarette butt hung on McManus's bottom lip. The ever-silent Seamus O'Shea was again slouched in the chair with steepled fingers, except now his long black coat lay open, revealing a gun holster strapped to his left thigh and an array of knives strapped to his chest. The gun was a very large and very shiny semiautomatic pistol.

"Now," McManus said, taking the remainder of the cigarette from his mouth. "That was impressive."

"YOU SEE," COREY O'Shea said. "My brother may be skilled with a knife, but with a gun, he's a surgeon. As I said, if I wanted you dead, you would be and you'd never see it coming. Now, please *sit*?"

A coppery taste coated his tongue, and he reached up to touch his mouth, bringing away blood-smeared fingertips confirming the sting was a split lip. He locked eyes with Bianca. While he was pissed at his treatment, seeing her manhandled had his blood boiling. She smiled at him, letting him know she was okay. She looked more concerned about him than anything else. She took the seat to the left while he pulled up the chair on the right.

He needed a hit. He could feel the shakes starting in his fingers; physical exertion had depleted his reserves. He took another cigarette from his pocket and held it up to Seamus O'Shea just in case the sharpshooter had something against smoking.

Seamus shrugged.

McManus put the cigarette in his mouth and this time found his lighter. As he lit the tip, he watched the younger O'Shea brother out of the corner of his eye. The man might look as if he was bored, but McManus knew he was being watched right back.

After he exhaled, he turned to Corey O'Shea. "I take it you already know about your cousin."

The older O'Shea nodded. "Madam Lo called me." He leaned forward on his desk and clasped his fingers together. "So, Detective, what are you doing to find my cousin's killer?"

"Nothing." The cigarette had lost its flavor. McManus stood up, put it out in the ashtray on O'Shea's desk, and remained standing. "As you already pointed out, I've been suspended."

"Ah, but you're here." O'Shea leaned back in his chair. "So let's drop the pretense. You're a cop through and through. You're not going to let a little thing like a suspension stop you. If you're here to talk to me, then you either think I can help or I'm a suspect."

"Maybe a little of both," McManus said.

"So . . ." O'Shea leaned back and spread his hands wide. "Ask away."

"What do you know about your cousin's recent activities?"

"As I told you before, I haven't talked to Jimmy in a couple of weeks."

"Did you know he was involved with at least two of the victims who were killed recently?" McManus asked, and glanced at Bianca.

"You're talking about the Womb Raider, aren't you?" O'Shea frowned. "Why would Jimmy be involved in that?"

"That's what we're trying to find out."

O'Shea brought his hands together and placed the joined tips of his index fingers against his lips. "I'd say that it's a fairly big coincidence."

"A coincidence," McManus said, astounded.

Bianca stepped up beside McManus. "The first victim owed him money, and he got her a job in a nearby magic novelty store where she was murdered, then his girlfriend was killed in the safe house McManus had arranged after we found his body."

"That is a fairly big coincidence, isn't it?" O'Shea said. "But I'm sorry, I can't help any further. As I said, it's been weeks since I last saw my cousin. Now if that is all, I'll have you escorted back to the front gate."

"One more thing," Bianca said. "What is your involvement with the Hilden group?"

O'Shea looked at her and his frown deepened. "They're clients. Why?"

"We hear your company has made significant donations to a certain bid for a CHaPR appointment," she replied.

"There's no law against supporting a candidate, is there?" O'Shea asked.

"No," McManus said. "No law against it. But still it's interesting that you would be interested in the politics of CHaPR."

"My only interest is in my interests. I'll do whatever it takes to protect me and mine." Corey O'Shea's composure grew frosty. "Now if you don't mind, I have to get back to running a company." He nodded to the security guards. "Please escort our guests back to their car."

ON THE DRIVE back to the front gate, they passed the warehouse Bianca had mentioned on the way in. She stiffened beside him.

"Do you still sense something?" he asked.

She nodded.

"Then I think we should come back here and take a look in that warehouse later," he whispered in her ear.

She shot him a wide-eyed look.

26
Devil's in the Detail

How HAD SHE ever let McManus talk her into this? It seemed like the perfect idea when they'd left the O'Shea office this afternoon, but now, either way she looked at it, it was still breaking and entering, and still illegal. Not that it would matter if Corey O'Shea caught them. Not if he was even half as dangerous as McManus kept telling her.

He was right about one thing, though—they had to make sure the stolen babies weren't hidden away in that magically protected warehouse.

Bianca signaled right and checked the review mirror to change lanes, catching a blur of movement in the back.

"What the—" She quickly glanced over her shoulder into the backseat, catching another flash of blue.

"Come out where I can see you," she said.

Kedrax's head popped up between the seats, looking rather shamefaced.

"Get in here." She indicated the front seat.

The little dragon slunk up over the middle console and into the seat beside her. Then Vincent's head replaced Kedrax's between the seats.

"You too?" she said in amazement. "Come on."

The two of them sat side by side on the passenger seat, looking up at her—sheepish guilt written all over their little faces.

"What the hell are you two doing here?" she asked.

Vincent glanced at Kedrax and started cleaning himself. *Great avoidance tactic.*

"We were worried about you." The dragon lowered his head and looked up with soulful eyes. "And you'll need my help to get past that concealment enchantment. I need to be nearer for that."

He was right damnit. She sighed. "Why didn't you just ask?"

"Vincent thought you'd still say no."

The cat stopped cleaning himself and made a funny little noise as he looked at the dragon. Bianca could swear he was frowning. *Could cats even frown?*

"All right, *I* thought you would say no," Kedrax said, and the cat resumed licking his fur. "But Vincent agreed with me."

Hang on . . . back it up. "He understands you?"

Kedrax glanced at the black cat and tilted his head to the side. "Of course he does."

"How?"

The dragon's head tilted to the other side, his expression puzzled. "Because we bonded."

Right. Of course that explains everything.

"Okay, but you'll stay in the car, and don't let anyone to see you," she ordered. "Understood?"

Kedrax brightened. "Understood."

He crouched down on his stomach, crossed his front paws and relaxed. Vincent lay down beside him. The dragon was catching up to his size faster than she would've believed.

The two animals climbed into the backseat as Bianca pulled in behind McManus half a block from the OFL complex entrance. McManus leaned against his car smoking a cigarette while he waited for her. He threw the butt on the ground and stomped it out.

Like her, he wore all black, including a beanie to cover his sandy blond hair. It was strange to see him dressed in any-thing other than a suit, especially in such ill-fitting clothes.

"Yeah, I know," he said, plucking the T-shirt at least two sizes too big. "I didn't have much time and this was all they had in black."

Bianca tried to remain serious as she grabbed her bag of tricks out of the car, shutting the door quickly before he could look inside. "Let's get on with it, then."

"What've you got in there?" he asked, pointing to the bag.

"You don't think we're going to get in on your charm and my good looks, do you? We need something to disarm that concealment enchantment, and I have just the toys to do it."

"Of course you do." His smile turned serious as he picked up his own pack and slung it over his shoulder. "I got here early to scope out the best way into the complex. I think I've found a hole in their defenses not far from the hangar."

They moved through the back streets until they got to a twelve-foot chain-mail fence with razor wire on top. It looked like something out of those old prisoner-of-war-camp movies on late night TV.

"You don't seriously expect me to climb that, do you?" she asked him.

"You brought your tools, I brought mine." McManus pulled a pair of wire cutters out of his pack and began at-tacking the fence.

He made his cuts straight down from about a foot and a half off the ground, then as he neared the bottom, snipped at the wires on a right angle with the first cuts. When he'd cut another foot and a half, he pulled the wire back from the bottom corner, which left an opening big enough for her to crawl through.

She pulled the fence wire inward from the other side, looking around as he squeezed through.

"Okay, this way," he whispered, and led her toward the private tarmac at a crouching run.

"I'm surprised by the lack of security," she whispered as they stood flush against the wall of a warehouse and McManus peered around the corner.

"When you have canian security guards and enchantments, what else do you need?" He glanced at her in the darkness. "Besides, anyone dumb enough to break in and steal from Corey O'Shea is going to end up in a shallow grave or at the bottom of the harbor."

"So," she said. "What are we doing here again?"

"I never said I was smart, and I have no intention of stealing anything." He glanced around the corner again. "Ready?"

"Yes."

He started around the corner, then shoved her back against the wall as light from a vehicle flooded the road.

Kedrax entered her head. *Use a concealment spell now.*

She closed her eyes and concentrated, visualizing an invisible shield cloaking her and McManus.

"I heard something, I tell you," a security guard growled. "It came from over there, but it's gone now."

She froze and stared at McManus.

"We'd better take a look," a second voice said.

Footsteps crunched in the gravel, heading in their direction. Something brushed against her leg then shot around the corner.

"Hey, look man, it's just a cat," the second guard said.

"It didn't smell like a cat," said the first.

"From the looks of that old black tom, he's been living rough. See, he's only got one ear. Maybe we should put it down."

Bianca's heart stopped. *Vincent.*

I'll look after him, Kedrax said.

"No, keeps the rats down. Come on, Fido, let's go get a coffee," the second voice said.

"Stop calling me that or next time I shift, I'll bite you."

As the vehicle pulled away, she unclenched her fingers from McManus's forearm.

I told you to wait in the car, she thought to the dragon.

We did—for a few minutes at least, Kedrax's reply entered her head.

"Shit," she spat.

"That was close." McManus checked around the corner again. "Right, we're clear. The hangar is just behind this building. You ready?"

"Go," she said.

McManus disappeared. With her heart thundering in her chest, she followed, sticking to shadows close to the wall. She was so intent on looking for a black cat and small dragon that she almost ran into him where he'd stopped at the other corner.

"What's wrong?" she whispered. "Are there more guards?"

"No." He looked around, confused. "It's just I don't think this is the right way."

"It's part of the concealment spell protecting the warehouse." She pulled a thaumaturgic disruptor out of her pack and flicked it on.

"So you'll be able to remove it?" McManus said. "Like the one in the magic shop."

She held up the disruptor. "No, it's very different from that spell."

"Is that significant?" he asked.

"I don't know," she said, then frowned, suddenly certain. "McManus, this isn't the place. It feels too different. He doesn't have the babies in there."

McManus placed his hands on his hips and looked around. *He knew already.*

"Are you sure?" he asked, not even acting surprised.

"Positive."

"Since we're here anyway, we may as well take a look. He's still hiding something in there."

She sighed. "Okay, but this had better be worth the risk. I should be able to punch a hole with this if I can find the right place."

"How about there?" He pointed at a blue metal door about twenty feet away.

"Perfect."

She set the disruptor to create a field in a six-foot arc and placed it at the foot of the door. Nothing happened. It was too strange and too strong, neither familial nor druidic magic. Kedrax was right; the enchantment was much too powerful, and too different for her instruments.

Can we boost it? she asked.

I think so, Kedrax returned.

Bianca felt the thaumaturgic energy fill her body. She folded and wove it before directing the new energy pattern into the disruptor, boosting the power of the field to push a hole through the spell.

"Okay, it's disabled," she said to McManus, "but the door is still locked."

"Leave that to me." McManus pulled a device from his pack and attached it to the number pad.

"You're a bit of a surprise lately," she said.

"I told you my past wasn't all innocent; some skills you never lose." The door mechanism beeped and clicked open. "After you."

She picked up the disruptor and entered a small dark room. As soon as McManus closed the outer door, she turned the disruptor on low and placed it on the ground. "Just in case we need to make a quick exit."

She felt different, like she was missing something. *Are you still with me, Kedrax?* Her thought was met with silence. The spell must've formed a barrier between them, which meant she wouldn't have access to any more thaumaturgic energy in here. For the first time since their bonding, she realized how much a part of her Kedrax's presence had become.

"This looks interesting," McManus said as he stood in front of a pressure-sealed door and turned the large wheel in the center. The red light above the door changed to green and a seal hissed.

A breeze hit her in the face, smelling like loam and cinnamon. "Holy Mother Goddess," she said staring open-mouthed at what appeared to be an indoor old-growth forest.

27

Fantasy in Green

McManus could not believe his eyes. The trees grew so high they blotted out the ceiling. An eerie, ethereal glow lit the forest. Flowers and ferns grew in the leaf-littered loam soil around the enormous tree trunks. Butterflies, dragonflies, and other insects buzzed around, and birds sang sweet songs from the trees. It was like something out of a fairy tale, one of the most beautiful forests he'd ever seen.

"Now we know what he was hiding." Bianca's voice was little more than an awed whisper.

McManus stepped out onto the trail leading off through the undergrowth, but Bianca grabbed his arm. "I don't know if this is such a good idea. There's something strange going on here."

"You think?" he said. "Because I would've thought forests grew in aircraft hangars all the time."

She gave him that play-nice look. "There's something different here . . . different to anything I've ever felt before."

"How often do you get a chance to visit a secret forest like this? Come on, what can it hurt?"

She raised both eyebrows. "Are you kidding?"

"Come on, just a quick look." He needed to see what was

in there. Maybe this is where the O'Shea brothers cooked their drugs. *But in a forest?*

She sighed. "Okay, just a *quick* look." She reluctantly stepped onto the path beside him.

The otherworldly glow shone from above, through the trees, dappling the ground with shadows and light. A few feet in, the door and wall were no longer visible through the foliage. The climate was as temperate as a perfect spring day. After a few minutes a small clearing appeared off to the side and Bianca stopped. A fat rabbit hopped out from the undergrowth to nibble on some grass or roots or whatever it was rabbits ate.

A strange noise came from the bushes, almost like singing. Beautiful singing, and goose bumps peppered McManus's arm. The rabbit lifted its head and looked in the direction of the sound, still chewing. It sniffed, wiggling its little nose, and hopped a few steps closer, then wiggled its nose again. The singing continued and the rabbit moved closer still, sniffing the air, then disappearing into the foliage.

The bushes vibrated violently and a terrible high-pitched scream filled the air, stopping abruptly as a bloody tuft of white fur flew out and landed on the ground.

"Oh . . ." Bianca breathed beside him, eyes as round as saucers, filled with a mix of horror and revulsion.

"I need to see what it is," he whispered in her ear.

"No," she whispered back, gripping his arm tightly.

"I'll be careful."

He crept forward, keeping his footfalls as silent as he could. Curiosity outweighed his fear; after all, whatever it was didn't look that big, given the height of the undergrowth.

The vibration of the leaves had settled, and he swatted at the insect buzzing his ear as he reached to part the greenery.

"What do you see?" Bianca asked softly.

He put his finger to his lips to silence her and turned back to the bush. The annoying insect buzzed again. He batted at it, his hand connected with a satisfying thump, and he reached forward to part the undergrowth.

The rabbit carcass was already half stripped by many little creatures with what looked like glowing blue wings.

Little people?

He bent to get a closer look and a faint neon glow burst into full megawattage in front of face. It zigged and zagged at eye level, then flew straight at him, stopping mere inches from his nose. He stared at a three-inch female with translucent blue wings and a filmy dress. The others on the rabbit carcass all turned, their little hands and faces covered in the rabbit's blood.

"Fuck me," he said, falling back.

The tiny woman screeched in a high-pitched language he couldn't understand and appeared very, very pissed. She flew at his face, brandishing a tiny weapon she'd pulled from her belt and slashing at his cheek just below his eye. It was a surprisingly vicious attack, and his hand came away with a smear of blood.

"Protect your eyes," Bianca yelled at him as she raced to help him up, then froze as she got a closer look at what had attacked him. "A faerie?"

He swiped away the vicious little faerie female hard, and she slammed into a nearby tree trunk. Her glow grew even brighter as she flew at him with renewed vigor.

Persistent little thing.

A second glow joined her. This time a tiny male. Then a third. McManus held his arms in front of his face. They were only three inches tall, but they inflicted some nasty wounds. Already his cheek was open and bleeding freely.

Bianca screamed. McManus backhanded two of the flying creatures away and glanced over at her. Three more of what could only be faeries had yanked off her beanie, pulled her hair, and slashed at her arms.

Time to get out of here.

He smacked away a couple more of the flying pests. The little fuckers were tough; no matter how hard he hit them, they still got up. He grabbed Bianca and pulled her close.

"Run!" he yelled.

BIANCA FELT A moment of dizzy disorientation as she started to run. *Which way out?*

A buzzing horde of winged little warriors flew out of the trees to join the others. Most headed straight for McManus, who had his back to her, swatting at the half a dozen glowing blue sparks flying at him. She held out her hand and pushed the air at the oncoming onslaught, scattering the swarm before they could reach him. But she used up all the residual thaumaturgic energy she had left, and with her connection to Kedrax cut off, she had no way to source any more.

McManus fought through the swarm and ran toward her. "Come on, let's get out of here."

He grabbed her by the hand and pulled her back down the path she couldn't find a few moments ago. As the door came into sight, a glowing wall of blue appeared between them and their escape.

"This way," he said, turning right.

High-pitched laughter and taunting howls followed them as they ran blindly on. The amazement of this hidden enchanted forest had long worn off, and they'd be lucky if they made it out of there alive.

Another wall of blue appeared ahead of them. They turned. More faeries appeared, and she and McManus changed directions. The little creatures were playing with them, herding them where they wanted them to go.

McManus led her out into a clearing ringed by mushrooms and toadstools. Faeries were on all sides. They had them trapped and started to close in, primitive little weapons raised.

"STOP THIS," a strong voice boomed.

Everything stopped. They all turned toward the voice. Bianca hugged McManus's side. Several open cuts seeped on his face, and though his black clothing didn't show much, she could smell the blood on them.

"What is the meaning of this?" Corey O'Shea stood just outside the toadstool ring with three men and his brother behind him.

One of the faeries started to speak in a strange language, and Corey listened before calling out, using the same tongue. He held out his hand and the creature flew onto it, the blue glow now dimmer than it was before. It began to glow again as the tiny female launched into an animated tirade in the faeries' strange language, periodically pointing toward them.

McManus struggled to stay standing, and collapsed into a sitting position on the ground, clutching his leg around a small spear buried deep in the flesh of his thigh.

The tiny female's glow seemed to grow stronger the angrier her tirade got. Corey asked a few questions, which the faerie met with quick pointed answers as Bianca tried to follow. Even though she couldn't understand, she could tell it looked bad for them.

"Li-anis tells me you attacked them as they fed," Corey said to McManus.

"I did not," he answered. "One minute we were minding our own business—"

Corey raised an eyebrow and tilted his head to the right. "In a locked-down aircraft hangar that you broke into?"

"Ah, right." McManus shrugged and dragged a hand over the top of his head. "About that—"

"What are you doing here, McManus?" Corey asked.

"It's my fault," Bianca answered instead. "I sensed the power hiding something . . . but never in my wildest fantasies could I have imaged anything like this."

"It's something, isn't it?" Corey folded his hands behind his back and looked around. "It's been difficult keeping my subjects safe, both from humans and themselves."

It suddenly hit her. "That's impossible, you can't be."

He smiled and inclined his head. "Very good, Dr. Sin, I see you've worked it out."

28

The Faerie King

MCMANUS CRAWLED TO his feet holding his thigh. He was starting to think the only possible explanation was that O'Shea had slipped him some highly potent hallucinogenic. But the pain was real enough.

Very fucking real, in fact. And everyone but him seemed clued in.

"What the hell is going on here?" he asked.

Corey O'Shea addressed the faeries in the strange tongue, and the creatures reluctantly melted back into the forest. The little female that attacked him flew at his face and flitted her wings angrily before flying off to join the others.

When they were all gone, O'Shea looked at McManus. "The good Dr. Sin has worked it out. Ask her."

McManus shifted his weight. Warmth ran down the inside of his trousers and pooled in his shoe from the wound in his thigh.

"The O'Shea brothers are Unari, the first ones. The original magic wielders from which all castes are descended, though they were thought to have died out long ago."

O'Shea held out his arms. "As you can see, we're very much alive. However, while we still have some extraordinary talents in the outside world, our magical power is only confined to habitats like this."

"The faeries, they're the source of your magic," Bianca said.

O'Shea nodded. "Why we set up this habitat and several others like it."

"So, why did they attack us?" she asked him.

"The Fae are naturally curious but can become nasty when crossed. Li-annis said she was just trying to say hello, but when you went after her family while they were feeding, she attacked."

Unbelievable.

"So, let me get this straight," McManus said, his head growing light and dizzy. "You have an enchanted forest hidden in a hangar housing vicious Tinker Bells, and you're some kind of king of the faeries?"

Corey's lips curled in amusement. "I prefer Lord of the Fae."

"But you're supposed to be extinct," Bianca said.

Corey bowed at the waist. "As you can see, reports of our demise have been greatly exaggerated. Mostly by us. Misinformation is one of our greatest tools."

"You knew about them?" McManus said to Bianca.

"Only by legend and myth. When the tribes turned on the Dark Brethren, they disappeared," she said.

McManus could see it was the truth. "So are you going to tell us about Jimmy?"

Corey glanced at him. "Like I said before, we had a falling out. Jimmy was human, a cousin by marriage only, but he was still family. When he stole from me, I was furious, but I would've forgiven him in time as I had before. He knew this too." His expression took on a hint of regret. "But I have no idea what he was up to or who he was working for."

"If you find out, you'll let me know." McManus turned to Bianca. "Let's get out of here."

She nodded.

"Wait a minute. You broke into my property, saw things you shouldn't have seen, and you think you're just going to walk out of here?" Corey said, and crossed his arms. "Seamus here thinks we should dispose of you quietly. And trust me, he's been wanting that for years."

McManus tensed and turned. "If you wanted us dead, we already would be."

Corey O'Shea grinned and shrugged. "I see you've been listening, Detective. For now it suits me to let you go. I trust there's nothing you can do to hurt me." He leaned close to McManus. "Nothing. You can speak of this place, but no one will believe you. It's all part of the protection enchantment protecting this grove." He looked Bianca up and down. "Besides, I think you both have secrets of your own you need to protect."

O'Shea started to walk away, then stopped and turned. "I told you before. The only thing that interests me are my own interests." He held out his arms toward the trees. "This is my interest. If I so much as get a hint you are jeopardizing this, I'll let my brother loose on you."

Seamus O'Shea smiled—cold and deadly, his flat soulless eyes crinkling at the corners.

"Get them out of here," Corey said to a couple of his goons.

As McManus moved, the spear tip scraped against bone. He wrapped his hand around the shaft to pull it out.

"No," Bianca said, stopping him. "Not here, you could bleed out if you hit a vein or something. We need to get you to a hospital."

"Just get me out of here," he said.

LI-ANIS BUZZED OUT of a nearby tree and flew into a tirade of Faeish curses. Corey ignored her as he watched his men half drag the cop back through the forest. The witch followed uncertainly. He tilted his head, enjoying the way her ass swayed as she went.

"Do you think they know what they are," Seamus said quietly.

His brother never spoke unless they were alone.

"Not yet," Corey said. "The witch exudes power, more power than I have sensed in a millennia. The good detective—well, when he works out what he is, things are going to get very interesting. We're going to need them to finish this. So, they can't die. At least, not yet." He smiled at his brother and slapped him on the shoulder. "Besides, McManus is one of our best customers."

"We were lucky this time. If they'd discovered—"

Corey frowned and crossed his arms. "We can just be thankful they didn't. It would've ruined everything we've worked for. Now, for those security guards that let them in here—" He looked at his brother. "Fire them, permanently. And tell Tyrone Jordan to send us competent ones this time." He looked away from Seamus at the small building only visible through the trees because he knew it was there. "We've grown complacent, thinking our position protects us. Times are changing, my brother. The darkness is growing stronger."

29

the impatient patient

"I'M NOT GOING to the hospital," McManus stated as he leaned against his car. "There'll be too many questions."

"But you're pretty banged up," Bianca said. "That leg needs stitches."

"This isn't my first time. I have everything at home I need."

"Then at least let me drive you. We'll take your car." She held out her hand.

McManus opened his mouth then winced. "Okay." And felt around for his keys. "Shit, I think I lost them in the O'Sheas's warehouse. We'll have to take your car."

Kedrax, hide.

She pulled out her keys and hit the unlock button, still having no idea how the dragon and the cat had gotten out. Then she saw it. The broken rear window on the passenger side.

"Looks like you've been robbed," McManus said.

"That's what I get for parking in this part of town, I guess."

She opened the front passenger door and glanced inside to make sure it was all clear. There was no sign of either animal as she helped lower McManus into the car. She checked the back and saw a pair of golden eyes glowing low on the floor behind the seat. A pair of green feline eyes opened and blinked beside them.

"Sorry I'm bleeding all over your upholstery," McManus croaked. His skin had taken on a rather disturbing pallor. She had to get him home fast. Although hospital was probably a better idea, McManus was right about it raising too many questions.

By the time they reached his building, he looked even worse. She tried to help him from the car but he stubbornly pushed her away and hauled himself out.

His knees buckled and he put his hands out, bracing himself against the back passenger door. "Give us a sec."

"Okay, but the sooner we get you upstairs, the sooner we can get those wounds dressed."

"What the fuck is that?" McManus shouted, looking even paler as he hurriedly pushed away from the car.

She swallowed. "Where?"

"In there." He pointed to the car. "The blue thing with glowing eyes."

Different people saw Kedrax as different things. "What does it look like to you?"

"Some sort of lizard, or . . ." He tilted his head and leaned into the car, looking closer. "Any other night I would say that's impossible." He turned his head in her direction. "But it looks like a fucking tiny dragon?"

"What?"

Kedrax jumped up on the backseat. "He sees me, the real me."

"Whoa," McManus said, backing up farther. "It fucking talks too?"

"He hears me too." The little dragon looked perplexed. "This shouldn't be possible."

"Okay." McManus straightened. "I think I need a drink before you explain to me why you have a dragon in your car."

Vincent popped up onto the seat beside Kedrax.

"Come on, I need to get you upstairs and dress that wound," she said.

McManus dropped his head. "Well you can't leave that here, may as well bring it too. Both of them."

Bianca looked at him for a moment longer, then opened the back door. "Okay, let's go."

The two animals scurried out of the car and looked up at her.

We're sorry, Kedrax spoke into her head.

"It's okay," she said aloud. *Just behave.*

She shoved her shoulder under McManus's arm before he really did collapse, and this time he didn't fight her.

"I've lost my keys," he said as they walked toward the elevator. "The desk has a spare."

She leaned him against the wall and raced back to the desk clerk. "I need the key to Detective McManus's apartment."

"Lost them again, has he?" the clerk said, shaking his head, and unlocked a small cabinet on the wall. "That's the second time this week." Several keys hung on hooks. He took one and handed it to her. "Call the bar where you found him and they'll have them."

"Thanks," she said, and hurried back to McManus, looking around.

Kedrax and Vincent popped out from behind the potted plant and entered the elevator before them. McManus almost collapsed when they reached his floor and the doors opened, but clutched onto her shoulder and steadied himself.

His apartment was only two doors down from the elevator, but it still took several minutes to get him there. Bianca fumbled with the key while holding him up but finally managed to open the door, and they stumbled across the threshold together.

It'd been a while since she was last here. His apartment was clean, as usual. The first time she'd come she half expected to find empty bottles and old pizza boxes lying everywhere, but McManus kept his home clean and tidy, if somewhat spartan. No pictures hung on the walls, no plants decorated the corners, and the furniture was plain and simple.

He disengaged from her to shuffle into his tiny kitchen, and opened the cupboard above the sink. He pulled out a bottle, unscrewed the cap with a push of his thumb, took a swig, then practically fell into a chair beside the small kitchen table. He took another mouthful and reached over to turn on the gas cooktop.

Bianca filled a pot with water and set it over the naked flame. She grabbed a knife from the block and sliced open his sweatpants from the bottom of the leg to the hip. Fresh blood seeped around the shaft joining the dried stuff caked to the skin.

"Where is your medical kit?" she asked.

"In the bathroom."

"Watch him," she said to Kedrax and Vincent. "Make sure he doesn't move."

Kedrax jumped up on the table and dropped his head with a little snarl. She couldn't help smiling at the bemusement on McManus's face.

The bathroom, like the rest of the house, was neat and orderly. She opened the cabinet under the basin, grabbed the first aid kit and unzipped it. It had everything she needed, scissors, sterilized gauze, tape, bandages, but seemed short of antiseptic.

She opened the medicine cabinet above the basin and found some, but as she reached for the bottle, she spotted a small cellophane package of blue crystals. She dropped her head. The urge to grab it and throw it in the toilet lasted about a nanosecond.

She took the antiseptic, closed the cabinet, and looked at herself in the mirror.

It's really none of my business. "The fuck it isn't," she said aloud. "He's my friend, and one way or another I'm going to help him kick this shit."

"What did you say?" McManus called from the other room.

"Nothing." She picked up everything she needed.

McManus and Kedrax sat eyeing each other. Vincent lay curled up on the back of the sofa and appeared to be sleeping, though his ear twitched her way as she moved back to the table. McManus held the knife she'd used to cut his pants away to the flame on the gas stove as he drank more from the bottle.

"What *are* you doing?" she asked.

"Just a little street surgery," he said.

He set the bottle down on the table and with one sweeping movement yanked the spear shaft from his leg and placed the red-hot blade against the wound. The smell of burning flesh filled the apartment, and he bit down on a pain-filled roar.

Sweat blistered McManus's brow as he ground his teeth to silence his scream and picked up the bottle again.

"Give me that," she said, snatching it out of his hand and placing it back on the table out of his reach. "You shouldn't be drinking in your condition."

"It seems the perfect time for drinking to me," he said. "I need a little anesthesia."

"How could you be so stupid?" she asked as she looked at his wound.

Except it wasn't so stupid. The wound cauterized cleanly, and if she could stop the burn from getting infected, it should do nicely. She upended the antiseptic onto some gauze and cleaned around the wound.

McManus and Kedrax still sat staring at each other across the table in a Mexican standoff. Vincent had jumped up on the kitchen counter and sat watching them both.

Bianca placed a clean gauze pad over the wound and looked between him and Kedrax as she bandaged his leg. "You seem to be taking this surprisingly well."

He laughed derisively and threw up his hands. "I just found out there's a hangar full of carnivorous faeries. Why would a fucking toy dragon be a surprise? Besides, I'm still not convinced O'Shea didn't just slip us a Mickey and this is all just a hallucination."

"Hey," Kedrax said with real annoyance. "I'm not a hallucination, or a toy."

"Sorry, but you do look like a cereal box surprise." McManus snorted again and reached for the bottle. "Now I'm fucking talking to it."

So, not taking it as well as I thought.

"Remove your shirt," she said, changing the subject.

He raised an eyebrow but did it anyway as she walked around behind him. A multitude of scratches, grazes, and some rather nasty cuts covered his broad muscular back. Most looked superficial, but it was difficult to tell under all the blood. His discarded shirt was soaked in it. The deep cut running across his right shoulder blade worried her the most; it would need stitches.

Apart from all the fresh injuries, there were several old ones. Scars from bullet wounds, knife attacks, and a long puckered line under his left shoulder blade that looked more surgical than anything else. Bianca traced the scar with her fingertips, and McManus shivered under her touch.

She filled a bowl with some of the boiling water from the stove, added cold water and some of the antiseptic solution.

"So where did it come from?" McManus said.

Bianca glanced at the dragon. "*His* name is Kedrax and he's always been with me in a way." She smiled fondly at the dragon.

She slipped on a pair of latex surgical gloves from the kit, dipped the gauze in the solution, and began wiping away the blood from the wounds, starting with the nasty gash on his shoulder. Fresh blood welled when she wiped the deep cut.

"I'm going to have to stitch this, but you don't have any anesthetic."

"There's a needle and thread in there," he said, nodding to the kit on the table.

You can heal him with magic. Kedrax's words entered her head.

No, she answered. *He can't know.*

She threaded the needle and placed it in a kidney tray with undiluted antiseptic.

"You sure you want to do this?" she asked, needle poised.

"Hang on." He reached for the bottle of scotch and drained several mouthfuls before slamming it back on the tabletop. "Now, I am."

McManus sucked a breath in through his teeth as the steel bit into his flesh, but that was the only sign of pain he showed.

"Kedrax? Where did you get a stupid name like that?" he asked.

"*It's* my name." The little dragon's eyes flamed with anger.

McManus chuckled. "And it has a temper."

"Play nice you two," she warned as she finished the last stitch and snipped the thread.

As she moved around to his front, he looked up at her. "What do you mean he's always been with you?"

"Can't we just drop it?" Her hand went automatically to where her pendant used to be.

"That necklace you don't seem to wear anymore has something to do with this . . ." He tilted his head to the side and frowned.

Bianca didn't answer and kept her head low so she wouldn't have to look at him. She moved between his thighs and leaned over to dip fresh gauze in the antiseptic solution. His torso was even worse than his back. She lifted his chin to dab the cut on his cheek and his eyes met and held hers. A wicked smile played on his lips as he put his hands on her hips.

"Behave yourself," she said with a frown.

His hands moved to her waist and she smacked them away. "I said behave yourself."

"Oh I am," he said with a mischievous gleam. "If I wasn't,

I'd do this." He grabbed her around her waist and pulled her into his lap, his right hand resting on her thigh as his left trapped her against his chest.

She pushed up and out of his reach. "Be serious, McManus. I need to get these wounds dressed."

"Okay," he said, with mock contriteness.

Bianca tried not to look at him, but couldn't help it. She snuck surreptitious glances out of the corner of her eye. His muscular chest didn't have that over-worked-out look of body builders but was well shaped, and the cuts only seemed to enhance his physique. Artemisia had sensed his attraction to her. Thankfully, she'd learned to block the fact that she also found him attractive from her mother, and anyone else, including herself at times.

As soon as she came back within reach, he grabbed her again. She could've fought harder if she wanted. In that moment she didn't want to. After everything that had happened over the last few days, it was nice to be held. He looked down at her, the smile sliding from his face, and leaned forward to claim her lips. His mouth tasted of whiskey, which wasn't as unpleasant as she thought it would be. Hard muscular shoulders bunched under her fingers as he ran his hand down her thigh and the warmth traveled from her lips to her core.

McManus pulled back and looked at her. "Are you okay?"

All she could do was nod; his kiss had stolen her voice. Her fingers traced a raised surface above his collarbone. A mark, not a scar or a fresh wound, became apparent now that she'd cleaned the blood away. An oddly shaped purple birthmark sat just below where his neck joined his shoulder. She looked up at him and back at the birthmark.

"You know, this looks strangely like a—"

"Yeah I know," he said roughly only inches away. "Like a dragon."

She swallowed hard. "Please. Let me up."

"Why?" he asked. "Don't you like this?"

"You're drunk, McManus."

His face clouded over. "Do you think I only find you attractive when I'm drunk?"

"It's the only time you ever make a pass at me."

He ran his fingers down her cheek. "Oh, Sin, you are too beautiful for words," he whispered, intensely staring at her lips. "Too beautiful."

Then he let her go. "You're right, I *have* been drinking." Except now he sounded very sober.

With shaking hands, she continued to clean his scrapes and mend his cuts with butterfly plasters from the first aid kit. None of the others seemed serious enough for stitches, though.

"Bianca." McManus grabbed her wrist and swayed. "Suddenly, I don't feel so good." And he slid from the chair and fell to the floor. The blood loss wasn't that bad. Something else must be wrong.

"Kedrax," she yelled, and fell to her knees beside him.

The little dragon jumped from the table and sniffed at the tip of the six-inch little spear. "It's been poisoned, an old magical poison. You'll have to heal him."

She shook her head. "I don't know how."

Kedrax leapt off McManus onto her thighs. "Yes you do. Reach inside yourself, everything you need is in there."

"Corey O'Shea, he'll know what—"

"You don't have time for that. He'll die."

She nodded and wiped her hands on her pants, then held them over McManus's naked chest. Nothing happened.

"Reach down deep, it's in you," Kedrax said.

Bianca closed her eyes, concentrating harder, and looked into McManus to find the poison. She wove a spell to transform the poison particles into healing ones. Not just for his blood either, but to boost his immune system and speed up the healing process. She could feel the life flowing back into him.

When she opened her eyes, the wounds closed as if zipped from the inside, though the blood remained.

Confusion turned to accusation in his eyes as he looked up at her. "What've you done?"

She panicked. The magic, stronger than any she'd used before, backlashed.

Kedrax.

She kept hold of the energy to protect the dragon. Until a white light exploded behind her eyes.

30
cat's out of the bag

MCMANUS WOKE ON the floor staring at the ceiling. This wasn't the first time, and yet he didn't feel the nausea and foggy headache that usually accompanied his hangovers. He raised himself up onto his elbow. Bianca and her little creature lay beside him, both unconscious.

That couldn't be good.

It all came flooding back like some sort of bad dream; the O'Shea brothers and their freaky Alice in Wonderland aircraft hangar, the little dragon and Bianca . . .

She'd used magic, which meant she wasn't broken anymore. *How?*

The dragon. He had to be her familiar somehow. Bianca's cat meowed down at him from his perch on the kitchen counter.

"Worried about them too, puss?" he asked the feline. The cat answered with another meow and looked between Bianca and Kedrax.

McManus climbed to his feet and realized he was half naked. Dried blood caked his skin, but there was no pain. He ran a hand over his torso, checking his injuries. She'd completely healed him.

Bianca's low, shallow breathing worried him as he picked up her limp body and carried her into his bedroom. The dragon's hide seemed duller than before, and though cold, it felt soft and velvety instead of reptilian. He lay it down on the bed beside Bianca. The cat had followed him, and now jumped up beside the dragon. It meowed and gave the little creature a couple of licks. When the dragon didn't move, the cat lay down and rested his chin on his paws, watching over both it and Bianca.

McManus didn't know what to do. He suspected that her condition had something to do with the magic, but he had no idea where to start. Oberon DuPrie might, though. He pulled out his new cell phone, but had lost all his numbers when the old one was destroyed in the magic shop fire. He searched Bianca and found hers.

DuPrie answered on the first ring. "Hello?"

"Something's happened to Bianca. She's unconscious; I think it's some sort of magic thing."

"McManus?" DuPrie asked. "Where are you?"

"My apartment. It's—"

"I have the address. Be there soon."

He almost asked how DuPrie knew where he lived, but instead said, "Make it quick," and hung up.

"Watch over them, puss," he said to the cat, and could've sworn it understood, as it started cleaning the unconscious dragonette again.

OBERON ARRIVED TWENTY minutes later with the former medical examiner, Kitt Jordan, and McManus took them straight into the bedroom, where Bianca remained unchanged.

The cat purred beside them, half covering the little dragon. Kitt rushed to the bedside and pulled a stethoscope out of the black bag she carried. "What happened?" she asked, listening to Bianca's heartbeat.

"I don't know. I woke up and found her like that, along with the dragon."

Kitt frowned, pulled the stethoscope from her ears and hung it around her neck. "Is that the cat's name?"

"No," he said. "Not the cat, the other one."

Kitt tilted her head to the side. "Have you been drinking?"

"Yes a bit, but . . ." *Maybe I'm going mad.* "Never mind," McManus said. "Do you know what's wrong with her?"

"I'm afraid not," she said. "If it's something mystical, then it's beyond my field of expertise. You need another witch."

Using Bianca's cell phone, he called Artemisia. Why hadn't he thought of her in the first place?

"This is a funny time to be calling your mother," a somewhat irate female voice answered.

"Forgive me, but—"

"Detective McManus?"

"Yes, Your Honor?"

"Why are you calling from my daughter's phone? Something's wrong, isn't it?"

"We can't wake her," McManus said, looking down at Bianca. "Or her familiar."

"Familiar? Is this some sort of joke?" Artemisia sounded genuinely annoyed. "Bianca's unbonded."

"Not anymore, she has this . . ." What should he tell her? The truth, and have her think he was completely mad, like Oberon and Dr. Jordan already did? "You just need to get here as fast as you can."

A crash of light flashed behind him. "Bianca, honey."

"Right," he said, and hung up the phone as Artemisia Sin sat down on the bed beside her daughter, the white python wrapped around her shoulders.

"Where did you come from?" Kitt asked shakily.

"A mother can always sense her offspring." Artemisia unwrapped the snake from her shoulders and placed it on the bed. "Now, tell me what happened."

The snake hissed and slithered toward Vincent, who arched his back and spat.

"Matilda, behave," Artemisia commanded.

The snake stopped and curled up, keeping the cat within her hungry, soulless gaze.

McManus repeated the story about waking up to find Bianca unconscious on the floor beside him. He left out the bit about Kedrax, but Artemisia remembered what he'd said on the phone.

"So where is this familiar?" she asked.

31

LOST AND FOUND

IT WAS HER room, yet it wasn't her room. The one from her childhood, not the one she lived in now. Except it wasn't that either.

Instead of the floor there was a whiteness. The walls and ceiling were made of the same stuff. But the bed was the same one she'd slept in as a child. All her favorite toys were piled on the kitten-patterned quilt, just as they had been all those years ago. A rocking chair sat in what would be the corner of the room with the shawl her mother used to wear as she rocked and sang lullabies to her. The window with the lace bunny curtains hung to one side of the room, suspended in midair.

It was in her haven, her mind's safe place. The place she came to when she was scared. Nothing could touch her. Nothing could go wrong or hurt her. Everything here was right and safe.

But it wasn't all right. And she didn't feel safe.

Something was here with her. Something cold, something dark, something foreign. It moved beyond her vision, swirled in the mist. Stalking her. Soulless and hungry.

"Who's there?" she called out.

No answer came, though she sensed amusement.

"Who are you?" she asked again.

The room lost some of its brightness and all of its safety. Her bed and toys no longer seemed as comforting as a moment ago. The toys' smiles twisted into evil grins, chilling Bianca to the bone as the room began to spin. An amused chuckle filled the air.

"What do you want?" she screamed.

"YOU WITCH," a hollow voice intoned. *"YOUR POWER CALLS TO ME."*

The mist grew thicker. Bianca caught movement out of the corner of her eye, but when she turned her head in that direction, nothing was there.

"I CAN HELP YOU BE MORE POWERFUL THAN YOU EVER DREAMED. MORE POWERFUL THAN ANY OF THOSE WITCHES THAT LOOKED DOWN ON YOU."

A warmth ran up her arms, as if someone was caressing her. It fondled her hair, brushed her neck.

"JOIN WITH ME," it said seductively. *"YOU'LL NEVER HAVE TO BE ALONE AGAIN."*

"Who are you?" she moaned, feeling her will slipping away from her.

"MY NAME IS EALUND," it said.

Then Kedrax was with her. Not only nearby, but within her mind.

The presence shank back. *"NO,"* it hissed. *"IT CAN'T BE."*

Kedrax's aura surrounded her. *Leave her.* The little dragon's tone projected power. *NOW!*

The misty darkness withdrew, and when it was gone completely, Bianca opened her eyes to relieved smiling faces surrounding her, even if they had a ghost of worry.

Artemisia cupped her cheek with a warm hand. "Welcome back."

As she began to sit up, her head spun. "What happened?"

"You passed out," McManus said from the doorway, his face half cast in shadow from the bedside lamp.

"No I don't mean that . . ." She couldn't gauge his mood.

Kedrax stirred beside her and rested his leg on hers.

What happened in there?

We'll talk about it later. The dragon's thought entered her head. *It'll be better if I tell you when we're alone. They'll see something wrong on your face.*

Oberon and Kitt stood on the other side of the bed. Vincent jumped on her chest, purring and rubbing his head against her face, almost frantic to be near her.

She laughed and scratched behind his good ear. "I'm happy to see you too."

Kedrax yawned and stretched his wings. She looked around. McManus knew. So she wanted to let those closest to her know too. Especially her mother.

Show yourself to them. I want them to know.

Are you sure?

Yes.

Bianca watched her mother's face as a collective gasp filled the room.

"What in the holy hell is that?" Oberon was the first to speak.

"I can't believe it," Bianca's mother whispered, her hand going to her throat.

Kedrax sat up and looked at her. "Hello, Artemisia, it's good to see you."

"You know me?" Artemisia said, and frowned. "And why do I feel I know you?"

"You wore me around your throat until your daughter was born. You were strong, and there were times I thought you'd be the one to wake me, but your daughter is stronger."

Like Bianca, Artemisia's hand clasped at a pendant that was no longer there, and she nodded.

Sitting on the side of the bed, she took her daughter's hand in hers and looked at Kedrax. "This is incredible."

McManus stayed in the shadows, closed off and unreadable.

"Um . . ." Bianca said stroking Kedrax's velvet leathery wings. "I guess I have some explaining to do."

"I have to get back," Kitt said, and took Bianca's hand. "I'll call in on my way home later." She bent down and kissed her cheek. "I think he's totally cool."

"I'll put on some coffee," McManus said as he pushed away from the doorway.

Artemisia tucked a strand of Bianca's hair behind her ear. "Now tell me what happened. Both before and while you were out. I could feel your terror."

"I don't know where to start."

"She got scared of the magic and stopped," Kedrax explained. "The backlash of energy shut us both down. And while she was unconscious, the Dark Brethren tried to seduce her. Now they know I exist."

"Why was he so afraid of you?" Bianca asked.

Kedrax crawled into her lap. "Because dragonkind imprisoned the Brethren several millennia ago."

Her mother sat back and traced her fingers over Kedrax's hide. "I've heard stories of dragons, but I thought they were just that—stories. I mean, dragons . . ."

"I don't think it's a coincidence that Kedrax is here now, when the Dark Brethren are stirring," Oberon said.

"I think you're right," McManus said, coming back into the room with a tray of steaming mugs.

Bianca remembered his lips on her. But he wouldn't even meet her eyes now.

Artemisia stood up. "This means you can finally take your rightful place at my side."

Bianca shook her head. "I don't think that's a good idea."

"What do you mean? You've been licensed for years, it's only the lack of a bond that stopped you. I've dreamt of this from the day you were born. I'd given up hope."

"We can speak about this later," Bianca said. "Right now I think there are other things to consider."

Oberon crossed his arms. "She's right. We've had word

from someone high up in the CHaPR council that the Hilden coven are trying to force some major changes. They're buying votes and trying to get their own candidate elected to the Five."

"Gayla?" Artemisia said, seemingly unsurprised.

"Her son-in-law, Marcus," Oberon replied.

"Having Bianca remain off the grid could give you an advantage." Artemisia's brow creased at the thought, and she looked down as she paced. "There've been rumors of other covens aligning to the Hildens'. And not just familial either. But other castes." She looked up again, first at Oberon and then at Bianca. "Okay, I'll agree for now. But when the others find out you've bonded with a dragon, they'll be after you to either join them or . . ." She trailed off, her frown deepening.

"Or?" Oberon asked.

"Stop her from joining anyone else," McManus said, looking at her for the first time. "One way or another, Bianca is going to be the most powerful witch alive, and that kind of power will be coveted." It was still difficult for her to gauge his reaction.

"It's just as well no one else knows about it," Oberon said.

Kedrax jumped up on the table in front of Bianca. "That's not exactly true."

"The Dark Brethren presence from my dream," she said.

The little dragon nodded. "It was no dream. And now they know what you are."

"I thought they only went after the weak-minded and the insane," Oberon said.

"They also prey on the vulnerable," Artemisia said. "And with all you've been through lately," she said to her daughter, but looked pointedly at the little dragon.

"You know about the Dark Brethren?" Oberon asked Artemisia.

"Of course I do. There was a cult known as the Noire Apôtre that worship them but they haven't existed in nearly a century," she said. "However, there've been rumors of a new coven of the black disciples."

"Well, I'd say rumor confirmed," Bianca said, "and they're responsible for the recent deaths. McManus and I found their temple in the basement of a magic shop."

Artemisia looked at her sharply. "This is very bad news."

"Do you think this has something to do with the instability of the council?" Oberon asked. "Could Gayla Hilden's coven be responsible?"

"Highly unlikely," Bianca said. "Though I wouldn't mind the chance to see how they're taking this."

"That's going to be difficult," Oberon replied. "Since the deaths, all covens have increased security, and we no longer have jurisdiction over the case, so you can't just waltz in."

"Actually, that's exactly what you can do," Artemisia said to her. "The funeral."

Bianca looked at her mother. "Of course. It's today. And their emotions are going to be raw and exposed."

"Is that wise, I mean just turning up?" Oberon asked.

Her mother turned to him. "As for my daughter, it's expected she pay her respects."

"Then I'm coming with you," McManus said.

32

A prayer for the Living

THE DEEP PURPLE velvet coat was the closest thing to formal funeral wear, though probably not the best choice, given the warm day. Bianca took a deep breath and looked at McManus. "You ready for this?"

Without looking at her directly, he offered his elbow. They stepped through the front gate of the Hilden estate and joined the throng of guests dressed in similar shades of deep purple, the mourning color for witches.

News vans from all over the world blocked the streets along the estate perimeter. A death in the family of one of New York's most prominent families would've been newsworthy at the best of times, but to have such a brutal murder made it a world event.

Bianca kept her head down as they passed Trudii Crompton speaking animatedly in front of a WFTN camera, and loosely clutched McManus's arm as they walked across the lush lawns between the black and purple flags flapping on the late afternoon breeze.

"You could've told me," he said, low enough for only her to hear.

He'd avoided her for hours, wouldn't even look at her, and

he wanted to do this *now*. "Really, McManus? Not exactly the best time."

"Maybe not." He pulled her behind the trunk of a large, leafy oak tree. "But how can I trust you when you lied to me?"

"I didn't lie," she said. "I just didn't tell you."

"Why?"

She searched his face, the hurt and betrayal raw in his eyes. "It's been less than a week and I'm still trying to come to terms with it myself, let alone ready to share it with anyone else. Besides, you've made no secret of how much you hate magic."

"No," he said, frowning deeply. "I hate witches. There's a big difference."

"How?" She stopped speaking and smiled politely at a couple who drifted close. "Blessed be."

"Blessed be, sister . . . brother," the woman said, linking her arm through her partner's as they walked in the same direction as the other mourners.

McManus waited until the couple was well out of earshot before speaking again. "Tell me why you weren't so keen to join your mother's coven."

"Like I said, I think it's best to stay—"

"The real reason, Sin, not the excuse you gave your mother."

She sighed. "They would've had expectations and put restrictions on—" She looked up at him. "Oh . . ."

He nodded. "That's what witches do, they control, they bend and twist things for their own purpose, and you'd be powerless to stop them. But you're right about one thing," he said, taking her arm as another couple of mourners drifted close. "This probably isn't the right time."

"So, you're okay with this?" she asked.

"No!" But he didn't say any more as they continued across the grounds.

Okay, maybe time to change the subject. "Have you ever been to a coven funeral before?"

"Only when one of the Sisterhood passed away. There were three funerals in the Sanctum while I was there."

"This will be different, very different. Weddings, births, and deaths are spectacles for my people," she said. "One thing you must remember is to stay out of the ring of white stones around the funeral pyre. Only the family members or those of the same coven are allowed within the grief circle."

"Thanks for the tip," he said. "Anything else I should know?"

"Just take your cues from me."

He nodded without looking at her and his eyes narrowed as they crested the slight hill. Several hundred people gathered in the valley below filled with tents, food, music, and a sea of purple. It looked more like festival than a funeral, but that's how her people did things.

"Holy shit," McManus whispered. "I didn't think there'd be so many."

"I tried to warn you. Given the family's rank, there'll be representatives from covens all over the world. The highest ranking will be closest to the pyre, the lowest will be at the back. And given that the Sin coven is ranked second in New York, we'll have ringside seats."

It took more than twenty minutes to make their way through the crowd, and she found the Sin pavilion set up just outside the circle. Not even Gayla Hilden's animosity would've displaced their position.

Relief relaxed Artemisia's features as Bianca leaned forward to kiss her on the cheek. "I was starting to wonder if you'd changed your mind."

"No, just had trouble finding a parking space."

"Go, say hello to your grandmothers." Artemisia turned to McManus and held out her hand. "Welcome, Detective."

Bianca left him with her mother and bent to kiss an impeccably dressed woman. "Hi, Grammy."

"Hello sweetie," her grandmother said, patting her on the cheek.

Bianca turned to her great-grandmother and squatted to eye level in front of her wheelchair. "It's so good to see you, Gi-Gi."

"Child." A smile split the old woman's face as she reached out and stroked her hair with cool shaky fingers. "It shouldn't take a death for us to get to see you."

"I'm sorry, Gi-Gi." She squeezed her great-grandmother's hand gently. "I'll make an effort to come visit more often."

"And you can bring that new pet of yours too," Gi-Gi said, looking to where McManus stood with her mother.

Bianca's eyes widened in surprise.

Grammy smiled. "She's right, he's quite the specimen. Artemisia, bring Bianca's new boy over here so we can get a better look."

Bianca's cheeks heated. "Grammy, he's hardly a boy."

Artemisia laughed, taking the detective's arm and leading him over. "Detective McManus, I would like to introduce you to my mother, Leticia Sin, and my grandmother, Bianca's namesake."

McManus took Leticia's hand. His eyes went wide and Bianca could swear he was blushing.

"Fine specimen indeed," Bianca's grandmother said.

"Mother!" Artemisia pulled McManus away. "And Grandmother. Behave yourselves. This is Bianca's colleague, not her lover."

"Why not?" Gi-Gi asked as she stroked his hand with her ancient arthritic fingers. "He's got a good body under that suit, strong agile hands." She looked at Bianca. "What's wrong with you, girl? Where's your Sin passion?"

"Gi-Gi," Bianca complained. How could they embarrass her like this?

"Well, it's very nice meeting you anyway, Detective." Gi-Gi smiled widely.

McManus just grinned and winked at the elder Sin. "The pleasure is all mine, ladies."

A sharp horn blast interrupted any further conversation, and people took up their positions around the ring of white stones.

33

Life, Death, and Rebirth

McMANUS GLANCED TO his right and caught Bianca's grandmother watching him again. She winked and he looked away with a smile. Who'd have guessed Bianca's family was filled with such lusty women?.

Bianca had told him about the circle of white stones and the pyre, but he still wasn't completely prepared for the wooden dais adorned with flowers and ribbons sitting over a pile of kindling and firewood. They were actually going to burn the body in front of all these people. Surely there must be some sort of law against this kind of disposal of human remains?

A hush fell over the gathering as two women appeared in flowing white shifts, each of them holding a bouquet of wild flowers, with more woven into their long flowing hair. They chanted as they started down the path leading to the white stone border. Two more followed them, then two more, until a procession made its way to the circle, their voices filling the air with haunting beauty. As they carefully stepped barefoot into the circle of stones, the two lines split, heading in opposite directions, following the inside circumference of the white stone ring.

.

Bianca glanced at him and leaned closer. "The women of the coven are creating the circle to represent life, death, and rebirth," she whispered out of the side of her mouth.

"I thought purple was your color of mourning?" he whispered.

"Not for the family or coven. It is white for purity of life."

As the circle was completed, two lines of men appeared from the same place, balancing a platform on their shoulders. Like the women, they were barefoot and dressed in loose white clothing and proceeded down the path. Flowers filled the platform, Tiffany Hilden's body nestled among them. Her hair lay in dark ringlets threaded with flowers and she was dressed the same as the other women of the coven. Her face looked fresh and flush with life. None of the horror of her death marred her beautiful features, but she was dead, and nothing could change that.

Tiffany's father led the procession, his face set in a stony mask as he bore the burden of his daughter's body. The men carried the platform to the dais and carefully placed it on top, each stepping back and out of the circle.

"According to tradition, women are the bringers of life and ushers of death," Bianca explained in a whisper. "The men must take their rightful place behind them."

"Rightful?" McManus asked under his breath.

"I told you we were a matriarchal society."

At the head of the path an ancient woman appeared, pushing an even more ancient woman's wheelchair. They were followed by an elderly woman, the Domina, and Astrid Hilden.

"This is the matriarchal line of the deceased coming to bid farewell to their lost daughter," Bianca whispered. "The first is Tiffany's great-great-great-grandmother, who is a hundred and fifty-six years old, followed by her great-great-grandmother, her great-grandmother, then the Domina as her grandmother, and finally her mother."

"Witches live a long time."

She chuckled softly and looked over at her own forbearers. "Yes we do."

"What's wrong with Astrid?"

Artemisia leaned over. "I hear she's taking the death of her daughter extremely hard. They've had to keep her sedated since the night of the murder."

The woman stumbled. The Domina stopped, her face pinched with disapproval as she helped to her steady her daughter. McManus glanced at the dead girl's father, whose expression matched the Domina's.

A little harsh, since the woman just lost her only child.

They weren't the only ones looking on with interest. Another group just beyond Marcus Hilden whispered behind their hands, seeming to take delight in the poor woman's stumble.

"Who are they?" McManus asked, nodding to the group.

Bianca glanced at them. "That's the Manov coven. Should the Hilden coven fall out of favor, the Manov would be one of the forerunners to take their place."

"'One' of the forerunners?"

"There are three contenders," Artemisia said. "The Manovs—Marcus's former coven; the Bruun; and of course us."

"Your family is a rival coven?"

Bianca glanced at her mother and nodded.

Any one of them could be responsible for knocking off a rival family member. And yet, stolen fetuses didn't really fit well into that scenario.

Several other groups had pavilions around the circle. Some were dressed in more normal clothing, while others were dressed in full-on Wiccan robes. "What about those other groups?"

Bianca frowned and looked around. "They're the representatives from the other castes."

The singing stopped suddenly as the five Hilden women took up positions around the pyre.

"Where are all the animals?" McManus asked.

"All this emotion upsets and confuses the familiars," Bianca explained.

A solemn hush fell over the gathering. The Domina took her a place at the head of the funeral pyre and started to speak in a language McManus didn't understand. Bianca sat up straight, her attention riveted on the proceedings. McManus took his cue to shut up, but couldn't turn off his inner cop. He watched the crowd, every twitch, every nuance, trying to catch the unguarded look that may give away some hint of guilt.

There was a lot of awe and respect for the Domina, and there was also a lot of fear and hate. The old adage of keep your friends close and your enemies closer embodied this atmosphere.

Bianca and her elders kept reverent silence during the rite, but others whispered behind hands, and cast disapproving glances. As the head witch spoke the words, she also watched those around her. He could see her eyes resting on one then another, as if committing them to memory. She was arrogant, but she was no fool.

When she stopped speaking, the oldest of the witches rose from her wheelchair and pulled fire out of the thin air. The flames danced in their hands as it was passed from mother to daughter down the line, until all five witches stood before the funeral pyre, blue fire dancing on upturned palms. Tiffany's mother stood the closest to where McManus sat, with her back to them.

As the sun disappeared on the horizon, the witches each flung a stream of fire at the wood and kindling, engulfing the platform completely with the blue blaze. It burned bright and brilliant and then, as if all the air was sucked out from underneath the fire, the flames folded in on themselves and went out. The body looked untouched, her pale complexion still vibrant against her dark hair. Then, suddenly, it disintegrated into dust and fell to the earth, as if each particle that made the flesh had let go. Out of the ashes a pure white dove flew high and fast up into the darkening sky.

As the dove disappeared, the dead girl's mother stumbled backward across the white stones and collapsed in a heap. Bianca was out of her seat instantly, McManus a step behind her. Everyone else seemed to be watching the bird. Astrid Hilden roused, her eyes opened as Bianca pushed the hair back from her face, and seemed relieved to see her.

"Please, help me," she whispered to Bianca. "You have to stop them. They won't let me—"

"Astrid?" the Domina yelled, rushing over to her side.

The witch glanced at her mother and then to her husband, who stood behind the Domina. Her eyes went wide, filling with fear as she tightly clutched Bianca's hand and whispered, "Please."

The coven members surrounded them, quickly lifting Astrid up. As they whisked her away, Astrid glanced back at Bianca over her shoulder, desperation filling her drawn features.

"Astrid is having a difficult time," Gayla Hilden said to them. "Please forgive her behavior."

"There's nothing to forgive," Artemisia said. "I can only imagine what it would be like to lose a child." She squeezed Bianca's hand.

The Domina nodded quickly and turned to follow Astrid.

34
paradise lost

BIANCA WAITED FOR McManus in the foyer of NYAPS. Astrid Hilden's desperate expression had haunted her since the funeral the day before. She couldn't erase the image of the witch's grief-stricken distress as she pleaded, clutching Bianca's hand almost with desperation.

Who or what did she want stopped, though? The killer, the coven, or the deaths?

Bianca jumped with a start at the touch to her shoulder.

"Hey!" McManus said. "You away with the pixies?"

"Not this time." She smiled. "I was just thinking about what Astrid was trying to tell us."

He nodded, his face solemn. "I've been doing the same. I wish we could've questioned her."

"Come on," she said. "Let's go see what Tones has for us." She turned to the elevator.

"Before we do," he said, catching her by the arm. "About the whole witch thing—I just need some time."

"There's no need—"

"Yes there is." He pushed her gently against the wall, his face mere inches from hers. "Do you know how happy I get when there's even a hint of parahuman activity and I have to call you in on a case? But now everything's different . . ." He glanced down.

She put her hand against his chest. "I know, for me too. All of a sudden I have something I never thought I'd—"

Her cell rang, making her jump.

"What's taking you guys so long?" Tones asked.

"We'll be right there," she said, and hung up. "We have to go, we can talk about this later."

In the Bunker, Tones had three smart screens set up in the conference room.

"Right, what have you got for us?" Bianca asked, taking a seat.

"I've pulled down all I could find, records, notes, missing person files," Tones said. "So let's start at the beginning. This is the first victim, known simply as Angel." He dragged the picture of the dead girl in from the side with his finger and placed it in the first of four columns set out on the board. Small droplets of blood splattered her pretty, pale features. The head shot didn't show the gaping wound in her stomach, which he rectified with the next couple of images.

"Any luck in identifying her?" McManus asked.

Tones shook his head. "She's not on any missing persons' list that we can find. Even though you said she may have been a hooker, no charges of soliciting or anything else were ever brought against her. She was completely clean and, as of this moment, untraceable. However . . . I had a little more luck with this one." Tones pulled in a couple of pictures of the first crime scene Bianca had attended in this case. He dropped the pictures into the second column. "This is Crystal Daniels, the niece of Nilifa Daniels, the famous 'apothecary to the stars.'" He summarized in points with the special blue smart pen as he spoke and added a high school photo of the girl.

McManus frowned. "What was she doing on the streets?"

"Apparently, she was researching a thesis paper called 'The Invisible Population'," Tones said.

Bianca crossed her arms and leaned against the table. "So she wasn't homeless?"

"Far from it. She lived with her mother on the Upper East Side when she wasn't studying sociology at NYU," Tones said.

"Damn, it's surprising the press hasn't jumped all over this," McManus said.

Tones smiled. "VCU haven't released the information yet. Besides, the media sharks are still in a feeding frenzy over the Hilden story."

McManus leaned on the table beside her, his shoulder touching hers. "Tiffany Hilden is next."

Tones dragged the girl's pictures into column three, and then dropped Myfanwy's pictures as the final victim into the last column on the first board.

"Hmm." Bianca picked up the red smart-board pen and tapped it against her palm. "So we have an unknown, an apotheke, a familial witch, and a druidess. It almost looks like the killer is targeting young witches from each of the thaumaturgic castes. So our first was either from the divination or the necromancy path, and we can expect another set of murders."

"You're right." McManus straightened. "I think VCU have it completely wrong when they say the murders of the males on the same night are just coincidence or just a case of wrong place, wrong time."

"I'd agree." Tones pulled in a photo and placed it in the second column. "I've done a bit of digging and found out the pre-med boy murdered the same night as Crystal was her date the previous night. Tiffany's boyfriend and Fast Jimmy were killed in an identical fashion as the premed kid."

"I think the male—or at least his blood and death—is part of the spell to induce the pregnancy," Bianca said. "Is there anything else that could tie this all together?"

"I would've thought worshiping the Dark Brethren was a pretty big motive," Tones said.

"I agree, but why these girls and why now?" Bianca wrote the name on a second board. "Astrid Hilden knows something. Did you see the fear when she looked at her husband and mother?"

"There's definitely something going on there," McManus said.

"Do you think they'd kill their own flesh and blood?" Tones asked.

McManus nodded. "When it comes to power, some people will do anything."

"Let's list some of the other persons of interest," Bianca said, and stepped up to the white board. "What does VCU have?"

Tones grinned. "Nothing as usual. They're still assuming this is a black market baby ring."

Bianca stepped away from the board. "Okay, we have several rival covens that could benefit from the Hilden fall, but what would that have to do with the other witches?"

"If we're counting the familial covens," Tones said, "we have to be looking at the other castes as well."

"And add the O'Shea brothers," McManus said. "I'm convinced they're involved somehow. Any luck finding out who owned that magic shop?"

Tones shook his head. "It's listed as a concern of an umbrella company owned by another umbrella company based in the Cayman Islands. I'm still tracking the paper trail."

"In summary, we have nothing," McManus said, looking at the names on the board. "Nothing at all."

35

HELL BOUND

NANETTE'S HANDS SHOOK and she dropped the keys. Again. She picked them up and tried to make the slim shaft of metal enter the lock, which seemed impossible with his hot breath burning the back of her neck.

His hand closed over her wrist. "If you don't hurry up," he whispered darkly against her ear, "I'll just do you right here in the alley."

A shiver ran down her spine. The key slid home. She unlocked the door and twisted in his arms. The door opened inwardly and they fell through, smashing against the wall behind. His breath was hot and heavy as he pushed her against the table, ripping at the front of her shirt.

"Slow down," she said, trying to catch her breath. "We have all night."

Dajon looked around nervously. "Are you sure your grandfather is gone?"

Nanette laughed. "He really scares you, doesn't he?"

"Fuck yeah," he said. "All that crazy voodoo shit."

"Come on." Nanette took him by the hand. "We can go and check, just to make sure."

Several chickens popped their heads up in cages and

clucked softly. Snakes slithered in their tanks, black tongues darting out. Dried chicken feet hung from a rack suspended above the counter. Skulls and bones of all shapes, sizes, and species were stacked on the shelves behind the cash register. The mummified remains of birds, insects, and reptiles hung from the ceiling along with an array of colorful bric-a-brac. All the things used in necromantic spells could be found here. Nanette's grandfather was the shaman of their congregation.

Dajon was human and didn't understand the ways of her people. Which was exactly why her father and grandfather didn't like him. Anything that pissed off the old bastard was just fine by her.

"Come on," she said, giving him a coy smile. "I know exactly where I want to do you." She took his hand and led him into the back room.

"What is this place?" Dajon asked.

She turned, taking both his hands. "I guess you'd call it our church."

"You want to do it in a church?"

She nodded and smiled as she slid her zipper down a few inches. "Ah-ha."

His eyes dropped to watch her slowly pull the zip down a little more, his pink tongue darting out to lick his thick brown lips. "Now?"

"Hell yes." The naughty thrill of it sent her nipples hard, and she opened her top all the way.

She wore nothing underneath, her large breasts aching for his touch.

"God, I've never been this turned on," she whispered in his ear. The thought of doing it in her grandfather's church really had her hot, so hot she was ready to come.

Dajon moved in, his palm cradling her left breast, the pad of his thumb brushing her nipple and sending a shock through her body. His other hand snaked around behind her and pulled her close. Real close. His hand reached under the flouncy shorts she loved and squeezed her cheek as he pressed his arousal against her. She wanted him. Needed him.

Now.

She reached down and fumbled with his belt, desperate to feel him inside her. He pushed her back against the table. Holding her face with both hands, he sucked on her bottom lip, traced along her jawline with gentle playful nips. He pulled back a little to look into her eyes, his lips so close to her yet not touching as she pulled the air he exhaled into her own lungs.

He pushed her top off her shoulders and his gaze fell to her breasts. He lifted her leg, snagged her panties with one finger and dragged them over her hips. Nanette wriggled her butt to help him. Keeping her eyes locked with his, she kicked them off when they reached her foot, then leaned forward and fumbled for his belt buckle. "I need you in me now," she whispered.

He claimed her mouth and gently pushed away her hands so he could get his pants off himself. She leaned back on her elbows and watched as he dropped them to his ankles and enclosed his erection in one big, strong fist.

She almost came at the sight of him touching himself. She was wet and ready as he guided the tip to her opening, and filled her completely with one hard thrust.

She cried out and gripped his shoulders. The rough wooden table bit into her buttocks. She'd have splinters in the morning, but right now the pain only intensified the mind-blowing sensation of him inside her.

Dajon swept the offerings off the table and pushed her back as he climbed on, barely breaking his rhythm.

She rose to meet him but just couldn't get enough of him inside her. She wanted more.

"I want to ride you, baby," she whispered.

He stopped, buried deep inside, and looked at her. "What?"

"I want to be on top, I want to ride you all the way."

He grinned and deftly flipped them so he was under her. Then slipped his hands behind his head and watched as she positioned herself above him.

"Oh, baby," he whispered hoarsely. "I'm so close to coming."

"Then come, baby," she said, so close herself. "Come for me."

She closed her eyes, feeling him beneath her as she rocked back and forth, picking up the rhythm. He shuddered suddenly, making a strange gurgling sound in the back of his throat as he came, but she wasn't about to let that stop her. Almost there . . . *almost* . . .

She threw back her head as her orgasm shattered through her body her, and then she ground her last shudder against him.

"Whoa, baby," she said with a laugh, leaning forward and sliding her hands over his chest. "That was amazing."

Dajon was still under her, his skin slick with perspiration . . . *and sticky*?

"Baby?"

He didn't answer, not even with the grunt he usually gave when their lovemaking had sapped all his strength. The room was dark. All the candles had gone out and she hadn't even noticed. But it couldn't be the wind. Everything was locked up tight.

"Dajon, baby," she said again, a bad feeling starting in the pit of her stomach. "Say something, you're scaring me."

Something moved. But not Dajon. Something else touched her on the stomach. A strange heavy sensation bloomed deep within her womb. She lifted her hands closer to her face, unable to see in the darkness. It smelled familiar, like . . . *blood.*

All the candles burst into life at once. Nanette looked down at her lover. He stared sightlessly at the ceiling, eyes wide with shock, blood spilling from his throat, pooling on the floor, covering his chest and . . .

All over her. Her stomach, her hands, and even her breasts.

The scream ripped up her throat and out of her mouth, her lungs contracting painfully with the force of it, but it died as a figure in a white robe appeared out of the smoky darkness. The ghostly figure floated across the floor, toward her, chanting in a language from a world long gone, powerful words, dark words, words that spread a chill up her spine.

She tried to climb off Dajon, who was still buried inside her. But she was stuck. Her legs were paralyzed and her womb heavy and tight. Nanette looked down as her stomach bulged and swelled. She placed both hands against the tightening skin trying to stop it when something moved.

Then the screams returned.

36
Death Follows Five

HERE WE GO.

McManus hoped breaking into this crime scene would not end like the last. It wasn't off to a good start. Déjà vu. Disturbing knickknacks, bones, and dead things hung from the ceiling, covered the counter, and filled the shelves.

"This place gives me the creeps," he said. "All this black magic."

"It's not black magic," Bianca said, tilting her head. "Necromantic practices are often misunderstood. They deal with death, yes, but use the spirits to help heal, find things, or just plain get messages from the other side. Most of it's benign or even beneficial. It only becomes black magic if they use the death energy as a way to harm or kill. Even a hex can be seen as somewhat gray, depending on the intent and the outcome."

"I'll never understand witches and your politics. Come on, we don't have much time for Witchcraft 101."

Bianca ducked under the yellow crime tape crisscrossing the doorway to the back area where the local necromantic parishioners held their services. Blood stained the floor, the table, and splashed the altar bearing offerings of foodstuffs, candles, and other macabre looking items. It still all appeared rather evil to him.

"I can't see the Dark Brethren symbol," he said.

"I can." Bianca pointed to the ceiling.

"Well, that's different," he said, looking up. "Have you tried to reconnect to that Dark Brethren thing again?"

"Ealund? No." She squatted beside the bloodstain on the wooden floor. "Apparently the line's been disconnected."

"Probably for the best anyway."

She gave him an ironic smile. "That I'm sure of."

"So what do you think?" he asked. "Is it our guy?"

"It's our guy all right." Bianca nodded. "And if it's five castes they're after, then I think they now have everything they need. But this is just the preparation for something big. I'm sure of it. I fear these babies are the elements to a greater spell. And they have five—one from each magic caste."

"Too bad we can't trace them like a phone call," he said.

Her face lit up. "McManus, you're brilliant."

"I know, but why?"

She tossed up her hands. "I've spent most of my adult life finding a way around magic, that I didn't even think of it . . ." She stopped and looked at him. "I need to talk to Tez O'Connor and get my hands on some blood samples."

"What're you thinking?" he asked.

"Come on, I'll tell you on the way."

"SURE I HAVE samples," Tez said, her hands buried in the chest of an elderly man.

"I have an idea," Bianca said. "I don't know if it'll work, but it's worth a shot."

The medical examiner looked up, a knowing smile on her lips. "You're going to scry for them."

"Actually, I'm going to have an old friend scry." Bianca swallowed. She could handle the blood and open body cavity . . . but the smell. It was like death hanging in the air, refusing to leave. Even the antiseptic and ammonia couldn't hide it.

McManus didn't seem to have any issues with the corpse or the smell and watched with interest as Tez worked.

"What'd he die of?" he asked.

"Don't know yet." Tez stepped away from the body, peeling off the two pairs of latex gloves, then threw them into the bin. "He's one of yours, Bianca. They found him dead in his greenhouse, with no obvious signs of foul play. I think I'll have to wait for pathology on this one." She rinsed off her hands and dried them. "I'll get you those samples."

Bianca moved closer to the body. He seemed familiar. Very familiar. Tez said he was one of hers but she just couldn't quite place him.

"Here you go," the medical examiner said, handing her a small wrapped package. "I hope this helps."

"Thanks, Tez," Bianca said. "And if anyone asks, we weren't here."

Tez winked. "No problem."

BIANCA KNOCKED. GODDESS, this brought back so many memories. The door opened and Lucinda's smile reached her dark eyes. "Hello stranger."

Bianca stepped into her old friend's hug. "Hi, Luce. You look good. Motherhood really agrees with you."

"So does divorce." Luce's smile lit up even more as she looked at McManus. "Well, hello there."

"Sorry," Bianca said. "Lucinda, this is my associate, Detective McManus from Homicide."

"Detective," her old friend said, holding his hand a little too long.

Bianca recognized that look too. She'd seen it enough in high school. And he didn't exactly seem in a hurry to let go of the dark-haired beauty's hand either. In fact, he was making eyes right back.

"Are you ready?" she asked, feeling pissed at her child-hood friend and McManus for some strange reason.

"Right." Luce raised an eyebrow. "Should we get started?"

"That would be great, thanks," Bianca said.

Breaking off contact with McManus, Luce turned back to Bianca. "Come on in. I have everything ready. Did you bring the blood?"

"Right here." McManus held up the package Tez had given them.

She led them into the living room. It hadn't changed much since they were both in grade school and Luce's mother was the local seeker. Photographs lined the mantel, including pictures of her and Luce when they were kids.

Bianca picked up a photo of a smiling teenager and a little girl with no front teeth. "Amy has grown up so much, and Hannah looks just like you did at her age."

"You can't be old enough for a teenage daughter," McManus said.

Luce laughed and pointed to the little girl in the photograph. "Hannah's my daughter. Amy is my baby sister. Well, half sister. Though she does feel more like my daughter. She's been with me since she was eight, after my mother died." She turned to Bianca. "Can you believe she turns sixteen in two days?"

"You're kidding. Already?"

"I gather from Bianca you two have been friends for a long time," McManus said.

"Since birth, actually. Our mothers were friends and pregnant with us at the same time. Bee was born two days after me. Which makes *me* her elder." Luce winked.

"A fact she never lets me forget," Bianca added with a laugh.

There was another girl in some of the pictures, older than Bianca and Luce.

"Who's this?" he asked, pointing to the unsmiling girl.

She glanced at the picture and frowned. "That's my sister, Ursula."

"She doesn't look very happy."

Luce shrugged. "No, she rarely was."

A map of the city covered half the living room floor, and heavy black curtains were drawn across the windows. The subdued light of flickering candles kept the room in half darkness. Luce knelt in front of a low table holding five crystals, each tied with a different colored piece of string.

Bianca sat across from her friend, watching her reverently touch the tools of her trade as she prepared for the scrying process. When they were kids, they used to sit together on this very sofa and watch Luce's mother perform the same rituals.

She held out her hand for the package. "Give me the blood."

McManus passed it to her and carefully stood back so not to step on the map, but he watched intently.

"Please, Detective, stop hovering. Sit that tight little tush of yours over by Bee and let me prepare," she said, and unwrapped the package.

"I like your friend," McManus told Bianca as he sat down.

"Even if she's a witch," she whispered back, a little more sarcastically than she'd intended.

"I'm going to search the New York State area for close relatives of the victims," Luce explained as she removed a rack of tiny labeled test tubes from the insulated box, each with less than a quarter inch of crimson in the bottom. "Shall we start with the first victim?"

"Sounds great," Bianca said, pointing to the first test tube. "It's this one."

Using a thin metal tool, Luce scooped out a small amount of the sample, no more than a few drops, and smeared it onto the crystal with the yellow string. A pale yellow glow bloomed in the center of the stone.

"Here goes," she said, hanging the crystal by the string

and with a slight movement of her wrist rotating the glowing stone over the map.

Nothing happened.

"Hmm, that's not a good start," Bianca said.

"It's not working?" McManus asked.

"Or there's no living relatives in the area," Lucinda said.

Bianca sat forward. "Why don't you try the latest victim? We know she had plenty of family."

Luce nodded. She selected another vial and repeated the steps, this time using a crystal with a purple string. As soon as she started circling it above the map, little purple glowing dots appeared on the paper, some brighter than others.

"Whoa," McManus said, leaning forward. "But how do we tell who they are? I mean are they male or female, brother or sister, aunt or uncle?"

"It doesn't work like that," Bianca said.

"Each dot represents a blood relative," Luce explained as she increased the circumference of the swinging crystal, more dots appearing on the map. Most were clumped around the neighborhood where Nanette lived with her parents. "The brighter the glow, the closer the relative is. But that's all we can tell. Blood calls blood."

"Why don't I make us some coffee," Bianca offered as Luce prepared the next crystal. "McManus, can you give me a hand?"

She knew that her friend needed to concentrate, and didn't need McManus distracting her with his questions.

He followed her into the kitchen. "Look, I don't see how uncovering all of the victim's blood relatives is going to help. If there's nothing to distinguish one from another, how's that going to help?"

"Patience, McManus," Bianca said scooping coffee into a filter before sliding it into the coffee maker. "Let's just see what happens when she's done. Now shut up and give me a hand. Cups are in the cupboard above your head."

"So, tell me about your friend," he said.

Bianca looked around the kitchen. "This was my second home growing up, same as my house was for Luce. I haven't really seen her much in the last couple of years. We've both been busy—me with the Academy, her being a single mom and running the practice. Time just flies."

"The practice?"

"Sure. A seeker serves the community, kind of like a doctor. Her mom was the seeker here, when we were in grade school. When her mom died a few years back, Luce took over the house and the practice."

"I think I'll go see if she's found anything more." Mc-Manus slid his hands into his pockets and smiled. "But I'll promise to keep my mouth shut this time," he said as he walked back into the living room.

This old house brought back so many memories. Bianca leaned against the counter while she waited for the coffee to brew. Luce had kept everything the same after her mother died. It was comforting and disturbing at the same time, like being in a time warp. Even the coffee mugs were the same ones they used to drink cocoa from after school. She smiled and took some cookies out of the barrel to put on the tray before she carried it back into the room.

McManus was leaning forward on the edge of the sofa when she walked in, his elbows resting on his knees and his hands clasped between them as he stared intently at the blue dots appearing under the swinging crystal.

Bianca put the tray down on the sideboard in between the candles and glanced down at the purple, green, and blue dotting the map on the floor.

"Wow, you *have* been busy," she said. "Wonder why it didn't work the first time?"

"Actually it did," Lucinda said, and placed the crystal she was holding on the table. "If you look closely here."

Bianca leaned in to where she pointed. A very faint yellow dot stained the map, only a shade or two darker than the paper itself.

"This has to be a distant relative, maybe a great-aunt or -uncle or distant cousin."

"But no baby?" Bianca asked.

Lucinda shook her head. "Afraid not."

"Maybe it's been shipped off somewhere," McManus said.

"Maybe," Bianca said, looking closer at the map.

"Tiffany Hilden is the last one," Luce said, picking up the final crystal with a crimson string and priming it with the blood from the last tube.

"This is what you were hoping for, wasn't it?" McManus asked, pointing to a spot where three different colored dots sat together. "That could be where the kids are."

"Do you know the area?" Bianca asked.

"Not really. But if a red dot appears when Luce does her thing, I think we should check it out immediately." He took a small notebook from his pocket and jotted down the address.

Bianca held her breath and watched carefully as Luce dangled the final crystal above the map.

"Ready?" she asked.

Bianca nodded and the seeker began to twirl. Red dots appeared on the paper. The Hilden family was vast. One spot appeared with the other three, then another. Two dots.

What did that mean?

McManus reached for his cell phone. "We gotta get to that address, and quick."

"Thanks for your help." Bianca took Lucinda's hand. "I'll be back in a couple of days. I want to be here for Amy's coming of age birthday."

"Amy would love that," she said, pulling Bianca warm hug. "So would I. Now, go. Save those babies."

37

HUNK A BURNING LOVE

McManus pulled into the street and his heart sank. Fire engines, police cars, and paramedics blocked the street in front of a blazing inferno.

"We're too late," Bianca said, voicing what he was thinking.

He pulled the car in beside an empty open ambulance. Debris littered the street; glass shards glinted all over the ground, reflecting the flames from the burning house.

"Looks like it didn't just catch fire, but exploded," McManus said beside her.

Shell-shocked onlookers stood watching firefighters finally winning the battle against the flames that had already completely gutted the house.

"Hey." The fire chief walked up to them and placed his hands on his hips. "You can't park there."

Bianca pulled out her ID. "Dr. Bianca Sin, Forensic Thaumaturgist. This was a residence of interest in a case about possible black thaumaturgists working in this area."

The chief pushed back his helmet and looked at the fire. "Sorry ma'am, but I doubt you're going to find anything much once we're done here."

"How did it start?"

"Not sure yet, ma'am. Could be a gas explosion, the way the house went up, but there's no way to tell just yet. And we'll have to wait until the fire is out before we can determine if there are even any fatalities."

"Do you mind if my assistant and I talk to some of the neighbors?" she asked, handing over her card. "I'll give you any pertinent information we find out."

"I'd appreciate that Dr. Sin, and as soon as we have any news I'll do the same." The fire chief half turned, paused with a frown and looked back. "Aren't you Detective McManus from Homicide?"

"Yes," McManus said, extending his hand to clasp the chief's.

The man nodded. "I did a stint at the Forty-ninth a few years back. You're a long way from your jurisdiction, Detective."

"Like Dr. Sin said, I'm only here to assist."

"Okay, but if you need anything, just ask." The chief walked away and started yelling out orders to his men.

"Let's see if the neighbors saw anything," she said to McManus. "Maybe they saw something we could use."

"How about them?" McManus nodded to a group of three women, watching the house burn as they chatted among themselves. One was older, while another had a young child about a year old on her hip.

"Why don't you let me talk to them, and you sound out the firemen about what the scene was like when they arrived."

"Good call," he said.

Bianca approached the women. "That's some fire."

The dark-haired woman in the middle smiled cagily. "You should've been here when it started."

"Are you a reporter?" asked the older of the three.

"Yes," Bianca said, going on gut instinct. "I'm a freelancer looking for a real juicy story. You know you could really help me out if you could tell me about the people who lived here."

The three women exchanged glances, and then the one in the middle, who seemed to be the unspoken leader, held out her hand. "Tally Mason, I live here." She indicated the house behind them, immediately next to the fire. "Agnes Walker lives on the other side."

The older of the three shook Bianca's hand.

"And Macy Johnson here lives across the street."

The young mother swapped the baby to the other hip to shake hands.

Bianca smiled at the infant. "Looks like the firemen got this under control enough to save your houses. Can you tell me what happened?"

"Well," Tally said, "I was just tackling the weekly wash when I heard this massive 'bang' and the whole house shook. I thought it was an earthquake or something."

Macy nodded. "I was putting the baby down upstairs when it happened. I came down to find all my windows smashed, glass everywhere, and the house across the road alight."

Agnes didn't say anything, just nodded at what the others said.

"So who lived here?" Bianca asked.

Tally looked at the others before answering. "We never really met them. We tried to when they moved in, only the girl wouldn't let us in."

"The girl?" Bianca asked.

"Yeah, about nineteen or twenty." Agnes spoke for the first time. "A sweet young blond thing, said she was sorry but her mother wasn't well enough to receive visitors."

"There were the babies there too," Tally added.

Agnes nodded. "At least two that I saw, but I swear I could hear more than that crying in the night."

"And that big black car that used to stop by, only you couldn't see who was in it, as they always parked in the garage before they got out."

"Yes." Tally nodded. "I was starting to think we had one of those bloodsuckers living next to us."

Bianca raised an eyebrow but said nothing. She hated the intolerant term. "So did you ever see this girl's mother?"

"Only as a shadow in the window," Tally said, and Agnes agreed.

"They have a body," someone yelled closer to the fire.

All three women craned with ghoulish glee to see. It was too much for Bianca. "Thanks, ladies," she said.

They ignored her as a firefighter carried a blanket-wrapped bundle from around the side of the ruined house.

As she walked away, McManus joined her. "The fire department thinks it might've been a bomb. They found a body blown into the backyard by the force of the explosion."

"Let me guess . . . a young girl, blond, about nineteen or twenty," she said.

He cocked his head and frowned. "The neighbors tell you?"

"She was the only one they saw, but they did hear the crying infants. This was where they kept them. But what happened?"

"Maybe they were tipped off," McManus said. "Maybe they somehow sensed the scrying."

"Oh my Goddess, McManus." A cold hard knot of fear settled in her chest and she grabbed his arm. "Lucinda!"

38
sacrifice

BIANCA KNOCKED AGAIN, more frantically this time. "Please, Luce. Open the door."

Something wasn't right—McManus could feel it in his gut. "Maybe she's in the kitchen and can't hear." He squatted before the letter slot and pushed it open with his finger.

A bloody handprint smeared the wall. A hand in the center of a sticky red-black pool lay half hidden in the doorway. His heart sank. They were too late.

"Stand back," he said, and slammed his shoulder against the door.

"Oh Goddess," Bianca said with a certain finality. "Luce—"

"What's going on?" A girl's voice said from behind. Two girls with school bags over their shoulders looked at them in confusion. "Aunt Bee? Is that you?"

Shit. No kid should ever see what was in the house, and neither should a childhood friend. He had to get them all out of here before he went in.

"Sin," McManus said, taking her arm. "Go and look after the girls, okay?"

He could see the grief in her eyes, but she hid it as she

crossed the porch to meet the girls. "Hi, Amy," she said to the older one, and dropped to one knee in front of the little girl. "You've gotten so big since I saw you last. Do you remember me?"

Hannah shrugged and looked up at Amy. "I think so."

Amy took the little girl's hand and looked between McManus and Bianca with a worried frown. "You remember Aunt Bianca, Hannah-Bannah, she gave you Pookie-bear for your birthday."

"Oh yeah." Hannah's smile lit up, but disappeared when she looked around Bianca at McManus.

"That's a friend of mine, he's a policeman." Bianca stood up again.

"Where's Lucinda?" Amy said. "The car's here, so she can't be far."

Smart girl. "We need to get inside to make sure she's okay. Do you have a key?"

Amy nodded vigorously, tears welling as she unclipped a key ring from her school bag. McManus descended the stairs to take the keys from the girl. He held her hand for a moment. "I want you to be brave and take Hannah over to the neighbors and wait for us there, okay? Can you do that?"

The girl nodded again, and led Hannah back down the path to the front gate. She looked back at them with one uncertain terrified glance before turning left and walking purposefully away from the house.

"Poor kid." Bianca's voice was hollow. "This happened to her before when her mom died."

"Stay here," he said.

She shook her head, her face void of any emotion. "I have to do this."

"No you don't. Actually, why don't you go and wait with the girls. Keep them calm."

"I can't," she whispered, a tear sliding down her cheek.

"Okay, but don't come in until I call you."

She nodded blankly.

The hand in the doorway belonged to a young man in his early twenties, a bag of groceries spilled on the floor beside his body and his throat opened from ear to ear. *All too familiar.*

It took a moment for McManus's eyes to adjust to the dim candlelit living room where Lucinda had performed the scrying. When they did, he wanted to close them and block it all out. Lucinda had been so full of life a couple of hours earlier. Now she lay with clouded eyes staring blankly at the ceiling. The colorful dots on the scrying map under her were obscured by the Dark Brethren symbol painted in blood.

"Luce!" Bianca said softly behind him, and he turned to find her staring at her dead friend's body.

"I told you to wait outside." He wrapped his arms around her, trying to shield her from the scene. "You don't need to see that," he whispered against her hair.

"Oh Luce," she whispered again, and balled his coat in her fists.

Bianca trembled as the shock set in. He pulled her face into his shoulder and led her from the room, carefully trying to avoid the blood and other evidence spread over the floor. She felt like a rag doll in his arms, as he sat her down on the step. She stared ahead with a silent glassy look, which scared him even more than if she screamed hysterically.

He sat down next her and pulled her cold shaking hands into his, but she didn't seemed to notice. "Are you okay?"

Stupid question.

Finally, she turned to him. "No." A single teardrop slid down her cheek. "No I'm not."

McManus wiped the tear away with his knuckle.

"She was my friend. My best friend—" Her voice hitched in her throat. "And now she's . . ."

"Gone," McManus finished for her; he just couldn't bear to hear her say *dead*.

She nodded. More tears escaped. Then she stiffened against him. "They picked the wrong one this time."

She looked him in the eye, her eyes steeling as she swiped away her tears. "I don't care what it takes, I'll do anything now to find them and make them pay for this. *Anything*."

39
home sweet home

McMANUS REACHED FOR the keys in her hands. "Here let me."

"I'm okay, really," she said.

"I know. But let me do it anyway."

Vincent and Kedrax sat just inside the door, waiting. The dragon was now as big as the cat. His growth rate was amazing.

"I sensed something was wrong," she heard Kedrax say through her numbness.

McManus led her inside. Kedrax jumped up onto the arm of the sofa as she fell into the seat. McManus sat and turned sideways toward her, one hand resting along the back of sofa and the other on her knee.

"Her friend was murdered today," he said.

It took her a moment to realize he was actually talking to the dragon. Wonders would never cease. Kedrax jumped into her lap, placed his front paws on her chest and rubbed the top of his head on her chin. Vincent rubbed against her shoulder.

She wanted to cry, ached to even, yet now the tears wouldn't come. "Stop treating me like I'm made of glass," she said in frustration. "You're as bad as my mother."

"She cares about you, that's all." McManus pulled her into

his arms. "It was good of her to take Lucinda's girls home with her."

"Luce was family. And it's only until they can get in touch with Ursula. Though I still find it hard to imagine that woman bringing up a teenager and a young girl."

As comfortable as she felt in his arms, she placed her hand against his chest and pushed him away. "I'm fine, really. You don't need to babysit me."

"I don't think you should be alone," he said.

"Do I look alone?" she asked, stroking Vincent's head.

McManus's face set with determination. "I'm not leaving, Sin, deal with it. You need to talk about this."

She shook her head. "No I don't." *That's the last thing I want.*

"Tell me about Luce," he said gently.

She sighed. "You really aren't going to leave me alone, are you?"

He shook his head.

"Can I at least have a shower?" she asked.

"That's a good idea, I'll make some coffee."

BIANCA WOKE AND stared at the ceiling. A numb ache filled her. Where was the grief, the devastation? Why wouldn't the tears come? Instead, she felt this big empty nothingness. Like someone had come along and sucked out all her emotions.

McManus had been gentle and attentive. He'd listened all night to her talk about growing up with Luce, until she left him on the sofa around dawn to come to bed. She'd almost been tempted to invite him to join her. If only to make her feel something for a little while. In the end she couldn't use him like that.

Her cell phone rang beside her bed. Her mother's ring tone. She didn't want to speak with anyone right now, especially not Artemisia. But she wanted to find out about the girls.

"Darling, I just wanted to check on you." She could hear the grief in her mother's voice. Just as Lucinda had been like a sister to her, she'd been like another daughter to Artemisia.

"I'm fine," was all she could manage. "How're the girls coping?"

"As well as can be expected. Hannah slept with Amy and they both cried themselves to sleep. Why don't you take my advice and come home too?"

She sighed. "I told you I can't, I need to be here for the case."

"Hang on," Artemisia said, and there was a pause.

"Bianca, this is your father." Her mother was bringing out the big guns.

"Hello, Daddy." She closed her eyes again and pinched the bridge of her nose. "Welcome home."

"We're worried about you, sweetheart. Why don't you come and stay in your old room, let us look after you for a while? I miss my little girl." His warm masculine voice made her feel a little better.

She smiled. That was her dad. He let her have freedom to do what she wanted, yet was ready to give her a hug whenever she needed it.

"Not yet, Daddy, I have to work on this."

He was silent for a moment. She could almost see him smiling. The same smile she heard in his voice. "I know, sweetheart. You do what you have to. But remember where your home is should you need us. We're here for you. *Any time*. Day or night. Okay?"

"Thanks, Daddy. I love you."

"Theron, don't tell her that. Make her come home," her mother said in the background.

"I love you too, sweetheart. And don't worry about your mother," her father said. "I'll take care of her."

"Give me that phone, Theron," Artemisia demanded.

"'Bye sweetheart." Her father hung up, cutting off her mother's objections.

Bianca allowed herself a little smile. Her mother was all emotion and sexual energy, where her dad was down to earth and filled with logic. Total opposites, yet they fit together so well and loved each other more than life itself.

The phone rang again. "Mother, I need too—"

"Bianca, it's Tones."

She sat up straight. "Sorry, Tones. What've you got?"

"I traced the house to a small company that specializes in leasing properties to corporations. The company is a subsidiary of the O'Shea conglomeration."

Bianca felt the charge building in every molecule of her body. She couldn't stop it. It burned from within, filling her with more power than she'd ever felt before.

"Bianca, did you hear me?" Tones said.

A white light exploded behind her eyes.

40
HELL HATH NO FURY

CLANGING PIERCED MCMANUS'S skull like a thousand hot pokers, and he kicked the almost empty bottle as he stumbled to his feet, sending the final dregs onto the floor. He looked around and realized he was still in Bianca's apartment. The bottle was what was left of the awful absinthe stuff he drank after she'd left him for bed. The urge to follow her had been so strong, he'd needed something to take the edge off.

"I'm coming," he croaked to the white-hot noise coming from his cell, but the torturous instrument ignored him. Finally, he picked it up, cutting off the skull-splintering agony.

"What?" he growled.

"Thank God you're there," a man said.

"Who's this?" he asked, trying to shake off the nausea and feeling like a dragon had shit in his mouth.

"Tones."

His mind went blank. "Who?"

"You know, Antonio Geraldi. I work with Bianca and Oberon."

"Oh, yeah, sorry man." McManus picked up the bottle from the floor and drained the last mouthful. "What's up?"

"I can't get Oberon. I have no idea how to stop her, and she's not answering her cell," Tones babbled with what seemed like a single breath.

McManus had trouble keeping up. "Stop who?"

"Bianca." The near panic in Tones's voice finally snapped McManus awake.

"What happened?" he asked, gripping the phone so tight his fingers ached as he raced into her bedroom, to find it empty.

"I told her who owned the house destroyed yesterday and some sort of electrical feedback came through and fried my phone." Tones's voice took on a sharper edge. "Oberon told me she has a familiar."

"Fuck," McManus said, scrubbing his hand across his face. "Who owns the fucking house?" But he already knew the answer.

"I traced it to a subsidiary company owned by the O'Shea Freight and Logistics conglomerate."

His gut bottomed out, and it had nothing to do with the hangover. McManus hung up the phone, cutting off Tones, and patted his pockets. He slid his arms into his coat and snatched up his keys from the kitchen counter. For the first time, he realized the dragon was missing too. He had to stop Bianca before someone got killed.

Because if either of the O'Sheas harmed a hair on her head, he'd kill them himself.

THE BOOM GATE lay splintered on the ground and the guardhouse appeared empty. The place seemed oddly deserted as he drove over the broken boom and into the complex. Bianca's car sat in front of the admin building, the driver's door hanging open. He pulled his gun from his underarm holster as he climbed from his car.

Several bodies littered the ground, and he looked up at the broken window of the top floor. Blue light flickered and sparked from inside the building. He turned over the first body with his foot and an electric charge zapped up his leg. McManus squatted beside the fallen man in a black suit and laid two fingers at his throat. A pulse beat strongly beneath his fingertips, but the man was out cold.

The others were the same. How could they have fallen from that height and survived? The inside of the building was just as deserted as the exterior. The stairs were a safer bet at this point, and he started to climb, constantly looking up, keeping his gun cocked and ready.

McManus kicked the door at the top of the stairs and froze. The scene before him was pure chaos. Bianca stood in the middle of the room, her hair flying around her head, blue electric energy crackling around her body. The dragon sat perched on her shoulder, and she held her arm out toward Corey O'Shea, who was pinned against the wall with the same blue charge. His brother, Seamus, hung suspended horizontally in the air, his head slumped forward with blood dripping from a gash in his forehead.

Bianca and Kedrax turned to McManus as one, and his breath died in his throat. Both had identical glowing eyes that shifted like molten gold in a smelting pot yet were as cold as ice.

"Stay back, McManus," she said in a flat tone, and turned to look up at the drug lord, her head tilting to the side. "He's going to tell me where they are."

O'Shea's composure seemed to be holding—only just. "I've got no idea who or what she's talking about."

One of his men burst through a door, and Bianca flung her free hand out, engulfing the would-be assailant in a ball of smoky blue energy, flinging him out the nearest broken window.

McManus took a step toward them.

She turned those golden eyes back on him. "Unless you want the same treatment, I'd stay where you are."

He slid his gun back into his holster and held out his hands as he took a step back.

"You lied to me," she said to O'Shea. "Now tell me . . . where are they?"

"Again . . ." O'Shea raised an eyebrow. " . . . who are *they*?"

"You own the house on Maple Street?" McManus asked.

O'Shea frowned. "I don't know, it's possible. We own lots of property."

"The one that burnt down yesterday," McManus said.

O'Shea's eyes widened. "Yes, I know the one, it was on the news. A girl died in the fire."

Bianca squeezed her hand, and the crackling blue energy increased. "So where are the babies that were in that house?"

"I don't know," the drug lord said. "But if you let me go, I'll find someone to look into it."

"Listen to him," Chancellor Rudolf said from the corner. "He's not the one you're looking for."

Bianca's features creased in confusion. "But—he owned the house."

"What are you doing here, old man," McManus asked. *Something funny is going on.*

"I came to see Corey and his brother about a personal matter. Trust me, they're not the ones you want," the old man said, walking toward her.

"They know who we are," Corey managed to croak.

"If you know," Rudolf said to Bianca, "then know they definitely would *not* benefit from the Dark Brethren coming back into the world, seeing they were the first to turn against them."

McManus's head swam and his vision blurred. His hand shook as he tugged his sweat-soaked shirt away from his skin. He had been so focused on Bianca he'd missed the signs. What he'd mistaken for just a hangover was actually a Neon Tears comedown.

He stumbled and fell to one knee as his sight dimmed even further to a dark fogginess.

"McManus?" Bianca called. For the first time since

he'd walked in, her voice carried a hint of emotion. Then she turned back to the suspended drug lord. "I'll heal him myself when I'm done with you."

"No you won't," he heard O'Shea say. "He's going into Neon blindness and you can't heal that with magic. You have no idea what the drug is."

"Bianca," Rudolf pleaded, "please listen to me. You have to let the O'Shea brothers go."

"The withdrawal is happening fast," O'Shea replied, sure and confident. "His vision is going, the sweats will turn to tremors, and if not treated he'll lose his sight, which could become permanent due to his prolonged use. You can't help him with magic, but I can."

"Shut up," Bianca said, but the force had gone out of her words. "This is just some kind of trick."

McManus stumbled forward.

"Watch out," she yelled.

He turned just as Rudolf threw a burning lighter at him and his clothing burst into flames.

41

Baptism of Fire

THE FIRE BROKE Bianca's concentration, and the spell crumbled. The elder O'Shea landed lightly on his feet, strode purposefully across the room to yank the fire extinguisher off the wall and turned it on McManus, quelling the flames.

When the fire was out, McManus lay shivering on the floor covered in retardant foam—his clothes burnt and tattered. Corey O'Shea snagged up an expensive looking rug and covered him.

"Why would you do that?" Bianca asked Rudolf.

"I knew it wouldn't harm him," he replied.

"It was like he was covered in accelerant," O'Shea said. "So I guess this proves you're right, old man. I just wish you could've done it without ruining my carpet."

"What is he?" she asked.

"Let's get this all sorted out first and I'll tell you all about it," Rudolf said.

Corey moved to his brother and lifted his unconscious head. Bianca had given him that gash in self-defense but still felt the guilt squeeze her heart as the wound wept. Kedrax jumped from her shoulder and ran to McManus's prone form.

"Help McManus first," she said to O'Shea. "Then I'll heal your brother."

"Stop talking about me like I'm not here," McManus croaked from the floor.

"Go find *her* and ask her to come," Corey said to one of his men who nursed an injured arm.

The man gathered himself off the floor and made a quick exit out the door. Bianca sat down and pulled McManus's head into her lap. He trembled and she reached for his hand, squeezing it. He smiled a shaky little smile and squeezed back, his milky white pupil-less eyes staring into nothingness. Kedrax sat beside her with one paw on her thigh; if she wasn't mistaken, the little dragon was just as concerned about the detective as she was.

"He's a long-term user," Corey said in a matter-of-fact voice. "The eyes only cloud over this badly from heavy use."

"I said, stop talking about me like I wasn't here," McManus said, but she could hear the shame in his tone.

The drug lord lifted the edge of the rug to check McManus's injuries. He looked up at Rudolf and took a knife from his pocket to cut away some of the ruined clothing. "Nothing. Not a mark on him."

"Sorry to disappoint you, O'Shea," McManus croaked.

"Oh, Detective, I'm far from disappointed," O'Shea said. "Trust me. Anyway, I knew you were too stubborn to die."

The drug lord's eyes flicked to his brother, fear and concern flaring for the briefest of seconds. Bianca could see the long-haired assassin was Corey O'Shea's Achilles' heel.

"Kedrax," she called, and rose to feet.

The dragon climbed onto her shoulder as she dropped to Seamus's side and reached out. The energy entered her and she wove it into a healing spell slightly different from the one she used on McManus. His eyes opened and in a flash he flowed to his feet, drawing a large handgun from inside the long black coat and pointing it to her head.

The cold steel of the gun muzzle pressed against her left temple and her heart beat wildly.

Corey placed a hand on his brother's gun arm. "Put it away, Shiz."

It seemed Seamus hadn't heard, but then his cold killer's eyes left her and he glanced at his brother. He said nothing. He didn't need to. She could tell exactly what he thought about her. Corey whispered something in his ear. Seamus's eyes flicked back to her as he lowered his gun. The drug lord didn't *have* to save her. So why had he*?*

Corey took out his cell phone and dialed. "Get me the detail on that house in Maple Street . . . Yes the one that burnt down . . . I need to know to who leased it and I need to know five minutes ago."

He hung up just as two men entered the room. One carried a small pet carrier that he set down on the nearby coffee table before opening its door. A faerie stepped out and sat down in a huff, her arms and legs crossed, the tiny bottom lip poked out sullenly. Corey spoke to it in the strange language he'd used the other night. The creature saw McManus lying on the floor and let loose a stream of incomprehensible babble, shaking her head and gesturing wildly.

"Enough, Li-anis, do as I say," he ordered, and addressed her in more of the same strange tongue.

Bianca realized that not only was it one of the faeries from the other night, but was the one who started the fight. The female faerie came to her feet, and stubbornly shook her head. Bianca had no idea what such a tiny thing could do to save McManus.

"Mistress Li-anis," she said, not having a clue what she was doing, but she had to at least try. "Please help us if you can."

The faerie stopped mid-babble and turned, tilting her head with a quizzical frown. Bianca bowed. She'd dealt with enough witch politics to see when someone's ego needed stroking. Corey smiled and nodded encouragement. The faerie puffed up and crossed her arms again. Even if she didn't speak English, she clearly understood it. The faerie spoke to Corey. He replied quickly in the same language.

Li-anis stared at her a moment, then turned to Corey and nodded, fluttering her wings. He walked over to the cupboard by the wall and pulled out a small vial with an eyedropper lid, similar to the one McManus always carried.

He put it down on the table beside her and removed the stopper. She perched on top of the vial and urinated a few drops of bright neon blue into the vial.

"Oh my . . ." Bianca whispered.

How could she ever tell him where his drug of choice came from?

"What?" McManus asked, worried.

Kedrax jumped onto the table beside the faerie, crouched with head down and tail flicking. As the dragon pounced, the tiny female took flight and landed on Corey O'Shea's shoulder.

"Hey," O'Shea said to Kedrax. "Don't even think about it."

O'Shea sucked liquid into the eyedropper and placed a drop into each of McManus's eyes. The detective's face screwed up in pain. Bianca grabbed his hand and squeezed, letting him know she was here. He held on tight. Brilliant incandescent azure replaced the milky whiteness. The color slowly dissipated to reveal his normal blue eyes. He blinked a few times, looked up at her and smiled.

"What happened?" he asked.

"Um . . . Mistress Li-anis here helped . . ." She pointed to the faerie on Corey's shoulder.

He pulled himself onto his elbow. "How?"

O'Shea grinned widely. "She pissed in your eye."

"No really." He turned to Bianca.

She glanced down and picked at her fingernail, trying to keep her smile from bursting into a laugh.

"He's fucking kidding, right?" McManus took her hand, drawing her eyes to his. "Right?"

Bianca opened her mouth, but still she had no words. She looked away before she broke down into giggles.

"Neon Tears, in its purest form, is a by-product of the Fae," O'Shea explained. "Faerie sight, they called it, or the *kiss* of the Fae." The drug lord reached his hand out to Lianis. She climbed on and he placed her on the table beside the pet carrier. "Thank you, my sweet lady, there'll be an extra treat tonight for you and your people."

"Kitten?" she asked in perfect English, her tiny wings fluttering in anticipation.

"We'll see," Corey replied.

The faerie made a strange little excited noise and stepped into the pet carrier.

Bianca smiled. "So, they like kittens?"

"Oh yes," Corey said. "It's their favorite meat."

A sick feeling settled in her stomach. "No!"

"What? You didn't think they played with them, did you? Actually, now that I come to think of it, they do, but it's rather disturbing to watch."

McManus rose unsteadily to his feet. Although more than a little singed around the edges, with clothes almost completely destroyed, he didn't seem all that worse for wear.

O'Shea sat behind his desk and looked around, surveying his ruined office. She'd made quite a mess. Papers were strewn over the floor, paintings hung crooked on the walls or had fallen altogether, and furniture was overturned.

"I think it's time we talked," Rudolf said.

"About why you tried burn me to death, old man?" McManus growled. "And what the hell are you doing here in the first place?"

"In answer to you second question first . . ." Rudolf straightened his shoulders. "I came here to talk to Mr. O'Shea about what Marcus Hilden promised him in return for his support. And to the first, I knew you wouldn't burn."

"McManus, why don't you go with Michael and clean up a little," O'Shea said. "You look like shit."

The detective looked down at his ruined suit, and his eyes appeared even bluer with his soot-blackened face. "Okay, but I'll be right back." The head of security, still nursing his broken wrist in a sling, led the detective from the room.

"Dr. Sin, please take a seat." O'Shea gestured to one of the fat comfortable chairs still upright.

Kedrax crawled into her lap and curled up. Almost without thinking, she stroked him. He closed his eyes and purred like a cat. For the first time since Lucinda's death, she felt calm.

Luce!

Then the grief landed on her, and tears that had been building behind her eyes threatened to erupt. *No here, please, not here.*

"You know," Corey O'Shea said, "I could sense you were different, but I had no idea how different." He steepled his fingers and leaned back in his chair. "It's been a long time since I've seen a dragon, even one that small."

Kedrax's head rose from his paws and glanced up at her and then to the man sitting behind the desk.

"You can see him?" she asked.

"Of course. I'm Unari."

The ringing phone on his desk cut off any further conversation. He listened for a moment and then said, "Interesting," before hanging up.

McManus came back wearing a borrowed suit. It stretched tight across his broad shoulders and was a little snug over his thighs. His face was clean except for one charcoal smudge near his left ear.

"I know who leased the property," O'Shea said.

She spun to look at the drug lord, coming out of her seat. "Who?"

He sat there looking at them for a moment longer, then shook his head. "Do either of you know how miraculous you both are?"

"Cut the shit and tell us who rented the fucking house," McManus said, his old menace returning with full force.

"You shouldn't be here, either of you," O'Shea continued, ignoring him. "You're relics of a long forgotten past."

"We can go into that in a minute, Corey," Rudolf said. "I'm quite interested in the answer myself."

Bianca held her breath. Something inside her shivered with anticipation, not only because of what he knew about the house, but also of what he knew about them.

He looked at the old man and nodded. "The Hilden Group has held the lease for the past three years."

The air rushed out her lungs as if she'd been sucker punched. "No, that can't be right." But it made sense. They had seen two close relatives of Tiffany Hilden at the address.

"Come on," McManus said, taking her arm and pulling her to her feet. "Let's go and talk to the Domina."

"We can't just barge in—"

"Did you know the last dragon witch died over five thousand years ago?" Corey O'Shea said before they reached the door. "My grandfather used to tell me stories about them. I never thought I'd meet one myself. But to find one with a warrior of the dragon elite, well that was a real surprise."

McManus frowned. "What the hell are you babbling about, O'Shea?"

"I think it's probably best to just show you," Rudolf said. "Lord Sagen," he called aloud.

42

DRAGON HEART

A BLINDING WHITE light surrounded McManus, and the ground fell away from beneath him. When he landed, he stumbled in darkness until his eyes cleared and adjusted. He found the darkness wasn't as complete as he first thought. He was in what appeared to be an underground cavern about the size of a baseball stadium. He'd never seen anything more beautiful. Columns and pillars were carved into the walls, and beautiful scrollwork had been etched into the rock but was worn by centuries of warm moist air.

Strange orange bulbous plants, or some sort of giant fungus, ringed a natural crystal-clear pool that filled a third of the area below. He got the impression there was nothing natural about it. A glow coming from the pool painted the surrounding white walls with a surreal watery light.

He stood near Bianca and Rudolf by the pool that cast a luminous glow over their features. The tiny dragon still clung to her shoulder. He moved to the edge. The water rippled and shimmied every now and then, almost as if something moved just beneath the surface. But nothing was there—the water was completely pristine.

"Where are we?" he asked, and wrinkled his nose at the

scent of corruption and rotting flesh. There was something else too, but he couldn't quite place it.

Bianca looked at him with an odd expression. "I don't know."

"You have brought me something." A deep rumbling voice resonated off the cavern walls around them.

"Yes, my lord," Rudolf yelled up into the cavernous darkness. "Something very special."

Torches burst into life, momentarily blinding him. A deafening snap cut through the still air, followed by a heavy downward gust and a loud whapping noise, like giant bat wings flapping. An enormous shape descended from above and landed by the pool, crushing some of the pale orange fungus trees and sending an orange cloud of spores into the air.

Metallic blues and greens flashed across the colossal beast's hide as it moved, though they seemed somewhat duller than Kedrax's. The giant head, as large as a small car, lowered, and the diagonal slit in the huge yellow eye contracted in the torchlight.

The creature turned his head and looked at Bianca. "I see you have brought me a snack."

McManus pulled her behind him and reached into his jacket for his gun. Except all he found was an empty holster. "You can't have her, dragon."

"Then I'll have you." The dragon's terrible jaws opened to reveal a mouthful of razor sharp teeth and a large grayish blue tongue.

"Try me, but I warn you, I'll give you such a bellyache."

"No," Bianca cried, clutching his jacket. "You can't do this."

A booming rumble rebounded off the walls, and the dragon sat back on his hind legs, his massive body shaking. "Such a bellyache . . . this one has spirit. Do not fear, little witch," it said shaking its head. "You are in no danger from me. Neither are you, my brave warrior."

"You're just joking?" she asked, incredulous.

"Sorry." The huge creature landed back on all four feet, this time not so gently, and seemed to wince. "There is little to amuse me down here, but your meat is far too sweet for my taste."

"Lord Sagen has been a guardian against the Dark Brethren for several millennia," Rudolf said, indicating the pool.

"And most of it spent slumbering in this cavern as the Dark Brethren's jailer," Sagen said. "But now I grow old and weak."

"My lord, the Unari have agreed to help if they can."

The dragon lifted his massive head a little. "This pleases me greatly."

Rudolf bowed. "Yes, but their race is diminished, they're not as powerful as they once were."

"Why?" McManus said. "They're running drugs, committing crimes, and killing people."

Rudolf smiled. "Actually, their reputation has been highly exaggerated. That brother of his is deadly with weapons, though, and his reputation well earned."

McManus remembered the drug lord had said something similar.

Again the dragon chuckled low and deep. "The Fae are like children. Selfish, self-centered, and undisciplined. But they bring magic to the world. The Unari are much like their charges."

"So why are we here?" McManus asked. "What's the point? You're talking about prison cells, dragon jailers, and Fae, but what does it have to do with us? "

Sagen turned in a slow circle and moved his massive head closer to McManus. "Are you sure this one is a warrior elite, fit for the Draconis Nocti? He seems much too angry to me." Dragons were condescending. *Who* fucking *knew?*

Sagen sniffed at him. "He's not ready."

"You're damn right I'm not ready. In the last few days

I've found out I've been putting faerie piss in my eye and now there are fucking dragons. Not just little toy ones like Bianca's—"

"Hey," Kedrax said.

He'd almost forgotten the little dragon was there. "I feel like somehow I've just woken up and the whole world has been turned upside down." He tossed his hands in the air. "Next thing you know, angels will descend from heaven and demons will crawl up from hell."

The dragon tilted his giant head. "Angels and demons are myths, devised by humans to give their actions consequences."

McManus laughed. How ironic. An icon of the biggest fairy tales creatures had just proclaimed the foundations of some of the largest religions in the world as mythology.

"Good," Sagen said. "The stench of your fear grows less offensive."

The dragon was right. He was afraid, and he hated feeling that way almost as much as he hated helplessness.

Sagen turned back to Bianca. "I see you have my gift. Come to me little one."

Kedrax climbed from Bianca's shoulder and scampered closer to Sagen. The larger dragon lowered his head to his tiny counterpart, who purred loudly and rubbed his cheek against the scaly hide. They started speaking in some strange language that felt oddly familiar.

The dragon looked up. "I'm happy to see the spell worked well. Kedrax says there has been some pain with his accelerated growth, but nothing he can't handle."

"You did this?" Bianca asked.

"Yes, young witch. I woke the dragon tear when I sensed its presence through you. I will have need of this little one to find a replacement for me. I feel I only have eight or nine hundred years left in me. I must train my replacement."

"This has to be some weird-ass dream," McManus whispered under his breath. "There are no such thing as dragons."

"And yet here we stand," Sagen said. "Trust me, young warrior. Dragons live, but most slumber as I have, to stay out of the way of humans."

The pool rippled and shifted. A distinct hand impression pushed against the surface. Sagen's face crumpled in pain. A strange sensation twisted McManus's gut and he doubled over with a grunt.

As the sensation subsided, the dragon moved closer and the pool returned to crystal calmness. "You felt it too?"

Sweat beaded on his brow. "Oh God, I felt like my insides were being squeezed like a tube of toothpaste."

"Maybe you are more ready than I thought," Sagen said with a tilt of his car-sized head. "The Dark Brethren grow stronger much faster than anticipated. The spark renewed my life force, but my strength is returning more slowly than I'd like."

"I told you, McManus," Rudolf said. "Long ago, when the dragons were lords in this world, they were served by human such as us."

"How do you know so much about it?" Bianca asked.

"Because I served another like Lord Sagen several centuries ago," Rudolf said. "And I was the only one near when my lady died, leaving me the recipient of her dragon light, or soul, so to speak." He opened his shirt. A visible glowing heart beat within the center of his chest. "However, I was not a warrior of the elite. Even though I was given centuries upon centuries of extended life, I could never be a true warrior of the Draconis Nocti, as I didn't have the gift to withstand fire or the ability to wield it."

"Are you saying that's what I am?" McManus asked.

Rudolf nodded.

Bianca shook her head. "The Draconis Nocti are a highly trained black ops team. We have just resurrected them."

"The original Draconis Nocti served the dragons long before the name was borrowed in the modern incarnation," Rudolf said. "But their purpose is the same. When the dragons started to retire from the world, the warriors disappeared."

Another ripple in the pool brought McManus to his knees.

"The longer he's in your presence, the stronger your connection," the old man said to the dragon.

McManus's heart continued to beat fast as the pain subsided. "There've been a rash of ritual murders," he said. "Bianca thinks they're preparing some kind of spell that has to do with this Dark Brethren."

Sagen nodded. "Yes, I've felt them stirring, getting stronger. How is the ritual performed?"

"Dark thaumaturgy is used to generate a mystic pregnancy that grows a fetus to term in minutes," Bianca explained, "where it is harvested from the mother's uterus, killing her."

The dragon's head tilted, like he was listening to something they couldn't hear. "Are the mothers all from different castes of the craft?" he asked.

Bianca nodded.

"The ritual of Inok," the dragon said to Rudolf.

The old man nodded sadly. "I was afraid of that. If the ritual succeeds, they'll open the portal to the Dark Brethren prison. The last time the ritual was even attempted, the Mayan civilization disappeared."

"So how do we stop it?" McManus asked.

The dragon didn't even flinch. "Kill the infants."

McManus reeled and shook his head. "No!"

Bianca clutched his arm. "You can't just murder innocent babes."

Sagen rose up, looming above them, full of indignation. "They're the by-product of the blackest magic. It's the only way to prevent the ritual from succeeding."

Bianca shook her head. "There has to be some other way."

McManus could've sworn the dragon shrugged. "It's the surest way. Take away the means and the spell can't be performed. The infants are the means."

"What would stop them from performing the ritual again and creating more babies?" she asked.

Rudolf frowned. "I think there is something special about these infants, something that would be difficult to recreate. That's why they did a dry run first."

"What do you mean?"

"Angel," McManus said. "We didn't find her baby on the map because it was of no use and they killed it. Practice on a homeless girl before risking it with the real ones. That makes sense now."

"Blood is the key," Sagen said.

"How do you know?" McManus asked.

The dragon practically smiled. "Blood is always the key."

"The babies are linked by blood?" McManus mused aloud. "They're born of blood, do you think that could be it?"

"We have to get out of here," Bianca said. "I must stop my mother from handing over the girls to Ursula. She's the only family Luce had except Amy and Hannah."

"And someone from the Hilden family too, but which one?" Rudolf added.

"I don't know," McManus said. "But I think Astrid Hilden does."

"You're right," Bianca agreed. "I have to talk to her, and I think I know a way."

"Close your eyes," the dragon said. "And I'll send you back."

43

The Gift of Sympathy

"THANKS FOR COMING with me, Artemisia," Bianca whispered to her mother as they sat in the Hilden family home waiting for their host.

A girl entered carrying a tray loaded with cakes and coffee. She smiled at them, inclining her head as she put the tray on the low coffee table, and left again.

"Are you sure about this?" her mother asked. "I mean I've had my issues with Gayla but I just can't imagine she'd be involved with anything like this."

"It makes sense," she said. "If—"

Gayla Hilden's personal assistant, Mistress Tesha, entered the room and sat on the edge of the sofa opposite. "The Domina will be with us a moment. But while we wait—can I offer you some refreshments?"

"Thank you," Artemisia said. "You're most kind."

Bianca was in no mood for tea but accepted anyway. A veneer of politeness was the essence of witch culture. Tesha's full-lipped smile never reached her large ebony eyes as she poured tea into delicate porcelain cups from the matching teapot.

"So." Artemisia took a sip and placed the cup back on the saucer. "How's Astrid been since the funeral?"

"As well as one can be expected." The witch's eyes flicked to the side. "When one has lost a daughter."

Bianca could almost taste the lie.

"The family is lucky to have you here at a time like this," Artemisia said, taking another sip of tea. Flattery had always been one her mother's best weapons. "You must be such a welcome comfort for the Domina."

"I do what I can," Tesha said, and this time the smile did reach her eyes.

"I can only imagine what she must be going through." Artemisia took Bianca's hand and patted it. "If I lost my Bianca, I don't know what I'd do. Would we be able to pass on my condolences to Astrid in person? I know we haven't been that close in years, but—"

"I don't think that will be possible." Tesha's gaze flicked nervously to the door, an almost impossible-to-detect flush coloring her dark skin. "Mistress Astrid is not really up for visitors right now."

At that moment the Domina swept into the room. "I'm so sorry to have kept you waiting."

The three women came to their feet. Gayla and Artemisia greeted each other with the traditional double cheek kiss, then the Domina sat on the sofa opposite and invited them to do the same with a wave of her hand. "Thank you for stopping by to pay your respects."

"It is the least we can do," Artemisia said. "And if there's anything I or the Sin coven can do to help out in any way, please just ask."

To Gayla's credit, she inclined her head with seemingly genuine gratitude. "The covens have been most generous, thank you. I will take you up on your offer should circumstances present themselves."

Artemisia picked her cup up again. "I was just saying I

would love the opportunity to pass on my personal condolences to Astrid."

The shutters dropped in the Domina's eyes and her features turned stony. "That's impossible. Astrid has taken Tiffany's loss hard and has been heavily medicated."

She's hiding something.

"I understand." Artemisia took Bianca's hand in hers. "I can only imagine what she must be going through." She clutched Bianca's hand tightly in both of hers.

It wasn't just for show. Bianca had always been able to sense her mother's emotions, particularly if they were strong. It was one of the links they shared, part of their succubus heritage. Right now her mother felt supreme sorrow, regret, and a large dollop of fear. For the first time, Bianca understood why Artemisia wanted her to come home. It was because her mother needed her close to make sure she was still here. She squeezed her mother's hand for reassurance.

"It has been hard on us all," the Domina said. "I appreciate your visit and your sentiments. But I'm expecting a call from London, so if you'll excuse me, my assistant will see you out."

Bianca and Artemisia stood with the Domina. Without any ceremony, Gayla nodded curtly and left the room so quickly that it bordered on rudeness.

"Follow me," the Domina's P.A. said as she led the way.

"Please pass on our best wishes to Astrid," Artemisia said as they stood in the entry hall.

"I will," she said. "Thank you for coming."

As soon as they stepped through the door, it closed behind them.

"Well that was short and not very sweet," Artemisia said on the ride down the long driveway.

Bianca glanced over from behind the wheel. "And pointless—we didn't even see Astrid."

"Look out," her mother yelled and gripped the dash with both hands as someone ran out in front of the car.

Bianca slammed on the brakes. The girl who brought in the tea placed her hand on the hood as the car skidded to a halt.

Bianca jumped out of the car. "Are you crazy?"

"I'm sorry," the girl said in a small voice, looking around nervously. "But this is the only point that can't be seen from either the house or the gate and I had to speak to you. I have a message." She reached into her pocket and pulled out a piece of paper.

Bianca opened it to find a hastily scrawled note.

They have locked me in my room and are holding me prisoner. Please help me. I'm so scared. A.

She passed it to her mother and looked up at the girl. "Did Astrid Hilden give you this?"

The girl nodded. "Please, I have to get back. If the Domina misses me . . ." She looked over her shoulder, fear blooming in her skittish little eyes, and leaned closer. "She got away a couple of times, but they always find her. They keep her drugged now and have a dampening spell on her room."

Bianca took the girl's trembling hand. "Okay, we'll figure something out. Now go."

The girl nodded and disappeared back through the bushes.

"Astrid has always been fragile," Artemisia said as they climbed back into the car and resumed their journey down the estate driveway. "It's one of the reasons Gayla picked Marcus as her daughter's husband. But it's hard to believe they would lock her up and drug her."

"It's very possible if Gayla is performing black magic and her daughter knows about it."

Her mother shook her head. "No, I can't believe she'd be involved in anything like that, especially since her grand-daughter was a victim."

"You said Gayla picked Marcus." Bianca glanced at her mother as she pulled up to wait for the estate gates to open. "Are you saying she was married to Marcus against her will?"

"No, not exactly," Artemisia said. "Let's just say Gayla vigorously encouraged the union. But if I were you, I'd look into this thoroughly before I acted. Especially Marcus Hilden. The Manov coven have been conveting the Domina-ship for a very long time."

Witch politics. Something she'd never understand. "Okay, how am I going to do that?"

"The Isis Foundation Alumni Ball?"

Bianca drove out of the estate and onto the street. "I thought that would be canceled this year, given recent events."

"No, I got the invitation this morning. And guess where it's being held?"

Bianca shrugged.

Artemisia looked back over her shoulder at the Hilden estate house.

She glanced at her mother again. "Why didn't you tell me earlier?"

Artemisia smiled. "I wanted to spend some time with you."

44

Behind Enemy Lines

McMANUS SLID HIS hands into his pockets and paced the confined quarters in the back of the SWAT van. "I still think it should be me going in there with you."

Bianca turned from the mirror where she fixed her makeup. "We've been over this a thousand times—you have get Astrid away once we get her out. Cody can help more in there by sensing out the emotions. Besides, he will be less conspicuous," she added, replacing the top on her lipstick.

"I don't know about that," Tones said with a laugh from the communications console. "Check out those shoes,"

"What's wrong with them?" Cody lifted his pants a little to reveal the surf sandals he wore underneath. "There's no way I'm putting a pair of those patent leather death skins on these feet."

"Amen." Tones gave Cody a high five.

"There's no way anyone will be looking at his feet," Bianca said as she straightened the bow tie on his tuxedo. He looked like one of those male model types, with his blond hair swept back neatly from his forehead.

McManus felt a stab of annoyance at how she smoothed

the jacket over his shoulders. "I thought he had to wear long velvet jackets or stuff like that."

"If he was a witch, yes, but since he's not, any formal wear is acceptable." She smiled and ran her palm over her own red velvet corset trimmed in gold over a black velvet skirt with a bustle. "How do I look?"

"Bloody hot," Cody said.

"Hell yeah," Tones agreed.

With white ringlets dropping from the intricate hairstyle piled on top of her head and a band of black lace, diamonds, and onyx surrounding her throat, she never looked more lovely.

While she smiled at the other compliments, she looked expectantly at him, waiting for his answer.

A knot caught in his throat. "You look *breathtaking.*"

Her smile blossomed, a self-conscious flush blooming on her pale cheeks, and she looked away. "Thank you."

"Too beautiful for a kidnapping," he added.

"A rescue, not a kidnapping." She tilted her head to the side and searched his eyes. "You really think I look good?"

He drew closer and twisted one of the pale ringlets around his finger. "Devastatingly good."

Tones cleared his throat. "I think it's time."

McManus scowled and stepped away. "I still don't have to like it, and to top it all off, I have to babysit the pets."

"Hey," Kedrax objected from the top of a cabinet where he sat with Vincent. "I'm the one who's doing the babysitting, flatfoot."

"Watch it, rat-breath, or I'll make a wallet out of you." McManus couldn't hide the smile. Since their trip into Sagen's lair a few days ago, the two of them had fallen into mutual lighthearted insult slinging, which seemed to work for them both.

The little dragon's voice had deepened and he now had the same sort of inner glow as Lord Sagen. He'd matured at an amazing rate, and now matched the cat for size. Bianca and Kedrax's bond also seemed to increase. But even more amazing was when the two of them were deep in one of their silent conversations, McManus could sometimes catch a snippet, half a word here, an emotion there, but never anything solid.

Vincent watched everything with his usual strange, almost human stare, from where he sat beside Kedrax. The little dragon alighted from the table with a graceful flap of his wings and flew to Bianca. McManus winced as the creature landed on her pale bare shoulder, afraid his talons would rip her flesh, but somehow he hung on by wrapping his tail around her upper arm and the claws never even marked her skin.

Bianca reached up and stroked the side of Kedrax's head. "You behave yourself."

Vincent jumped down and followed, his tail sticking straight up in the air to get his share of her love.

"So . . ." Bianca said. "Are we ready?"

"Okay." Tones rose from his terminal. "Put one of these in first." He held out a box of earpieces. "Cody, your lapel pin has a small audio visual device, as does one of the beads on your choker," he said to Bianca. "We'll see and hear everything you do and you can hear us."

"Here, let me," McManus said, taking the flesh-colored device from Tones.

She turned her head to give him access. Before he inserted the device, he leaned in close to her ear. "You be careful in there."

She looked him in the eye and smiled. "You're not going soft on me, are you, McManus?"

"Maybe," he replied, and gently tilted her head so he could slide in the earpiece. "Just don't do anything stupid. Okay?"

"Okay," she said softly, and placed her hand over his.

Cody held out his arm. "Let's get this show on the road."

Bianca took it with a smile. McManus felt another pang of anger and realized he was a little jealous. He wanted to be the one on her arm, and it had very little to do with the case. He closed the door after them and dropped into the chair next to Tones. The screens turned on one by one as Tones typed and McManus leaned back, putting his feet up on the desk. "So, you got the coffee and doughnuts?"

"In the cupboard and fridge behind you," Tones said without looking up from the computer. "Along with some vegan blood for me."

45

into the viper's nest

CODY PATTED HER hand on the crook of his arm as they stood in line for the ballroom and leaned in close. "We're almost there."

She smiled. Security was ridiculous. They'd had to pass through three checkpoints on the way in. There was also a dampening spell on the entire estate so no one could use any magic within the grounds. A very expensive precaution.

Just how the hell were they supposed to get Astrid past all of that? The entire Hilden family were lined up to greet the guests as they entered. Bianca sighed with relief when she saw Astrid standing next to her husband.

Finally, she stepped up, her grip tightening on Cody's arm.

"Thank you for com—" The Domina's eyes met hers and widened, her hand stopping for half a second as she extended it toward Bianca. Then the mask of politeness dropped again and she almost crushed Bianca's fingers in her grip. "I didn't expect to see you here tonight, Miss Sin."

"Dr. Sin, actually," Bianca corrected. "I thought it was about time I relented to my mother's numerous requests for me to come to a society function."

The Domina frowned and squeezed her hand, pulling her a little closer, suspicion written all over her face. "Why now?"

"A very close friend of mine was murdered in the same way as your granddaughter which has left Artemesia quite upset," Bianca said. "Something like that tends to change one's priorities."

The Domina blinked slowly, and Bianca almost regretted her words, then Gayla turned to Cody. "Thank you for coming," she said flatly.

Bianca moved down the line to Astrid Hilden. The woman was like an automaton, her face slack, her eyes blank, and her movements sluggish. They'd drugged her just like the girl had said. Her husband supported her by the elbow as he greeted guests with his own forced smile.

"Good to see you, Astrid," Bianca said, taking the woman's limp hand.

Astrid's blank eyes stared over her shoulder. She was about to move on when Astrid's grip tightened on hers and her gaze focused.

Marcus removed Bianca's hand out of his wife's grip and shook it. "Thank you for coming." And somehow he managed to make it sound more like a threat than a welcome.

This wasn't the time to rouse suspicion. "Thank you," she said, and moved on.

"Well, that was awkward," McManus said through her earpiece.

"Yes, very interesting," she replied softly as Cody grabbed two flutes of champagne from a waiter who glided past.

She accepted the glass, but didn't drink, and neither did he. The object was to blend in, and that's what they would do. The party mood in the ballroom seemed more normal as people drank and caught up with friends and family. Yet every now and then a forced laugh, a nervous titter, or guarded glance unsettled the mood a little.

"Hello, sweetheart."

"Hello, Daddy." Bianca spun to hug her father and then

kissed her mother on the cheek as Cody shook hands with Theron.

Her mother smiled. "At least Gayla can't criticize your dress sense tonight, darling, you look beautiful."

"Tell your mother she looks hot too," McManus said in her ear.

"Shut up," she said.

"What?" her mother said, a little taken aback.

"Sorry, not you, Artemisia," she said. "McManus is having a little word in my ear. He said to say how nice you look." She lifted her hair a fraction, as if showing her mother her new earrings.

Artemisia leaned in with a smile and touched the onyx jewels hanging from her lobe. "Hey there, hot stuff, I was looking forward to seeing you in a tux."

McManus chuckled. "Next time."

"Stop it you two," Bianca warned.

Cody and her father had their heads bent together, oblivious to what was going on. Bianca slipped her arm through her father's. "What are you two talking about?"

"Dr. Hunter was telling me about a tribe of cubii he found in the jungle of New Guinea," Cody said.

When they married thirty years ago, her parents had bucked tradition, with her father keeping his own name. It had caused quite a stir back then, but today it was a little more commonplace.

"A fascinating tribe living way up in the mountains," he father said. "Very isolated and totally untouched by modern living. They basically still live in the Stone Age."

As always, his face lit up as he talked about his work as a parahuman anthropologist. She'd gotten her love of science from him.

Artemisia put her arm around him and smiled warmly as he planted a kiss on her forehead. His passion for his work was only matched by his love for her mother.

Cody closed his eyes for a second. She didn't begrudge him the little snack he was having from her parent's emotions.

"So, what's your plan?" Artemisia whispered conspiratorially.

"Better you don't know," Cody said.

"Cody's right," Bianca said. "But when it's polite to do so, I'd get her out of here, Daddy."

Her father nodded.

The Hilden family finished greeting the guests and moved into the ballroom to join the festivities. Astrid glanced in her direction and their eyes connected. Marcus noticed where his wife was looking and said something to the Domina. This time Bianca could feel the full force of their disapproval. Marcus led his wife in the opposite direction, and Gayla turned to the building group of witches vying for her attention.

A pianist accompanied by a string quartet began to play.

"I think I'm going to dance with the most beautiful woman in the room," her father said, looking around. "Now if I can just find her."

"Theron." Artemisia playfully slapped him on the arm.

"Ah, there she is." He held out his elbow and led his wife onto the dance floor to join the rest of the couples swaying to the music.

"There's so many emotions flying around here," Cody whispered. "Most are just the normal happy ones you'd expect at an event such as this. But—" He stopped to take a canapé from a passing waiter.

"But?" she said when the waiter was gone.

Cody finished chewing and tucked in his chin as he glanced over at the Domina. "There's a hell of a lot of fear too. And I don't think you have to be an incubus to sense it."

Several people had worried expressions beneath their polite social masks. Even members of the Domina's own coven tossed cagey, surreptitious glances in her direction.

Marcus hovered close to his wife, heading off anyone who tried to get close to her. Bianca caught several guarded looks between the Domina and her son-in-law.

Something is definitely going on.

A prickle of tension skittered up her spine and tightened across her shoulders. If only she could just get to Astrid.

"Relax," Cody said. "Come on, let's dance."

A surfer boy from Bondi Beach, Australia, he might be, but Cody Shields was one of the most socially aware men she knew. That came with being an incubus, she supposed; being the son of a diplomat also helped.

He took her out and spun her onto the floor with a sweep of her skirts. She giggled.

"Hey, you're not supposed to be having a good time," Mc-Manus growled in her ear.

"Piss off and let us enjoy this dance," Cody said, and swept her up against him. "I think your detective is a little jealous," he whispered softly into her other ear, so their listeners wouldn't hear.

She pulled back and laughed aloud. "Don't be ridiculous." However, she felt a tingle of pleasure at the thought.

"Shhh." Cody pulled her tight against him again.

The music stopped.

"Excuse me," the Domina said from the small stage where the band played. "I would like to thank you all for attending this year's Isis Institute Ball. As you know, I've held this ball in honor of the institute for the last thirty years. And tonight was intended to be a special occasion with my . . ." She cleared her throat and straightened her shoulders. " . . . with my granddaughter attending the institute this year."

The Domina stopped and looked down at her daughter, who was silently sobbing into a handkerchief. "That was before the horrible tragedy that took her from us. I had considered canceling the ball this year, but since this event raises a lot of money that is used to fund scholarships for less fortunate young witches, I decided against it. With that in mind, I wish to announce the creation of the Tiffany Hilden Memorial Scholarship, which will be funded solely by the Hilden Group to allow yet another underprivileged witch to attend the Isis Institute. Please help me in honoring this great school by giving generously to the Isis Institute Scholarship Fund."

Applause filled the room.

"Again, thank you so much for your support, and please enjoy the rest of the evening." The Domina picked up her skirts with one hand, and her son-in-law helped her descend from the small stage. She said something to Marcus and Astrid, who started shaking her head at the words. Marcus nodded and led Astrid from the room.

"*Shit*, they're making her leave the party," McManus said in her ear. "Now what're we going to do?"

46

witch in the wardrobe

"YOU FOLLOW," CODY said. "And when you're ready, I'll create a distraction."

"Don't do anything stupid," McManus said in her ear.

She ignored him and slipped through the crowd just in time to catch Marcus leading Astrid up the sweeping staircase to the second floor. She watched until they disappeared and then followed, ascending the stairs as quickly and quietly as she could. She could hear them up ahead and crept into a small alcove near the top of the stairs, then peeped around the corner.

"Please," Astrid said. "Please don't lock me in there alone again."

"It's for your own good, my dear," Marcus replied, and caught her face.

"For mine or for yours?" she asked. "Don't think I don't know what you and Mother are doing."

"You're confused, my dear, you need your medicine," Marcus said as he opened a door. "Once the guests have gone, I'll join you."

"Will you at least send Mary up with some tea?" Astrid asked as she disappeared inside.

"I'll send her right up," he said, then closed the door again and locked it.

Bianca flattened herself against the wall, not daring to breathe, as he passed by. When she was sure he was gone, she crept down the corridor and tapped lightly on the door.

"Astrid, it's Bianca Sin," she called softly. "I'm going to try and get you out of here."

"Bianca?" Astrid replied from the other side. "You've got to help me. My mother and my husband are doing bad things." She let out a sob. "I think they killed my Tiffany."

She tried the door, but it was dead-bolted tight, and with the dampening spell she wouldn't be able to use magic to open it. At least it meant they couldn't use magic either, to set up any nasty surprises. "McManus, tell Cody to get my parents out of here, now."

"Already done." The frustration in McManus's voice came through loud and clear. He'd be going crazy right now in the van, feeling totally helpless.

Footsteps ascended the stairs with a clink of china. Bianca tried the room across the hall. It was also locked. However, this one had a simple old-fashioned lock instead of a dead bolt. She took a credit card from her little clasp bag and jiggled until she felt the lock give way. The door clicked open and she ducked into the room.

It was dark and her eyes took a moment to grow accustomed to the gloom. A thin stream of light from the window highlighted what appeared to be a pentacle on the wall to the right. She risked turning on the light for a better look and found herself in a man's bedroom staring at newspaper articles showing photos of the victims at each point of a pentacle denoting the caste of magic.

"Holy shit," she whispered. "Are you getting this?"

"Bingo," McManus cried in her ear. "We got the bastard."

"Mistress." A knock sounded faintly on Astrid's door. "I have your tea."

Bianca switched off the light and cracked the door open a

little. The girl who'd passed them the note the other day put a tray on a side table and fished inside her pocket. Bianca moved carefully out of the room and struck quickly, clasping one hand over her mouth before she could scream.

"It's okay," she whispered in the girl's ear, and turned her around so she could see her. "Do you remember me from the other day?"

The terrified girl relaxed a little and nodded.

"Good, now unlock the door," Bianca said, and removed her hand from the girl's mouth.

The girl produced a key from her pocket and unlocked the door. Bianca pushed her into the room quickly and closed the door behind them.

The girl raced straight into Astrid's arms. "I'm so sorry, I didn't—"

"*Shhh.*" Astrid smoothed her hair. "It's okay, she's here to help."

"That's right, to get you away from here," Bianca said, checking the hall.

Astrid nodded, appearing less glassy-eyed than she had downstairs. "They'll find me again, they always do."

"If you can get them out, I'll get them somewhere safe," McManus said in her ear. "But first you have to get past all that security."

"I know," Bianca answered. "Astrid, we have a safe place for you, but first we to get you out."

"How? My mother has security everywhere," she said. "Though, if we could get past them, I know a way over the west wall."

Bianca looked around, for something, anything, that could help, and found a blond wig on Astrid's dresser. She needed a disguise.

She turned to the girl. "Swap clothes."

"What?" Astrid said.

She picked up the wig. "You both exchange clothes and I'll sneak you out the back way through the servant's quarters."

The girl shook her head. "You can't just leave me here. Alone."

I don't have time for this. "I'll tie you up and they won't know you had anything to do with it."

Terror filled the girl's eyes. "They'll know."

"She's right, we have to take her with us," Astrid said, putting her arm around the scared girl and looking rather pale herself. "If they work it out, I'm afraid they'll kill her."

"No," the girl cried. "Please don't leave me."

Helpless, Bianca scanned the room again. She looked down at her own clothes, then went into Astrid's wardrobe. She found a tank top and a pair of pants, both black.

"Okay, here's what we're going to do," she said, starting to undress. "Astrid, put on the girl's clothes, and you—what's your name?"

"Mary," the girl said.

"Okay Mary, you'll put on my dress and go downstairs, where my friend will meet you and take you out the front door. McManus, let Cody know the plan."

"I'll get him to meet her at the bottom of the staircase," McManus said in her ear.

"Who's McManus and Cody?" Astrid asked.

"My partners," Bianca explained. "And they're close by."

"Okay," the witch said, still looking uncertain. "Let's do it."

The top and pants were snug but wearable, and Bianca pulled the hairpins securing the ridiculous hairdo and let her hair fall free. Thankfully, she'd worn comfortable boots under her dress—her one concession for dressing up.

Astrid laced up the corset on Mary, and though the girl didn't fill out the bodice as much as Bianca, it was passable. But the girl had dark hair.

Bianca grabbed the blond wig and put it on Mary. Hopefully, with the diversion Cody was about to create, they wouldn't look at her too closely.

When they were all dressed, Bianca went to the door. "Okay, tell Cody we're ready."

After a few minutes, the sound of yelling and arguments came from downstairs.

"Come on," Bianca said, herding the women to the top of the staircase, then stopping them to check that the way was safe.

Security guards rushed toward the ruckus in the ballroom, leaving the front door only lightly guarded. Cody waited at the bottom of the stairs and signaled them to come down.

"Mary, this is Cody and he'll take good care of you," Bianca whispered as they reached the bottom.

He took the nervous girl's hand and led her out the front door, joining several other guests who were taking the opportunity to leave.

Bianca took Astrid's hand. "Which way?"

"There." She pointed to a door almost hidden in the paneling. "To the kitchens and the back way out."

The kitchens were busy. Bianca pushed her way through, dragging Astrid with her.

A man stepped out of a door in front of them and looked surprised then glanced at the name tag on Astrid's uniform. He recovered and frowned. "Mary, where have you been? And who the fuck are you?"

Bianca didn't have time. She brought the heel of her boot down on his foot and shoved him back through the door he'd just come out of. Astrid ran. Bianca raced across the grounds after her, leaving the chaos behind.

Astrid pulled up and pointed off to the left. "Over there."

Bianca glanced behind for signs of pursuit, but only confusion came from the house. The witch led her to a wall of dense shrubs and pushed through. Bianca followed to find an eight-foot stone wall with a tall tree beside it. The cut branches up the trunk formed the perfect climbing holds.

"I used this tree to sneak out when I was a teenager," Astrid said. "I think Tiffany did too, though I could never prove it."

She climbed. The dress was not exactly conducive for tree climbing, and Astrid wasn't exactly a teenager anymore. But she reached the top of the wall and Bianca followed.

The street beyond the wall was dark and the pavement seemed such a long way down.

"It never used to seem so high when I was a kid," Astrid said, a quaver in her voice.

Car headlights appeared, creeping along the street and passing by.

McManus's car.

Bianca took a deep breath and pushed off, landing hard. Her ankle twisted, pain shooting up her leg as she struggled to her feet. Red brake lights lit up as the car stopped, then quickly reversed.

McManus jumped out and raced over to help her up. "Are you okay?"

"Yes, help Astrid down." She pointed to where the witch sat on the wall above.

Mary also climbed out of the car, still wearing Bianca's gown, and stood beside the car glancing around nervously.

"Jump—I'll catch you," McManus called up to Astrid.

"It's too high, I can't do it," she cried.

"Yes, you can," Bianca said. "And you must hurry or they'll catch us."

Astrid jumped, and just as he promised, McManus caught her.

"Good," he said, and gently set her down. "Get in the car and let's move before the Indians arrive."

"Don't you mean the cavalry?" Bianca said.

He winked. "No, we're the cavalry."

Astrid hugged Mary and held her away by the shoulders. "Thank you."

"Okay, let's go," Bianca said, and opened the car door.

"Please." Astrid grabbed her hand. "Make sure they catch my mother. I won't feel safe until they get her."

She's right. "I need to check on my parents anyway," Bianca said, and turned to McManus as Astrid climbed in the backseat behind the girl. "Get them somewhere safe."

"I know just the faerie forest."

"Oh, perfect. It'll shield them from any magic search."

"That's my thinking."

She smiled and looked at the women in the car. "Okay— text me when you get there. As soon as I'm sure my parents are safe and that the Hildens are in custody, I'll join you at the O'Shea complex."

As she turned away, he caught her by the arm and pulled her back, planting a quick kiss on her lips. "Be careful. Okay?"

She smiled. "You too."

BIANCA GOT BACK to the ops van to find the area swarming with police and men in suits. Agent Neil Roberts stepped out of the door and saw her. "There's one of them now. Where's McManus?"

"As I already told you." Oberon's deep rumble preceded his giant frame. "They have been working under my direction on—"

"Yes, yes, yes . . . a possible drug ring supplying the campus . . ." Agent Roberts turned on Oberon as he stepped onto the pavement. "Do you really think I'm that big an idiot?"

"Do you really want me to answer that?" Oberon replied, squaring his shoulders.

The top of Roberts's head didn't even reach Oberon's chin, and the bear of a man outweighed him by a couple hundred pounds at least. There was no doubt who would win in a smackdown, but right now Roberts had all the cards.

"Chief, we got something," the walkie-talkie on Roberts's belt squawked.

"What is it?" Roberts barked.

"You better come take a look; we're in a bedroom at the top of the staircase."

Roberts frowned and huffed. "I'll be right there." He turned back to Oberon and pointed a finger at him. "This isn't over—not by a long shot."

Oberon turned his back on the agent, lifted his right hand, and extended his middle finger. "Bianca, your parents are inside."

Artemisia leapt up from between Bianca's father and Cody and pulled her into a huge hug. Vincent rubbed his body against her leg, purring, and Kedrax landed on her shoulder.

"I'm okay, Artemisia," she said, hugging her mother back.

"So it looks like Marcus is our man," Oberon said as he closed the door. "Tones showed us the footage of the room again."

"Marcus doesn't shit unless Gayla tells him too," her father said.

"Daddy!" She'd never heard him talk like that before.

"Well it's true," Theron said with conviction. "He's always been a jumped up little coward."

"I should get you both home," she said to her parents.

"Oh no," Tones said from the communication desk, one hand clasping the headphones as he twiddled with the dials. "I just picked up something on the police channel. They've found McManus's vehicle . . ." His eyes widened.

"And?" Oberon prompted.

Tones took off the headset and placed it on the desk. "There's a body."

SQUAD CARS AND emergency vehicles blocked the road around the car. Bianca tried to get past, but Oberon stopped her. "Stay here, I'll find out what's happening."

Bianca craned to look at the scene beyond. "No, I need to see."

"Let the captain go first," Cody whispered, and wrapped his arm around her as Oberon strode over to the nearest cop.

Guilt immediately followed the relief she felt when saw part of her gown hanging from the covered gurney as the EMTs loaded the body into the open ambulance.

Cody squeezed her shoulder. "I know your succubus heritage makes you immune to my abilities, but if there's anything else I can do, let me know."

"Thanks," she said. "But until I know what happened here, I don't think anything will help."

"Maybe Oberon has found something out?" Cody said.

Oberon didn't look too happy. "The investigator says the car was found like that, the girl's body inside, with her throat cut. There's a lot of blood, more than could've come from the one victim. It looks like it could've come from both McManus and Astrid."

"So whoever was working with the Hildens now has them both," she said quietly.

Kedrax wrapped his tail tighter around her upper arm and a calm numbness crept over her. She turned and walked away.

"Where're you going?" Oberon asked.

"To question Gayla and Marcus Hilden."

"But they're in VCU custody," Cody reminded her.

"I don't care." She kept walking.

Oberon's brow furrowed. "They're not going to let you just walk in and talk to them."

She stopped and turned back to them. "Let them try and stop me."

Oberon crossed his arms and shrugged at Cody.

"Okay, but I'm driving," Cody said, taking the keys from his pocket.

THE VIOLENT CRIMES Unit was on the first floor of the Department of Parahuman Security building. Bianca stepped through the metal detector at the checkpoint and placed her hand on the facimorph test panel. It took every ounce of control not to charge ahead and rip the place apart to find Gayla and Marcus.

Kedrax flew in over the panels and the guards' heads. They were too busy dealing with Oberon and all his metal to notice. The clock ticked. She knew that every second they wasted was a second less McManus had. He might already be dead. But somehow she didn't think so.

I can still feel him.

Kedrax looked at her. *So can I.*

"Fuck this," she said, and turned for the stairs. "We don't have time."

Cody grabbed her gently by the upper arm. "Wait for Oberon."

"He'll catch up." She wrenched her arm away.

"Oberon hurry," she heard Cody say as she took the stairs two at a time.

Heads with surprised expressions rose from paperwork

as she strode through the VCU headquarters. Most of them she'd never seen before. Apparently, VCU had restocked with green recruits and burned out veterans

"Where's Marcus Hilden?" she asked the first fresh-faced VCU agent who stepped into her path.

"Sorry, visitors aren't allowed." He glanced at a closed office door with AGENT NEIL ROBERTS written in gold lettering, then down the corridor.

"I'm not a visitor," she said, pushing past just as Oberon and Cody came in behind her.

The young agent reached out and grabbed her arm. "I said you can't go in there."

Oberon was on him in a second, lifting him off the ground by the scruff of his shirt.

"Hands off, buddy," he growled.

She nodded. Not that she needed his help. The way she was feeling right now, she could crush this guy like a cockroach with just a thought. Thaumaturgic energy coursed thought her body, crackling off her fingertips.

The office door opened and Neil Roberts appeared. "What the hell is going on here?"

"I need to speak to Gayla and Marcus Hilden immediately."

He crossed his arms and smiled that vicious, vindictive smile she'd come to know so well. "Do you, now?"

She had just the thing to wipe the grin off his face. Energy tickled around her body and Kedrax growled in her head as her eyes began to burn. Agent Roberts frowned uncertainly and narrowed his eyes.

She felt the same power overload as at the O'Shea complex after Lucinda's death. This time she'd harness it instead of letting it control her. This time she'd be smarter.

"Detective McManus and Astrid Hilden have been kidnapped," Cody explained. "Marcus may know who has them and where they are." She could feel him trying to defuse the volatile situation with his incubus ability.

"That's unfortunate for Detective McManus," Roberts

said as his eyes flicked to Oberon. "But I'm afraid I can't allow you to see the prisoners." The bastard was using it to score points.

"Can't or won't?" the ursian said.

Roberts's smile deepened and he raised one arrogant eyebrow.

Enough.

Bianca lifted her hand where the energy built. Roberts's smile slipped. She flicked out her hand, letting a ball of energy fly toward him. He ducked, putting his hands over his head as the frosted wall into his office shattered in a deafening rain of tempered glass, sending chunks of the granular fragments down on him.

The entire office stopped and dozens of eyes turned on her in jaw-dropping surprise. Even Oberon and Cody froze.

"Do I have your attention now?" she asked in a controlled tone.

Roberts dropped his arms slowly, his petrified expression giving her some small satisfaction. "You can't do this, you don't have the right."

She threw another ball of energy into another glass wall with the same explosive result. He ducked again, even lower this time.

"Okay, okay," he said, holding his hands up in surrender. "You can see them."

Roberts nodded to one of his men, who raced off down the hall and swiped a solid door with a card.

"This is your fault," Roberts spat at Oberon.

"Hey." Bianca could hear the amusement in her boss's voice. "I'm only here to make sure she doesn't kill you."

As the three of them followed the agent through the open door, Oberon leaned in. "Fuck me, Sin, when did you go get all badass?"

She smiled to herself for a split second and then dropped it. She couldn't let her guard or concentration drop. McManus's life depended on it.

Marcus Hilden sat on one of the three metal chairs at the metal desk in the stark interrogation room. He rose to his feet as she entered and his eyes immediately went to Kedrax, perched on her shoulder. "Good Goddess," he whispered, and dropped back into his seat.

"No use hiding anymore," the little dragon said.

Bianca placed her hands on the desk and leaned in. "Where are they?"

"I don't know," he said. "We've been searching for them for weeks."

She straightened and took a step back. "But they've only just gone missing."

Now it was Marcus's turned to look confused. "Who?"

"Astrid and McManus," she replied.

His face turned a pale shade of gray. "Oh no, you've lost her."

"Don't say anything, Marcus," Gayla Hilden said from the door, her hands restrained in front by handcuffs as they moved her into the room.

"They've lost her," he answered in a small voice. "She's gone."

Gayla's composure slipped and she dropped onto the metal chair next to her son-in-law. "What have you done?"

Bianca leaned forward. "Tell me where your people would've taken her. And if they live, it will go better for you."

"My people?" Gayla said. "But they aren't my people."

Something's wrong. Bianca suddenly felt like she'd missed an important piece of the puzzle. A sick feeling rose in her stomach.

"Don't you see what you've done?" Gayla asked in a scared little voice.

Things started to fall into place like dominoes in her head. The way Astrid quickly recovered from the drug fog once they got out of the house. The way Astrid asked her to stay. And the way Astrid guided Mary into the front of the car.

She had her throat cut from behind.

The blood drained from her face and her scalp tightened. She sank into the chair opposite the Domina.

"It's Astrid. It's always been Astrid." Gayla reached out and clasped her hand in desperation. "We've tried to stop her, but she always managed to get by us. She killed Tiffany. She killed her own daughter."

48

Darkness Awakens

McMANUS OPENED HIS eyes, or at least tried to. His head felt heavy and his face ached. The taste of blood filled his mouth and several of his ribs felt like they could be broken. The darkness pressed in, compounding his disorientation as he tried to gain a sense of where they held him. The aching pull on his shoulders stiffened as he attempted to move again. He realized he was tied up on some cold floor, and he could hear chanting somewhere nearby.

Be still, Sagen's voice said in his head. *Don't let them know you are awake yet.*

He didn't need to see to know where he was. Beside the presence of the dragon, the mix of sulfur and decay told him this was Sagen's cavern.

How many are there?

Too many.

Can't you destroy them or something?

No. Sagen's reply was definite and final.

It suddenly all came back to him, making him dizzy.

He'd been halfway through dialing Corey O'Shea's number when he heard a strangled cry to his right and found

Astrid leaning over the backseat, holding a curved knife to Mary's throat.

"Thank you, Detective McManus, for helping me escape," Astrid said in a cold voice. "Now pull over the car or I'll kill her."

When he pulled the car over, she sliced the blade deep and Mary's blood flowed. She'd killed the girl anyway.

Astrid Hilden had done it all. How could he have been so stupid? A groan passed between his lips before he could bite it off.

"He's awake," a deep male voice said.

The chanting broke off.

"About time." Astrid's voice no longer carried any trace fear or insecurity. "Remove the blindfold."

"I don't know why you blindfolded him in the first place. He was already out cold," another woman said.

So, at least one man and two women.

"You have no appreciation for theatrics, Ursula," Astrid said. "You never did."

Ursula? Where had he heard that name before?

The tightness loosened and dropped from his eyes, but he still had trouble opening them. Finally, he was able to crack one eyelid a little.

Two burly men stood nearby. Obviously muscle for hire. As soon as he saw the woman he assumed was Ursula, he knew where he'd seen her before.

"You killed you sister," he croaked. "How could you leave her little girl orphaned like that?"

"That's your fault." She looked down at him sourly. "It was supposed to be Amy when she turned sixteen, but you forced our hand and we had to act sooner. Besides, Lucinda found us, so one sister was a good as another."

Pain stabbed through his eye as an inhuman scream cut the air. But the pain wasn't his. It was Sagen. They had bound the dragon in silver chains that crackled with ice blue energy. Astrid pulled the sword imbued with the same energy from Sagen's eye. The pain seared through to the back of McManus's skull as the black blood oozed from the dragon's now empty socket.

Silver tears slipped from Sagen's remaining eye, and Ursula captured them in a large glass vessel. Astrid drew back the sword and plunged it deep in Sagen's side. McManus's cry mingled with the creature's as pain stabbed under his ribs.

He gasped, trying to drag oxygen back into his burning lungs while his heart struggled to keep beating. McManus felt his own tears wetting his cheeks as he watched the dragon's remaining eye turn to him in pain. Again Astrid plunged the sword into the dragon, this time lower. The pain seared McManus's stomach.

She handed the sword to Ursula.

"And you killed your own daughter?" McManus said to Astrid.

Ursula nodded to one of the guards, who delivered a heavy blow to his gut with the definite crunch of a rib snapping. "You dare to address the Alto?"

He laughed through the pain, which was difficult given his lack of air.

Astrid's humorless smile never reached her cold eyes. "My child fulfilled the sole purpose for which I gave birth to her. It was always her destiny to be sacrificed to the Dark Lords. We have all made such sacrifices."

He looked at the faces of all the witches, burning them into his brain so he'd know who to kill once he got free. A dark-skinned man would be related to the girl who was killed in the voodoo shop. The others he could only guess.

Broken ribs screamed as he craned to see, but he ignored the pain. "They've all killed their blood for this. Why?"

An infant cried, and a soothing voice crooned softly as one of the witches picked up a tiny newborn from a baby carrier by the pool.

"To return the rightful rulers to us. The world has grown overcrowded and chaotic, and the Dark Lords will bring back order." Astrid's maniacal grin deepened.

She's totally and completely off her freaking rocker.

"The dragon's almost ready," Ursula said.

"Excellent," Astrid replied. "Prepare the vessels."

As the others moved away, Astrid looked down on him. "I'll really have to thank Bianca Sin, before I kill her. I couldn't believe my luck when she turned up to rescue me. I mean the plan I had for my escape would probably have worked, but she gave me something even more precious. You. A dragon warrior, the perfect way to into Lord Sagen's lair."

"Eat shit and die," McManus ground out through gritted teeth. Not very original, but pain and his need for a fix were not exactly conducive to clever comebacks.

The witch ignored his attempted insult and smiled that evil smile he was really starting to hate. "Of course, that meant I had to sacrifice that odiously loyal Mary earlier than I'd planned. Her essence was to be a feast for the masters when they arrived. But since I have you, it was a price worth paying."

Ursula returned dressed in a hooded white robe and carrying a swath of crimson fabric across her arms. Astrid's crazed violet eyes never left his face as the other woman held it up behind her.

"There is an added bonus to you being here," she said, slipping her arms into the robe. "When the dragon breathes his last in the presence of a dragon warrior, it must trigger the release of the dragon spark. He could have died holding onto it if not for you. And now I'll make it mine." Her eyes darkened and she took a step toward him.

"It's time, Alto," one of the other witches said.

She glared at him, then spun to storm back to the pool. She looked every bit her mother's daughter in that moment. He lifted himself to his feet to get a better look.

They all extended small glass vials over the pool.

"Water of my blood," they intoned.

Then Astrid picked up the glass container Ursula had used to collect Sagen's tears. "Water of the dragon."

As Astrid poured the contents into the pond, the crystal clear water turned a milky swirling silver. Ursula picked up the sword and followed her mistress to the dragon's side. The blade was now blacker than the blackest obsidian, as if the dark dragon's blood had imbued the very metal itself. Astrid took the weapon, her manic gleam returning as she moved to the dragon's side and placed the tip carefully against the hide, then thrust.

McManus's chest seemed to explode as Lord Sagen's scream filled his mind and the cavern with a white-hot pain.

49

ENEMY MINE

THE VCU AGENTS took Gayla and Marcus from the room, and Bianca leaned back in the chair.

"How could I have gotten it so wrong?" she said. McManus was missing and Mary dead because of her. Because she helped Astrid.

"All of us did." Oberon put his hand on her shoulder. "I'm going to talk to Roberts, see if we can mobilize to find her."

Suddenly, the dragon screamed and passed out, falling from her shoulder.

"Kedrax," she cried, catching him before he hit the floor and drawing his unconscious little body to her chest. Though his heart beat strongly, it was a little too fast.

"Is he okay?" Cody asked.

"I don't know," she replied in a near panic as she laid him down on the interview table.

The dragon's eyes opened slowly and he roused from his side, lifting his head to look at her with molten gold eyes. "Lord Sagen's in a lot of pain and McManus is there with him."

Her heart stopped beating. "Is he alive?"

"Yes," the dragon, said climbing unsteadily to his feet. "For now."

He lives. Her heart started again and she sighed and closed her eyes as relief flooded through her. "Lord Sagen!" she called.

Yes, witch. Sagen's voice filled her head. *I'm here*.

Kedrax's talons dug into her forearm on the table, though not hard enough to hurt. He'd heard the voice too.

"Can you bring us to you?" she asked.

No. Sagen was silent for a moment. *I'm too weak*.

She closed her eyes and used her mind. *How's McManus?*

He's alive but in bad shape.

Is it Astrid? Are they there?

Yes, they used my own arrogant complacency against me, the dragon said. *I didn't see the ruse until it was too late. They sent a man with a gun to kill me . . .*

"A handgun couldn't harm a Great Dragon," Kedrax said.

Precisely. The man was the weapon. The moment I bit into him, I felt the poison enter my system. So, when the witch turned up, I was helpless to stop them. They're preparing to open the . . .

Sagen went quiet. She could sense the pain he was in.

The little dragon trembled, out of fear or anger, she couldn't tell. In her case, it was definitely anger. She had to stop Astrid. She had to stop them all.

"What if I meet you partway? If I can get to the caverns below the subway? Will you have enough strength then?" she asked.

Maybe. They still have to prepare before they are ready to complete the ritual. But hurry.

"I'll get there as fast as I can," she said, as Kedrax climbed on her shoulder.

Cody stood silently through the entire exchange, but as she picked up her keys, he placed his hand over hers and gently pried them from her shaking fingers. "I'll drive."

THE PACKED SUBWAY station buzzed with people crowding the platform. A train screeched to a halt and several sets of doors opened in perfect synchronization. Commuters swapped in and out of the cars, providing little actual relief to the press of bodies. Cody used his mojo to guide people out of the way and open a path to the tunnel at the far end. Just as Bianca reached the edge of the platform where the tunnel yawned ominously before her, Sagen's presence entered her head and the now familiar blinding white light overwhelmed her.

Whatever she expected to find when she got there, this wasn't it. Nothing could've prepared her for the sight of Sagen's massive body secured to the stone floor with large magic-imbued silver chains. His wings were tattered beyond flight, black dragon's blood oozing from dozens of wounds, and his hide so pale it was almost colorless. He lay half in darkness, looking beaten, both physically and emotionally.

Kedrax shifted on her shoulder as she glanced around for Cody, but it was only the two of them.

I couldn't bring your friend, Sagen said in her mind. *I only have enough energy for defensive spells.*

Two men stood near a mound of rags with their backs to her. She hit them with a quick knockout spell before they could turn and catch her. They both froze to the spot. No one would notice unless they looked too closely. She could hear chanting voices, but the dragon's body hid them from sight.

Sagen shifted, pain burning deep in his eye. Tears welled in hers as she lay against him, her body lifting with each labored breath as she listened to his dangerously slow heartbeat.

"What have they done to you?"

He lifted his head as much as the chains would allow, more black blood seeped through his jaws.

"He's dying," Kedrax whispered.

I know. "Don't move," she cried softly, the tears flowing freely down her cheeks now. "Just lie still. Where's McManus?"

He's over there—Sagen's breath stopped as he hitched —*by the men.*

What she had mistaken for rags moved. She raced to his side and slid to her knees. His face was a mess, with one eye swollen shut, the other only half open. Dried blood crusted his puffy split lips, and his clothes were torn bloody rags.

"Be careful, they'll see you," he croaked.

She looked over her shoulder at the group of robed witches standing in a circle, chanting. If they looked this way, she'd be undone.

You are in a concealment spell, Sagen said.

That's why the guards hadn't sensed her either. Sagen protected her. He said he only had enough energy for defensive spells, and now she could see why. They'd taken an eye and almost killed him. How much of a toll was even the defensive spell taking? She had to save them. Both of them.

"Leave me," McManus said in little more than a breath as she worked the knots. "Stop them."

"I'll get you out of here first," she whispered back.

"No! Save the kids." His half open eye looked at her.

A baby's cry brought her attention back to five robed figures surrounding the pool, each now holding a naked baby. As they continued to chant, they pulled daggers from their robes. Bianca shot forward, drew all the energy she could through Kedrax and wove it into an energy ball.

"Blood of my blood," they chanted.

Before she could work out how to hurl the thaumaturgic energy without harming them, the five witches nicked the babies' heels and held them over the strange silver gray pool. Each of the infants' faces screwed up, red and howling, as they kicked out their tiny legs. Blood from each baby fell into the pool, turning the water crimson.

If she fired now, she'd risk the children. "Let them go," she screamed.

вloođ anđ waтer

McManus tried to suck oxygen into his chest as he worked on the knots Bianca had loosened. Breathing became excruciatingly difficult and he suspected his left lung had collapsed. Sweat beaded on his brow and his vision swam as his withdrawal meltdown crept ever closer. But he couldn't take his eyes off the most breathtaking spectacle he'd ever witnessed.

Bianca stood in magnificent splendor with the small dragon on her shoulder, his wings stretched out behind her head. White hair whipped around her head, arms held out at her sides, and smoky blue energy snaked around her entire body. Such a terrifyingly beautiful figure, his heart ached. He couldn't see her face, but he was certain her eyes would be just like Kedrax's molten gold ones.

The witches had finally noticed her. Astrid placed a naked baby back in the carry basket and said something to the others, who did the same before linking hands again and beginning to chant.

All except Astrid, who smiled and with a flick of her wrist lifted Bianca off the ground. She hung in midair, arms stretched out to her sides, completely immobilized, and so was Kedrax. Astrid picked up the sword she'd used to torture the dragon and advanced.

"Now," she said, approaching Lord Sagen. "Time for you to die."

McManus worked the knots faster. Ripping at them, even though the rough surface bit painfully into his wrist, he continued to tug his bonds. They loosened a fraction.

Astrid raised the black sword. McManus felt his bonds slip. The dragon lifted his head, his remaining eye filled with the certainty of his death, and he looked at McManus as Astrid thrust the sword deep in his side. She pulled the sword from the dragon's chest and captured the flow of dark blood in a challis.

Pain tore through McManus's heart, paralyzing him as his bonds finally gave way.

Don't grieve, I give you a gift, Sagen's voice sang in his head.

"No." McManus crawled to his knees. He couldn't breathe. The air rushed out of his lungs but he couldn't replace it.

He dropped to his knees, his chest heaving as he tried to draw breath. The pain subsided. Lord Sagen's chest constricted for the last time and a glowing ball of energy left with his final breath. Astrid hadn't noticed McManus was free, and the frenzied hunger twisted her deranged expression as she moved into the path of the dragon spark.

He'd be fucked if he was going to let her have it. His lungs burning with the need for oxygen, he drew on the last of his reserves to stumble to his feet and pushed the witch out of the way. The ball of light hit him square in the chest, lifting him into the air and surrounding him in a brilliant glow.

"Nooooo . . ." Astrid's scream slowed.

Time and space froze around him. A radiant light illumined the cavern. He felt safe and calm. The desire for Neon Tears left him, his wounds closed, his eyes opened, and the taste of blood left his mouth.

For the first time in his life he felt whole. Everything

became clear. He could feel Lord Sagen's presence. Fragments of the dragon's mind seeped through his consciousness, just beyond his grasp of understanding, but he didn't need to, not just yet anyway.

Everything came back into focus with a whoosh.

"... ooooo," Astrid's cry finished, and she hit the ground.

Normal time resumed. His transformation had taken less than a fraction of a second. He ripped open his shirt and looked down at the beating glow in his chest.

Astrid rolled to snatch up the challis from where she'd placed it and ran toward the crimson pool.

He had to stop her. "Astrid!" he yelled, reaching out for her, several feet ahead of him.

Flames shot along his arm and pooled in his hand. *Cool.*

She glanced over her shoulder and almost stumbled in surprise, but quickly regained her feet and threw the challis into the pool.

"BLOOD OF THE DRAGON!" she screamed.

McManus flung the ball of fire.

51
ground zero

BIANCA COULDN'T MOVE as she hung suspended above the ground, and Kedrax seemed just as helpless. The witches continued to chant as a mist flowed out of thin air to form a white robed figure. It advanced, raised a pale white hand, and pointed a pale white finger at her. Fear skittered up her spine as she looked at the four witches holding hands. For the first time she really looked at each of them, and stopped at the most familiar face.

Hate fired the rage, swelling the energy inside her. It rose up like a tidal wave, filling her with more power than she'd ever felt, and this time she didn't shy away. This time she gave into it. All of it.

Ursula.

She killed her own sister. *She* left Amy and Hannah homeless and orphaned. *She* had to pay.

Kedrax moved slightly and the spell broke. Bianca dropped to the ground just as Astrid ran past, screaming a curse and throwing something at the pool.

"Stop her!" McManus yelled as a ball of fire sailed past Astrid's head and shattered against the wall behind the pool, showering the ground with sparks.

The challis Astrid had thrown hit the crimson water, turning it black. Howling cries rose from inside the now shiny tarlike pool. The ground shook beneath their feet, everything trembled, and the babies screamed.

Then it stopped.

Just like that.

Five translucent figures emerged from the black pool, each different from the next but all the most ethereally beautiful beings she'd ever seen. Yet, their vileness corrupted the air until she almost choked. The portal was open and . . .

The Dark Brethren are free.

The mist figure melted away as all attention turned to the beings floating a few feet above the pool. An angelic form with disturbing azure eyes, waist length golden hair, and flowing pale robes floated toward Bianca.

"WE MEET AGAIN, YOUNG WITCH."

She'd never forget that voice. "Ealund."

He bowed with mock chivalry, and his smile chilled her deeply. *"IF YOU HAD JOINED ME, YOU WOULD HAVE LIVED. NOW YOU WILL DIE WITH THE REST."*

Cold foreboding iced her blood. She gathered strands of thaumaturgic energy, wove them into a lightning ball, and threw it at Ealund. The energy passed ineffectually through him, just as she suspected it might.

It was worth a try anyway.

A fireball flew from behind, passing through another of the Dark Brethren to shatter in a rain of sparks on the floor. She glanced over her shoulder.

McManus ran to her side, his shirt in tatters, and a heart of light beat strongly in the center of his chest, just like Rudolf. Heat radiated off him, warming her face. Fire flowed from his shoulder to form a ball on the palm of his hand, and he threw it at another of the floating Brethren.

"Wow," she said, laying her fingers on his chest. They almost sizzled.

"Tell me about it," he said with a frown, then turned his attention back to the Brethren.

McManus glanced over his shoulder at the large dragon's still and stone colored body. "Lord Sagen is dead."

The anger turned bitter on her tongue. "We must stop them."

Kedrax climbed higher on her shoulder. "The Dark Brethren had to leave their corporeal bodies behind. We can't touch them until they take human form."

"And how do they do that?" McManus asked.

Ealund hovered over the basket close to where Astrid stood to perform her part of the ritual. The baby howled loudly, the newborn's arms and legs flailing with distress. The Brethren descended, quickly entering through her nose and mouth. The infant became unnaturally quiet, blinking calm, and strangely ancient eyes, as she looked around.

Azure eyes. Ealund's eyes.

"That's why Lord Sagen told us to kill the kids," McManus whispered. "They're the way the Brethren enters the world as corporeal beings. But how can we murder babies?"

Another of the Brethren followed Ealund's example and entered the small dark baby girl. The voodoo priest beside the basket, probably Nanette's father or uncle, scooped up the basket and disappeared into nothingness as soon as the baby's cry stopped.

The other three Brethren forms approached the remaining infants. Ursula stood over the baby that must have come from Lucinda, almost drooling with anticipation. Bianca set off at a dead run and slammed into her, knocking the witch backward, and snatched up the baby.

"McManus, save the others," she yelled as the nearest Dark Brethren screeched in frustration.

He ran to the closest child and lifted the little bundle from the basket while a third Brethren entered the other infant before they could stop it.

"Take them both and go," Astrid screeched at a Druid, and pointed to the baby Ealund had entered.

The Druid nodded and picked up both baskets before disappearing like the voodoo priest.

Astrid tore Kedrax from Bianca's shoulder with a spell and smashed him into the far wall. The dragon's tiny form fell to the ground, his wings twisted and broken, his body unmoving.

Astrid laughed from where she stood over the two guards Bianca had disabled earlier. Their blood soaked the stone floor from their cut throats. Astrid must've killed them for the power.

The insane witch cackled. "Now what're you going to do without your little pet?"

Still holding the squalling babe to her chest, Bianca backed up until she hit Sagen's cold dead body. It felt like stone as she leaned against it.

"Bianca," McManus yelled, and placed his baby on the ground.

Ursula came up behind him, knife high above her head.

"Look out!" Bianca shouted.

He turned and Ursula buried the knife. Surprise rounded his eyes as he looked at the hilt protruding from his chest. Blood ran down his naked skin and his pierced, glowing heartbeat faltered.

"McManus!" Bianca screamed.

52

A HERO'S HEART

THE AIR IN Bianca's lungs hardened like stone as McManus's body crumpled to the floor. She didn't know what to do. Ursula had killed him. Kedrax could also be dead. She looked at the baby McManus had been trying to save. It was too late, the Dark Brethren had already entered it. A terrified witch scuttled out of the shadows, lifted the baby from the ground and disappeared, just like the others.

Astrid touched the two dead men's heads and they rose. Bianca's legs slid out from under her and she clung to Lucinda's screaming child. She'd failed. The Dark Brethren had escaped and now four of them had successfully taken over the infant's bodies.

Lucinda's child was the last one, and when they took her, all would be lost. It was futile. She and McManus had lost, and she felt her resistance ebb. Then her hand fell on something warm and metal. She lifted a black-bladed sword that lay on the ground beside her. The sword that killed Sagen—a dragon slayer. She'd heard of them in legends. They could defeat anything.

A Dark Brethren form descended on her, and she lifted the sword to meet it.

"Back off bitch." Bianca got the impression it was a she, though she couldn't tell. "You're not having this child."

The Brethren smiled, reminding her a little of agent Roberts. *"YES I AM,"* it said coldly.

As it reached out for her, the black blade brushed the Dark Brethren's arm and it hissed, drawing back with surprised fear as it rubbed the spot on its wrist.

The blade hurt it.

It might not be corporeal, but somehow the blade's touch had caused pain. Bianca carefully placed the baby on the ground beside her and rose to her feet, keeping the blade pointed at the translucent being. She advanced, forcing the Brethren to retreat.

"So you thought you were invincible too," she said.

Kedrax stirred. *Thank the Goddess.* He was still alive. He staggered to his feet, shook his funny little head and stretched out his wings, which popped back into place. Then the little dragon lifted off the ground and flew to her, landing lightly on her shoulder.

Bianca's happiness cooled as she looked at McManus's crumpled form.

"Get her," Astrid ordered her animated corpses.

They lumbered forward, and Bianca drew on thaumaturgic energy, pushing the force against Astrid's dead goons. They flew off their feet and landed on top of Astrid who screamed her frustration as she struggled under their dead weight.

Ursula tried to sneak in from the side.

"Don't you dare," Bianca said.

What now?

Maybe if she could just force this Dark Brethren back into the pool, she could somehow seal it there. *Only a few feet to go.*

The Brethren realized what she was doing and laughed at her. *"YOU CAN'T SEND ME BACK LITTLE GIRL."*

It lunged at her. The blade entered the creature's stomach, making it scream with an unholy sound, and she shoved backward, trying to get the creature into the pool behind.

As soon as the sword entered the pool, the black water hardened around the blade. Pinned by the blade, the Dark Brethren flailed wildly. The tarlike surface solidified into a black diamondlike finish, starting from the blade and rippling outward. Suddenly the Dark Brethren exploded with a pop, leaving nothing but a faint oily smudge behind.

The blade was stuck fast, buried deep in the shiny black surface.

"NO!" Ursula screamed as she pulled the knife from McManus's chest and raced at Bianca.

A shot rang out and Ursula crumpled.

Rudolf stepped over Sagen's stone tail with a gun in his hand. "Sorry it took so long to get here," he said. "It's harder to find when you don't have a dragon to guide you in."

53

winners and Losers

"WHAT HAPPENED?" BIANCA asked, looking down at the smudge marring the surface.

Rudolf joined her. "I'd say, being cut off from its corporeal form before it had a chance to take another destroyed it. Too bad we didn't work it out earlier."

Bianca looked at him, then threw her arms around his ancient frame, never more happy to see anyone in her life.

"You think you've won," Astrid said with an insane cackle as the two dead goons helped her to her feet. "But we still have four of the Dark Brethren children."

"It's going to be sixteen years before they're of any real use to you, though," Rudolf said. "You can't speed up their growth now, magic will no longer work on them. You'll have to wait for them to reach the age of enlightenment on their own."

Astrid's eyes darted and she frowned. "What's sixteen years, when we've waited centuries? But you won't need to worry about that, old man." She turned to her walking corpses. "Kill them."

The two dead men shuffled forward. Rudolf fired three shots into the head of the first but it barely even flinched.

Astrid's cackle filled the cavern. "You can't kill what is already dead."

Bianca wove the lightning spell and let it loose, missing the one in front and hitting the one behind just as a fireball exploded against the first.

McManus stood a few feet away, fire coursing along his arm and looking pale as he clutched his chest. The flame extinguished.

Bianca ran to him and wrapped her arms around his neck. "I thought you were dead."

"Careful, you might kill me yet," he said wrapping his arm around her waist.

"A normal blade can't kill one blessed by a dragon," Rudolf said. "But that doesn't stop it from hurting like a bastard."

"You're right there, old man," McManus croaked.

Rudolf nodded. "I knew you were of warrior blood, only they can be gifted with dragon fire."

Bianca looked at the bodies of the two dead men writhing on the floor as one burned to ashes and the other just shuddered and stilled.

Astrid howled in frustration and raised her hand to the ceiling, building energy around her. "If I'm going to die," she screamed, "then I'm taking you all with me!"

Rocks rained down from above and the earth shook beneath their feet. She was going to collapse the cave on them. A large chunk of rock fell from the ceiling, crushing Astrid, but the quake continued. Smaller rocks gave way to larger ones. A cloud of debris rose from the floor as the ceiling came down.

"We have to get out of here now," he yelled.

"I have to get the baby!" Bianca screamed.

"See if you can't slow this," Rudolf shouted above the din a moment before a heavy bolder crashed down from above and landed on the now solid black pond. "I'll get the child." And he disappeared into the swirling dust.

More rocks and debris rained down. Some larger chunks

of ceiling landed with enough force to knock them off their feet and cover them in dust.

Kedrax shifted to Bianca's right shoulder, as she held up her arms and formed a protective bubble over them, then moved it up and outward. The rocks bounced harmlessly off the invisible dome she'd made.

Then everything settled. The rumbling stopped. No more debris fell and the cavern seemed stable. McManus helped her to her feet, grabbed her face with both hands and kissed her on the lips. "You did it."

She smiled at him, exhaustion infusing every single muscle, bone, and fiber of her being, but all that fell away when she heard Lucinda's baby crying and Rudolf appeared, holding the tiny bundle in his arms.

"Please," she said, holding her arms out to him.

The old man placed the babe in her arms, and she looked down at the tiny face. The child was perfect. McManus leaned in as she opened her eyes, stared unblinking at him, then clutched his finger as he rubbed against her cheek. His eyes met Bianca's and a funny soft smile lit up his whole face.

"Come on," Rudolf said. "It's a long way back to the surface."

54
The End Begins

BIANCA BLINKED AGAINST the bright light and carefully looked around, disorientation making her dizzy as she tried to rise. *An ambulance?* Something smothered her and she reached up take it away.

"And leave that, it'll help you breathe easier and reoxygenate your blood." A kindly paramedic smiled down at her, patting her hand.

"Lay still," McManus commanded from the bench opposite, feeding a bottle to the baby.

"Am I dreaming?" she asked.

"No," he said with a smile. "It's all real. You collapsed just as we reached the surface. Dehydration and shock, they said."

A weight shifted beside her left leg as Kedrax roused and lifted his head. The little dragon closed exhausted eyes again and dropped his chin on her knee.

"How is the baby?" Bianca asked the attending paramedic.

"A little dehydrated too, but otherwise a healthy baby girl," he answered.

"She's perfect," McManus said as he looked down at the little girl with a goofy smile. "Just perfect."

The baby sucked on the bottle, never taking her eyes off his face. She seemed just in love with him as he was with her.

Oberon appeared at the back of the open ambulance, looking concerned. "How you doing?"

She grinned. "Fine. I think."

"Good, I've brought you something." He'd barely unzipped the top of his heavy leather jacket when a black, one-eared head popped out. "He wouldn't let me out of the apartment without him."

Vincent struggled with impatience for Oberon to open the jacket and leapt out as soon as he could get free. The cat raced straight up to Kedrax, his tail high in the air, and began to lick his friend clean. Kedrax seemed just as glad to see the cat.

"You big softy," she said to Oberon, and stroked the cat. "Thank you."

"Oh my baby." Artemisia pushed past Oberon and climbed into the ambulance.

Here it comes. Bianca braced for her mother's onslaught, but Artemisia went straight past her to the bundle McManus's arms.

Bianca propped herself up. "Artemisia!"

"Oh, hi darling. I'm so glad to see you're okay." Her mother sat down beside Bianca and brushed back her hair. "You did give us such a fright. But look at this tiny bundle of joy."

McManus's eyes crinkled at the edges, and Bianca gave him what she hoped was her best death stare. His grin just deepened.

"Mother!"

Artemisia looked at her again. "I'm sorry, darling. They said you were fine. I've just come from an emergency

CHaPR meeting. They just gave us permission to take little Lucy home."

"Lucy?"

Her mother's dopey gaze dropped to the baby again, with the same silly smile McManus had a few moments earlier. "Yes, that's what Amy and Hannah have called her. They're all going to live with us. The witch's council has concerns over Lucy's origins and agree that it's best she be watched carefully, and who better than the new Domina?" Artemisia looked up again. "Oh, did I tell you? Since Gayla resigned, I've been appointed acting Domina until a proper election process can be held. But that's just a formality."

"How long have I been out?" Bianca asked.

"Just over an hour," Oberon said from the back of the ambulance. "But the meeting was in full swing before you came out of the caverns."

"How are the girls?" Bianca asked her mother.

Artemisia's smile slipped a little. "Okay. But they're excited to see their new sister, so I'm going to take her home to them right now."

"Amy's her aunt."

"Aunt, sister, none of that matters now. We're all going to be one big family." Artemisia rose as Bianca's father appeared, wearing his usual smile. He held out his hand to help his wife down.

"Theron, we're going to have to stop at the store for diapers and formula . . ." Artemisia rattled off commands. "Oh and Bianca, stop by in a few days. The girls want to see you. You too, Detective McManus." And she disappeared into the crowd of emergency service workers.

"Sorry, sweetheart." Her father climbed in and kissed her on the top of the head. "You know how much your mother wanted another baby. It broke her heart when they told her she couldn't. Stop by in a few days if you can. I know you're going to be very busy with everything."

"I am?"

McManus shrugged at her father. "We haven't talked about that yet."

Her father's face grew solemn. "I understand. I'm just so glad you're okay." He backed out of the ambulance and shook Oberon's hand.

"What's going on?" she asked McManus after her father was gone.

He crossed his arms under the blanket around his shoulders. "Well, look at you, little Miss Independent all bent out of shape because she's not Mommy's baby anymore."

"Shut up," she said. He was being ridiculous.

Oberon climbed in and closed the doors behind him.

"So are you going to tell me what's going on?" she said.

Oberon hunched forward, trying to fit his seven-foot frame in the confined space. "The team as it currently stands has been disbanded. We're all being reassigned."

"I don't understand," she said, frowning. "I thought we worked well together."

"We did, but now things have changed drastically." Oberon held out his hands. "I've requested the change. It's not a bad thing."

"Well, I can always go back to just teaching forensic thaumaturgy at the Academy," she said, and turned to McManus. "And your suspension should be lifted now. You'll be a homicide detective again."

"Actually, I quit," he said.

She reached out and took his hand. "Oh, McManus."

"I encouraged it," Oberon said. "McManus has a lot to do, and so do you. We haven't been fired, just given more specialized roles."

Kedrax climbed onto her knee and looked at McManus. "Can you feel them?"

McManus nodded. "The dragons are stirring again. There are eggs to find and hatchlings to raise. You're not just *a* dragon witch, you're *the* Dragon Witch. The most powerful witch on earth, or you will be. Together, with Sagen's knowledge," he tapped his head, "and Rudolf's, we will bring back the lords of magic."

"Speaking of Rudolf?" Bianca said. "Where is he?"

"Still speaking to CHaPR," Oberon said. "It'll take years for children to grow to full strength, but the Dark Brethren are here and their effects will be immediate. If we can't stop them while they're still young, then we have to be prepared to fight them when they reach maturity."

"But there's only four of them," she said.

"They're the Dark Brethren." McManus leaned forward and took her hand. "War is no longer coming. It's here."

She removed the oxygen mask and reached out to move the blanket covering McManus's chest. His heart still glowed from within, beating steadily, though it fluttered when her fingertip brushed his skin.

"I'll leave you to talk," Oberon said, and left quietly.

"Are you sure about this?" she asked and looked up into his ice blue eyes.

"Never more so." He leaned forward and softly pressed his lips against hers.

Dark Brethren
Series References

Glossary of Terms

Abeolite: Worn by Animalians and Facimorphs, especially in urban areas, for the modesty of human society more than the wearer. The material is scientifically formulated to expand and stretch to great extremes to accommodate the changing shape. Mesh segments allow fur to grow through, and an overlapping split in the rear accommodates a tail.

Abomination: A child born to a woman embraced late in her pregnancy. Unlike a child born to Aeternus parents, who will awaken after twenty-five years, an Abomination will awaken after its first year, appearing to age only one year for every fifteen that pass. But most do not reach the age of one.

Alpha: The male leader of a Bestiabeo family. He is responsible for taking care of the day-to-day running of the clan or tribe of Animalians and enforcing the laws, but he answers to the Council of Elders.

Atropa wine: Despite the name, this is actually a distilled spirit, not a wine, made from the plant known as belladonna, otherwise known as deadly nightshade. While toxic to humans—especially the illegally distilled version known as belladonna moonshine—Atropa wine is one of the few substances that acts as an intoxicant on Animalians.

Alto: The head of a coven.

Awaken: A parahuman coming of age, which results in the activation of parahuman abilities. This occurs at different ages depending on the race.

Bloodsucker: A term usually used for a dreniac, but can be used as an insult to an Aeternus.

Blood-thrall: An extreme state of sexual arousal. In humans it's brought on by a small amount of Aeternus blood entering the bloodstream either by direct entry through a vein or cut or a few drops into an eye. Latents are more susceptible to its influence. If a human is in the throes of blood-thrall, the Aeternus responsible may also succumb to the effects. Once a certain point in the arousal is reached, it must be seen through to the conclusion.

Dark Sleep: A long dreamless state that can last up to one hundred years. An Aeternus can slip into Dark Sleep if feeding and resting cease for a period of more than a week. Only time and copious amounts of blood can wake the Dark Sleeper.

Death-high: The state of intoxication Necrodreniacs enter when they have drained a human to the last drop.

Domina: The head of several covens for a region.

Donor: A human who voluntarily donates blood through a donor agency to feed the Aeternus. A blood donation can be collected and bottled, or a live donation can be given, with the Aeternus feeding directly from a donor vein. Donors are regarded highly, unlike fang-whores, who are indiscriminate and little more than prostitutes.

Dopplar: A corporeal spell that looks and acts like a specific person. It feeds off belief, and as soon as there is doubt, the spell disintegrates.

Dúbabeo: Thought to be a myth, Dúbabeo are usually identical twins in the Bestiabeo world and have the ability to transform into both parents' animal forms instead of one or the other. In ancient legends the Dúbabeo served the Bestiabeo and were little more than prisoners in a gilt cage.

Elder: The oldest and wisest of a race. The Aeternus Council of Elders makes decisions regarding the Aeternus within the edicts of CHaPR. Positions are honorary, as the council's authority was superseded with the formation of the CHaPR. The majority of the Council of Elders now serve CHaPR.

Embrace: To change a human into an Aeternus or Necrodreniac through the eternal-kiss. A dangerous process often resulting in the death of the recipient human, with only one in ten embraced humans achieving successful transition. Humans who survive the eternal-kiss are known as the embraced. A human embraced by a Necrodreniac will automatically become a Necrodreniac, too, complete with an addiction to death-highs. However, it is rare for Necrodreniacs to exert the self-control necessary to embrace humans.

Eternal-kiss: A mix of Aeternus or Necrodreniac blood and saliva transferred from the mouth of the embracer to the mouth of the embraced. For an Aeternus to administer the eternal-kiss, permission must be given by the recipient, unless it is a life-and-death situation. Necrodreniacs usually don't ask—they just take.

Facimorphic test: A standard test in most government departments and private industry, especially high-profile ones, to guard against infiltration of a shape-shifter masquerading as an employee. The test checks for specific shifting markers in the DNA of the test recipient.

Fang-mistress: A human kept in luxury by an Aeternus in return for exclusive feeding and often a sexual relationship.

Fang-virgin: A human who has never allowed an Aeternus to feed from his or her vein.

Fang-whore: A derogatory term for those who sell themselves indiscriminately to any Aeternus for blood, and usually sex, in exchange for money and/or blood for spiking.

Humegitarian: A movement of Aeternus who will only feed on the blood donated freely by vegan or vegetarian humans, as they believe in not causing harm to animals. Many are also members of the PAAA (Parahumans Against Animal Abuse).

Latent: One born to parahuman parents who does not awaken in the designated year for their genus, instead continuing to live as a human.

Littermate: A Bestiabeo term for the siblings that result from the same pregnancy. Two progeny are the usual result of a Bestiabeo birth, one male and one female. While other combinations can happen, they are more the exception than the norm.

Mem: An Animalian endearment word for the Mother.

Necrodrenia: A disease that develops when an Aeternus completely drains a human while feeding, resulting in a death-high. Addiction is certain and immediate. Death is the only cure.

Neon Tears: A new designer drug to hit the streets, taken by dropping the liquidized crystalline drug into the eye. Side effects include a secretion of neon blue when the drug is depleted by the body, hence the name.

Orb or **orbing:** A crystal orb used by witches to capture images from a subject as they tell a story. Commonly used to reenact crime scenes, but because of the subjectivity of the witness or suspect, the evidence is not admissible in court. However, it can supply valuable insight into the crime, which can give investigators leads to pursue.

Primara: A midwife in the old sense of the word. The female who is the spiritual and cultural center of an Animalian clan and uses a mix of modern medicine and old herbal remedies to treat members of the community.

Seeker: A witch or thaumaturgist who finds things through the use of magic.

Sensitive: A witch or thaumaturgist who can sense spells or thaumaturgic energy.

Shadow-combat: Game in which individuals or teams, made up of human, parahumans, or both, are pitted against each other in mock-combat scenarios. First introduced in the Paris Academy of Parahuman Studies thirty years ago to help students hone their skills, it quickly gained popularity as a mainstream sport. The NYAPS state-of-the-art arena in the newly upgraded Venator training wing doubles as a venue for the sport.

Spiking: A human practice of mixing a couple of drops of Aeternus blood with a diluted amphetamine mix, which is injected intravenously. This increases the effect of the narcotic and "spikes" an extreme sexual high. Highly addictive and illegal, users eventually destroy their bodies' ability to produce white blood cells, resulting in death. A human who spikes is known as a spiker.

Tech or **Venator tech:** The technical support for a Venator. They monitor police channels and other avenues, looking for signs of dreniac activity, and support Venators with intel and environment monitoring when on a hunt. Many can also excel in weapons invention, computers, and communications support.

Thaumaturgy: The art of invoking supernatural powers, such as magic, which are created from life or death energy.

Troubles, the: Europe in the early nineties saw unrest among the Aeternus community, which almost caused a split in CHaPR. Assassinations were rife and Necrodrenia was on the rise through deliberate infection, causing major friction with humans. These events seemed to cease after the death of Dante Rubins, who was much later named as the supposed instigator, although this was not proven. The reasons behind the Troubles were never identified and seemed to die with Dante.

Venator: A type of bounty hunter who collects bounties for the capture or destruction of parahuman outlaws. Traditionally human, in recent years parahumans have joined the Venator ranks. Venators must be trained, licensed, and registered with the Guild before they are permitted to hunt. They gain this license by attending the Guild academy in their final year of training and passing a set of rigorous exams. Venators may specialize in various fields, including Necrodreniac destruction, hunting dark magic-wielders, or tracking down rogue Animalians. An Aeternus in the grip of Necrodrenia is known as a Necrodreniac or dreniac.

Wolfsbane (Aconitum vulparia or aconite): A toxic poison, especially to Animalians.

Races

Aeternus: A race of vampiric people—although not the "living dead" of legend—who must ingest human blood to live, the Aeternus have created a symbiotic existence with the humans that feed them. They are either born of Aeternus parents or created when a human is embraced (see *Embrace*). Those born to Aeternus parents live as humans until their twenty-fifth year, when they may or may not awaken to become an Aeternus. Those who do not awaken are known as Latents.

Animalians: Intrinsically, they are part man and part animal, but differ from shape-shifters. There are three main genera in the Animalians: ursians (man-bears); felians (man-cats); and canians (man-canines). Each genus is made up of several subgenera; felians, for instance, have families of tiger, panther, lion, cougar, etc. There is much infighting between the genera. Humans cannot be turned into an Animalian—they must be born. But it is possible for a human to mate with an Animalian, and then the child has a fifty-fifty chance of awakening to their Animalian heritage.

It is the same between the genera—the child of two different genera will not know its genus until it awakens.

The three main genera:

Family: A clan or family group of ursians.

Pack: A clan or family group of canians.

Pride: A clan or family group of felians.

Bestiabeo: Traditional name for what are more commonly referred to as Animalians.

Cubii: Collective term for the race of the male Incubus and the female equivalent Succubus. In centuries past they were used as sex slaves, agents of espionage, and sometimes even as assassins. When the CHaPR Treaty came into existence over a century ago, the race was freed from the enforced slavery it had suffered at the hands of humans and parahumans alike. Fearing their freedom would not last, they went into hiding. Only now are they starting to come out.

Dreniac: See *Necrodrenia*.

Faciabeo or **Facimorph:** Also known as shape-shifters or shifters, they have the ability to bend their form to mimic other shapes through the use of magic. Once changed, they retain their own consciousness and only take on the limited physical characteristics of the form they are mimicking—for example, flight when shifting into the form of a bird. Shifters do not become the animal they mimic, unlike Animalians, who are part human and part animal.

Glar-Achni or **Glarachni:** An ancient race made up of several clans that came to Earth ten thousand years ago. They adapted to their new surrounds by transmuting their DNA and mingling it with elements from their new planet. Each clan transformed into a different parahuman race according to the areas they chose to live in.

Mer-people: A little known race of parahumans who live beneath the sea. They have been known to mate with humans; however, this is rare and the hybrid offspring seldom survive.

Parahumans: Alternate humans that include the Aeternus, Animalians, shape-shifters, magic-wielders, and Mer-people. All begin life as human and change to parahuman in different ways, depending on their genus and race.

Shape-shifter or **shifter**: See *Faciabeo*.

Thaumaturgist (magic-wielders): Races that practice thaumaturgy to bend and use life-and-death energy—witches, Druids, shamans, etc. Each race uses magic in a unique manner and for a specific aim. For example, light witches use life energy for the benefit of others; dark witches use death energy for self-gain and chaos.

Unari: The first magic wielders, thought by some to be only a legend. It was said they harnessed magic in its pure form from the magical beings that inhabited the Earth long before humans and parahumans existed. They can manipulate all the casts of magic.

The five castes of modern thaumaturgy:

Natural: Use the earth, plants, and nature, including weather. Druids are one of the best known races in this caste and tend to focus on plants.

Familial: Use an animal as a conduit to pull in thaumaturgic energy to weave into a pattern to form a spell.

Divination: Can see the past, present, and future through divination such as cards, crystal balls, etc. Can also scry for missing people or items and can tell fortunes.

Focal: Focus thaumaturgic energy into or onto items. Users of focal magic produce magical potions and medical preparations (such as love potions, glimmer creams), and can also enchant items such as jewelry, charms, and talismans; an apotheke, for example, is like a magical pharmacist.

Necromantic: Deal with the dead. They contact spirits of the dead to help heal, to find things, to guide them, and speak to the dead. Also use the energy released from the death itself, such as animal sacrifices, bones, blood, feathers; for instance, voodoo.

Government and Organizations

Academy of Parahuman Studies: A tertiary institution of parahuman studies for both humans and parahumans alike. All potential Venators must spend three years at the Academy learning their craft and preparing for the final exams—a set of grueling mental and physical tests to determine a candidate's suitability to become a licensed Venator and what specialization they will undertake—be it Necrodreniacs, Rogue Animalians, or Dark Thaumaturgists. Other courses are offered, such as parahuman law, corporate thaumaturgy, and parahuman forensics.

Academy, the (NYAPS): New York campus of the Academy of Parahuman Studies—one of the first parahuman academies. Originally constructed in the early 1800s as an Aeternus stronghold, the complex has several underground dormitories and lecture halls connected through a large network of tunnels; years later, rooms and halls were built on the surface as well. When first converted to a center for learning, it catered only to parahumans, but in the 1960s, a period of integration for renewed human and parahuman relations, the Academy was opened to human students studying parahuman courses. In the early seventies the Guild moved its training and testing facilities to NYAPS to bring all parahuman studies under the one umbrella. Day and night lectures are scheduled to suit different student lifestyles.

Council for Human and Parahuman Relations (CHaPR): A council similar to the United Nations, consisting of parahuman and human ambassadorial representatives. The CHaPR passes laws that govern human and parahuman coexistence. It is governed by the CHaPR Treaty, established in 1887 after a bitter and bloody war between the Aeternus and an alliance of Animalians and humans. Since its inception, a majority of the other parahuman races have also signed the treaty and are bound by the laws.

Five, the: A small council of five representatives—each from a different race of parahumans or humans—that represents the wisdom of the combined population of the world. While they still have to answer to the rest of CHaPR, they have considerable power, especially in emergency situations.

Department of Parahuman Security (the Department): The umbrella group responsible for enforcing the laws handed down by CHaPR, the Department consists of many divisions and branches, including the following five: divisions are only some of those that make up the Department.

Necrodreniac Control Branch (NCB): Responsible for monitoring and setting Necrodreniac bounties.

Parahuman Intelligence Division (Intel): The Intelligence division of the Department, which gathers information (or "intel") on gangs and rogue parahuman groups, usually through the use of undercover agents.

Personal Security Branch: Provides bodyguard details to officials and VIPs.

Office of the Chief Parahuman Medical Examiner (OCPME): The office that performs the autopsies for the Department.

Violent Crimes Unit (VCU): A team that investigates serious violent crimes usually committed by or against parahumans.

Draconus Nocti: An elite black ops force, named after a legendary group of warriors. The earlier version of the modern Draconus Nocti went behind enemy lines and performed extractions and assassination as required by their employers (rumored to be the Elders of CHaPR). Now, Raven Matokwe is training new recruits specializing in black ops tactics in order to fight the Dark Brethren and their followers.

Guild, the: An organization founded by humans as a part of the CHaPR Treaty and as a form of protection against the parahumans. The Guild is responsible for Venator licensing. Once licensed, a portion of all Venators' bounty earnings go to the Guild.

Petrescu School of Training: One of the many small institutions that take a young human and train mind, body, and soul through regular academic studies supplemented with strong martial-arts regimes. This school has built a reputation for preparing its students to enter an academy for parahuman studies. This is not a Venator training facility, but those wishing to take up that line of work compete for a place in the school.

characters

Akentia, Princess: Aeternus. An ancient Aeternus and chancellor of the Five of CHaPR.

Crompton, Trudii: Unknown. Roving reporter for WTFN news.

DuPrie, Oberon: Ursian. Current head of security at NYAPS and former VCU agent. He is putting together a covert team of specialists to look into the possible recurrence of the Trouble of several years ago.

Ealund: Dark Brethren. An incorporeal being that thrives on violence.

Geraldi, Tones (Antonio): Aeternus. Former VCU agent. Oberon poached the computer expert to work on his team. Tones is a humegetarian and a card carrying member of Parahumans Against Animal Abuse.

Hilden, Astrid: Witch. Board member of the Hilden Group Corporation and Gayla Hilden's daughter.

Hilden, Gayla: Witch. Head of the Hilden coven, Domina of the Eastern Seaboard, and CEO of the Hilden Group Corporation.

Hilden, Marcus: Witch. Board member of the Hilden Group Corporation and Gayla Hilden's son-in-law.

Hilden, Tiffany: Witch. Gayla Hilden's granddaughter.

Jordan, Kitt: Felian. Former Chief Medical Examiner for OCPME. She recently resigned from OCPME to take up a teaching position at the New York Academy of Parahuman Studies and to join Oberon's Team.

Keith: Ursian. Personal bodyguard of Princess Akentia.

McManus, Lancelot: Human. Detective with the NYPD Homicide department. Burnt out, a drunk, and addicted to a new drug, Neon Tears.

O'Connor, Tez: Unknown. Medical Examiner at OCPME and occasional lover of Oberon.

O'Shea, Corey: Unknown. Freight and transport magnate and suspected drug lord.

O'Shea, Seamus: Unknown. Corey O'Shea's younger brother. A silent and dangerous man, rumored to be a crack assassin.

Petrescu, Antoinette: Aeternus. Ex-Venator and newly turned Aeternus. Oberon offered her a job after she was expelled from the Guild for threatening several members.

Roberts, Neil: Human. Agent in charge of VCU and the man responsible for having Oberon kicked out of the unit.

Rudolf: Human. An old human expert on the Dark Brethren, and chancellor of the Five of CHaPR.

Shields, Cody: Incubus. Head of Administration at NYAPS, he looks more like a surfer than an office worker. Oberon uses Cody to defuse emotional situations and as a liaison to external agencies.

Sin, Artemisia: Witch. High ranking witch and current Alto of the Sin Coven. Artemisia is Bianca's mother.

Sin, Bianca: Witch. Expert in forensic thaumaturgy and head of thaumaturgy at NYAPS. Bianca is a nonpracticing familial witch and often called on by city law enforcement agencies to consult on cases.

NEW YORK TIMES AND
USA TODAY BESTSELLING AUTHOR

JEANIENE FROST

FIRST DROP OF CRIMSON

978-0-06-158322-3

The night is not safe for mortals. Denise MacGregor knows
all too well what lurks in the shadows and now a demon
shapeshifter has marked her as prey. Her survival depends on
Spade, an immortal who lusts for a taste of her, but is duty-
bound to protect her—even if it means destroying his own kind.

ETERNAL KISS OF DARKNESS

978-0-06-178316-6

Chicago private investigator Kira Graceling finds herself in a
world she's only imagined in her worst nightmares. At the center
is Mencheres, a breathtaking Master vampire who Kira braved
death to rescue. With danger closing in, Mencheres must
choose either the woman he craves or embracing the darkest
magic to defeat an enemy bent on his eternal destruction.

ONE GRAVE AT A TIME

978-0-06-178319-7

Cat Crawfield wants nothing more than a little downtime with
her vampire husband, Bones. Unfortunately, they must risk all
to battle a villainous spirit and send him back to the other side
of eternity.

JFR1 0312